SHALOMAT

A Mad Run

A Crazy Riddle

Michael J Spyker

AgapeDeum

Published in Adelaide, Australia by AgapeDeum
Contact: agapedeum.com

ISBN 978-0-6486957-2-1

Previously published as *The Riddle of Shalomat*.
This renamed and revised edition published in 2020

Publication assistance by Immortalise
Cover design: Ben Morton

CHAPTER 1

THE RAIN WAS LASHING through the mountains and black lava rock glistened in the sparse light. Lightning strikes burst down the deep chasm beneath a retreat house that sat alone on a large ledge. Its isolation seemed absolute, a small but very exquisite building. Only few were privy to visiting there. Those who did, were concerned with influencing culture. Undercurrents in societies that remained elusive and effective.

The man watching through a large window felt a sense of foreboding in the wild weather. Try as he might, he could not shake it off. Their organisation had grown over centuries, its domination becoming established far and wide. The final steps towards absolute success were on the horizon. He simply knew that to be so. And yet, nothing was for certain. The next bolt of lightning made him shudder. He was not prone to shuddering, not in any situation. It simply added to his apprehension.

The man and woman, both sitting behind him in easy chairs, might have noticed his discomfort. Soft light outlined his back against the rain-blown glass and they were astute observers – a most necessary quality. They were also ruthless like himself, though not openly so. He had not spoken about his recent premonitions. That would now change. Time was of the essence. Turning away from the window he took the third chair, his mind made up.

'The Day of the Riddle is near.'

The silence became tense. This comment was a surprise, but his companions would never reveal that for it meant vulnerability. Faces remained blank, yet their eyes betrayed them. This news was disturbing.

'You've been told?' the woman asked.

'No, but I'm sure.'

In the Protectorate of *Cryslis*, which comprised the three of them, he carried the title Eminent. It was never used. It simply inferred that the mystical powers of Adlyn, the original founder of *Cryslis*, had been placed upon him. His spiritual sensitivity would guide the development of their organisation as many Eminent leaders before him had. This ability always offered insights. But today discernment was shrouded in a fog. That was bothersome and quite unexpected.

'When is this day?' the other man asked. 'What is required of us?'

'I don't know.'

These words came out with difficulty, which angered him, but he controlled his temper. 'All I can suggest is vigilance. It will become clear.'

The two nodded in understanding. 'It's been a long time in coming,' the woman suggested. 'That riddle remains a mystery, but we should be okay.'

This confident observation was typical of *Cryslis*. All conquering and positive. The Eminent man couldn't refute it, nor ever show his doubts. Those disturbed him most of all. Something was afoot. In the history of *Cryslis*, no leader had been confronted with what lay ahead. At least not to his knowledge. A threat was arising, against him and the whole *Cryslis* organisation. But not one sign of its approach was showing. The weekly reports from around the globe indicated nothing untoward. If the Day of the Riddle was near he might expect confusion. The dynamics involved would be very unpredictable. It had been foretold eons ago in a myth that Adlyn, had found in from Persia.

What about the Day of the Riddle's occurring on his watch, the man reflected. Had he been chosen to defeat their opposition once and forever? That would be a special honour. Making certain that the power of *Cryslis* increased to a point where its philosophy swept all before it. When world populations followed the *Cryslis* way without much interest in other ideas. It meant the psycho-spiritual control of humanity. For its own good. But there was opposition to that plan.

Always had been, from a cosmic realm beyond the earth. After years of successful work, a countermove was only logical.

Adlyn had been a German alchemist in the Middle Ages. He joined Italian merchants one day on their way to China. The journey followed the Silk Road. Adlyn was not interested in merchandise. He sought foreign stones and powders towards making gold. The unknown substances he had collected were never used though. Instead, Adlyn became the founder of a special organisation that for generations to come would bring people great wealth. His search after gold bore fruit. But quite differently from what he ever imagined. Not in his wildest dreams could Adlyn have foreseen that strange event in Persia.

The caravan of merchants became caught in an enormous storm one day. The heavens unleashed their maximum fury. Confused and with zero visibility Adlyn slid horse and all down a muddy slope. The wet earth helped in keeping them unhurt. Face down in the mud, Adlyn raised his head and noticed a glint not far away. It was a strange happening in that dark and violent night. He began to crawl to whatever was glowing in the muck and reached out. With a yelp he withdrew his hand. His fingers, burning with pain, were blistering. But for the cold rain the injury might have been much worse. Not easily discouraged, for alchemists were used to things burning up and exploding, he scooped the small object up mud and all into an earthenware pot. Adlyn hid his find in a saddlebag.

Once back in Germany he emptied the pot carefully onto a stone slab. Pouring much water over his treasure the caked-on mud washed away. It created clouds of steam. The result was startling. He saw a dark glass-like object that shone with a strange light. Not reflected light, but light that glowed from within. Staring at it intently Adlyn's spirit became agitated. He diverted his eyes and with a wooden ladle slid the small object back into the pot. The ladle was dropped into water for it was smoking.

Adlyn could not sleep that night. His spirit stirred in turmoil. The myth of *Shalomat* came to mind. A little story he had bought in a hurry in Persia. Having forgotten about it, he now felt an urge to find that story. A search amongst his papers soon revealed the old parchment and Adlyn began to read. It was how he discovered that the peculiar object in his workshop was called the *Cryslis*. A little glass-like pyramid with a triangular base and each edge of the same length. The *Cryslis* was ageless and originated from an unknown realm. Adlyn began to shake violently. A strange force dropped him into a deep trance. He woke up at dawn feeling different but had no idea in what way he had changed. It wasn't a bad feeling though.

Adlyn never spoke of what happened that night. He knew that a myth referred to something basic in human experience. But that a myth might have actual power independent of that experience, he had not considered. *Shalomat* was not just a story of significant meaning that highlighted aspects of human existence. It spoke of a force that could influence existence. Adlyn understood this from his mystical encounter that night. The realm of the *Cryslis* was able to interact with the world. It would be purposeful towards a specific end.

But someone was needed to start this process. Adlyn was that person. Ignoring the call would cost him his life. He submitted and began to meditate before the *Cryslis* every day. As his task unfolded, he found it in no sense oppressive.

Cryslis was about success and wealth. It ignored human qualities of deeper significance. Wealth and power appealed to people. The *Cryslis* offered them success with the support of spiritual influences.

Adlyn began to teach a number of suitable men. They met in secret gaining strength and inspiration from the small object that glowed with such a strange inner light. That centuries later these early beginnings would become a worldwide network of education and praxis, Adlyn never imagined. Advanced in years and sensing his task completed, he walked away leaving the

Cryslis to appoint his successor. His task was finished and his friends never saw him again. The future was left to those whom Adlyn had taught. They became very wealthy – every one of them.

The Eminent man's mind drifted once again towards the wild weather outside. I need to visit the Temple, he said after a while. It was the obvious step. His companions had expected it and their meeting ended.

CHAPTER 2

AHMED WAS ANGRY. But not so angry that he would crash the Porsche 911 he was racing through the English countryside. He pointed the car into a bend on the preferred racing line. Almost a year ago his father had given him the car as an unexpected present. It was not worth disposing of as a trade-in, Ahmed was told. He might as well race it. That was one perspective to take on wealth. Naturally, Ahmed had not complained. His Dad had bought himself a new Porsche for everyday use – another status symbol, besides the Bentley.

A Porsche was quite a present. More so, when you could race it with the bills being paid. Ever since receiving this hand-me-down Ahmed had been careful with his driving. He always remained within his skills. Exiting a sharp bend on the local track, he was acutely aware that it would be his last few laps for a while. Because not even a year later, the same hand that gave out Porsches would direct him towards a life without racing. Shit, Ahmed thought and felt his anger rise further. Right now, he'd better keep his mind on the enjoyment of driving fast. Soon it would no longer be possible. There was no race track at the *Cryslis*

Academy where he was headed tomorrow. Ahmed was so dark about it, that he felt to belt the tarmac extra fast. He restrained himself. It was too risky and the Porsche might crash. He would be back – one day.

His racing instructor had convinced his father that Ahmed at sixteen could handle the Porsche. That had been a great day, one of the best in his life. Those came sparingly. Rich kids are not necessarily happy ones. Ahmed knew his Porsche would not be replaced if he were to overreach and badly damage the car. The challenge was to drive excitingly fast without taking silly risks. Were he to become reckless, he would be back to racing his Ford Cosworth. Racing the Porsche fast and not making a bad mistake, it was a fine line. Ahmed's instant and instinctive reactions had saved him more than once. He wondered whether he could ever make the grade as a professional driver. He would surely like to try. But you had to race a lot and for him those days were over now. His stomach churned in pure frustration. He banged the steering wheel, quickly and hard.

The Porsche surged ahead destined to veer off the bitumen. The brakes were applied briefly just in time. The car felt alive with pent-up energy, growling like a hungry predator. As the Porsche sped over the top of a hill and Ahmed executed a left turn, he lost sight of the track for a split second, imagined being airborne. But the bonnet was dipping fast with the car plunging down the tarmac to the bottom. Ahmed found this sort of driving exhilarating. His blood was racing and heart thumping. The speed was heady, and he loved it!

At a sharp bend the Porsche needed a firm hand. Braking, gear changing, forcing the steering-wheel just enough and accelerating, all within seconds and with fluency for racing to be safe. Ahmed had done it many times but never in the company of other drivers tussling for position. That was a future he had hoped for. It would now never come. He had always raced privately and today was his last run for quite a while. Blast! He accelerated hard down the straight towards the next turn that banked to the right. Ahmed loved fast cars and high speed. There was nothing like it. He loved being alone in this metal monster that growled on his behalf, expressing deep frustration.

At every bend the entrance had to be just right for it determined where the car would exit. There was a perfect line for maximum speed and safety. Good drivers developed a rhythm around the course. Over time, Ahmed became proficient and began focusing on lap times. He was able to bring real feeling into his driving, an intuitive sense for car and course. That was when racing was most satisfying.

He decided to take the last few laps slower. Not fighting the car all the way and within his limits. It allowed for the fusion between man and machine at an almost spiritual level. United in harmony, the engine whining at perfect pitch and the semi-relaxed driver greedily following the bitumen. Heartbeats would be well up. Car and driver under pressure and capable. In this zone the mind and body were fully focused on optimum efficiency. It was difficult work and rather special. Ahmed didn't get close today. No surprises there. He simply was too agitated.

Rugger, their gardener, maintenance man and also chauffeur, was waiting in the pits. This nickname came from his rugby days when he got a broken nose a number of times and cauliflower ears. Rugger's given name was John and Ahmed never used it. Having been a handy amateur boxer as well, Rugger had taught Ahmed the fundamentals of that sport over the years. Not that Ahmed would ever place much of a punch on Rugger regardless of him being in his fifties. As Ahmed reluctantly climbed out of the Porsche, Rugger noticed the young man's foul mood and wisely said nothing. He took over behind the steering wheel and drove them home. Occasionally glancing sideways at his slumped down and sullen passenger. After racing practice it always grated on Ahmed to see his car restricted to suburban speed limits. Today, being very annoyed, it irritated him even more. He quietly chided himself for his foul temper. Why take it out on Rugger?

Surely not on this last drive together. But how the heck was he to snap free of it? Right now, it was beyond him. He hoped Rugger would understand.

As the Porsche crawled along in major traffic, Ahmed thought about home. Normally, he would reflect with wry amusement on his mother, a socialite who was always engaged with some project or other. His thoughts about her were not light-hearted today and a muddle of contradictions. Mother liked nothing better than to open her house for bridge evenings, dinners, fundraising and parties. It meant visitors, always visitors, far too many for Ahmed's liking, and too often. I feel like living in an entertainment centre, he had once chided her when every room downstairs of their large house was full of people. It doesn't feel like a home! he had said with some chagrin. But it was home – and now he was to leave it against his will.

Ahmed was fortunate in having such rich parents. Willing to admit that certainly it had major benefits. But having your face on the gossip pages of women's magazines as a son of the wealthy, he could do without it. On such occasions he felt to be living in a fishbowl; if a large one. Fortunately, such media exposure was scarce. Ahmed preferred to keep it that way. He valued his privacy and hated being talked about. Though he was internet savvy, he used it only sporadically. Most of the stuff on it was of little interest to him. Apart from car racing and rugby.

Though born in England, Ahmed was of Indian descent. His father was a wealthy businessman, who often visited the home country with extensive commercial interests there. Over the years Ahmed had met his Indian relatives regularly, which had been fun. He loved that busy and intriguing country. His next trip was not to be to India though, but to the Isle of Jersey. Not far from England, but many miles away from the life he had enjoyed to date. He felt sure of that.

That this change would come one day, Ahmed had forced from his mind for years. His father contributed much of his success to the training he received as a young man at a *Cryslis* Academy. In this, he had followed in his own father's footsteps. The dead grandfather Ahmed hardly remembered. Grandfather had started the Padhri business empire, which Ahmed was destined to enter continuing its success story. If only he was interested. The fact that he was not, no-one in his family accepted. The matter remained unresolved and not to be discussed. It should bring a confrontation, one day. It was too early in his life for that right now. As a young man Ahmed found himself in a no-win situation. The family business tradition was a formidable force.

On his father's desk at home stood a small *Cryslis*. The

way it was placed made ignoring the shiny object quite impossible. It was a fine copy of the real one in the Temple, dad had remarked a number of times. Like grandfather, Ahmed's father had visited that Temple and was proud of it. Admittedly, the *Cryslis* was quite beautiful and somehow typical of what the Pardhi business family represented. It was a shiny dark crystal pointy object, like a pyramid with a triangular base. It seemed to know exactly what it was about. The *Cryslis* would subdue all ideas or perspectives into its own realm and contained a strange power. Many would laugh at the notion of it having power, but not so Ahmed. He knew instinctively that his ideas about life differed greatly from those projected by the reflected light of this *Cryslis*. If it actually was a reflected light. The source of its energy seemed to come from within. Ahmed could not explain this. He disliked the small object deeply. It would easily fit into his hand.

His parents dismissed his noncompliant ideas as youthful enthusiasm. A romantic outlook. You will get on in life best with planning and dedication, the advice was. There was no need to be philosophical about that. Achievement comes through a singular focus. As a worldview that fell way short, Ahmed believed. He didn't want to dedicate his life to running a company and surely not to a power like *Cryslis*.

Thinking of the world and its struggles Ahmed felt that the problems were created by intolerance and greed. Somehow, he needed to get a personal handle on that idea and live it out. He should find insights on how to manage personhood. Create an existence less driven by wealth. Someone once told him that being rich he could afford such sentiments. That remark had stung because it was true.

Now Ahmed's turn had come, as a son of Pardhi, to enter a *Cryslis* Academy. He would leave tomorrow for Jersey Island, east of England and close to France. His stay would offer only the occasional brief holiday back home over the next two years. Not that he expected to feel homesick or even miss his parents much. Perhaps that was not fair. They had always cared and showered him with what money could buy. They would keep doing so. As their only child, they surely loved him. In spite of all the time consuming activities that shaped their busy lives. Still, they often annoyed Ahmed. How could he ever explain being at odds with their lifestyle? They wouldn't understand. Ahmed was not even sure he understood it rightly himself. He could feel so utterly alone. That is how young people were supposed to feel, according to a lecture he once attended. Fat help that, he thought, looking through the Porsche's windscreen.

The Porsche arrived at their driveway in Ascot near London. Rugger took a side turn to the garages which once had been stables. In the lush country around Ascot, with many large English trees and green hills, horse riding remained a popular sport. You would often find horses stepping away on the bitumen roads heading for the fields and tracks. There was still a place for horses at Ahmed's home. He was capable in the saddle and liked them. Their character and strength appealed to him, but he held no great love for the sport. Slowing to a crawl Rugger parked the Porsche in the workshop. He knew enough about cars to give it the needed attention after a short race. Ahmed took his leave from Rugger with a handshake. He hit the roof of the Porsche with a flat hand as goodbye and reluctantly walked away. It would be months before he would see his friend and his car again.

Only his mother was at home. Even this last evening together they would not be alone. Two people from a charity had been invited for dinner. It was well into the evening before they took their leave. Then his mother invited Ahmed to sit close for a while. 'Oh, my Ahmed boy,' she sighed. It was her usual way of starting a more intimate conversation. 'I will miss you, very much.' No doubt, that would be true. Ahmed wished he could return the comment with similar feeling. Perhaps, he could. But all he felt right now was being powerless. 'I'll miss you too, mum,' he said hiding his frustration. I am facing a waste of a year ahead. Two years actually, boring and tedious, learning stuff that didn't interest him. If only he knew how wrong he was.

***

At sunrise, on the other side of the world, a peculiar building threw a long shadow over the red desert. The Director of Education of *Cryslis* worldwide sat inside in deep reflection. He wondered about his disquiet. Hoped to find out why. Once clarity came, whatever problem ahead, it would be dealt with swiftly and well. Failure was not an option. But until he knew what was going on, he would be patient. Troubled and alone. No-one's business but his own. But for a few senior people and he had no idea where they were residing. It could be anywhere around the globe. He had kept his disquiet to himself. It had no substance and might fade away.

As the sunlight began to enter the building with increasing brightness, he got to his feet. His spirit was perturbed, but he'd better get used to it. That was all he knew.

***

Amsterdam is an old city with circular canals, many fine bridges and thousands of pushbikes. Jacq was pushing hers along hard because she was late. Ellie would be waiting at Het Leidse Plein, one of the famous city squares. They were to meet at De Balie. For a juice and then to visit the movies.

This popular venue was always busy. Ellie had secured a small table and was getting impatient. Her best friend Jacq was not usually late for anything. In fact, she was always so on time, you could set your watch by it. When I start going for auditions Ell, she had once said, being late would mean the end of my dreams. Jacq wished to be an actor, very much so, films preferably. But first she had to convince her parents. That it would be cool to have a famous daughter. They were not impressed and recently had a serious run-in about it. Jacq then had spent nearly two hours on the phone with Ellie. That was the good thing about Ellie, you could ear-bash her and she would listen. Unlike Jacq's parents.

They are never around, Ell, Jacq had complained. Whenever I want to discuss my future, they always have something else to talk about. Like, 'You will need to keep up your math Jacq, if you're going into science.' As if I want to be like them! Utterly boring! For ever they have their eyes glued to instruments looking at things no one can actually see! There is a whole world waiting for me and I want to be in it. Their talking had run out of steam and ended in deciding to soon meet at De Balie.

Ellie was about to text Jacq when she arrived. A slender, lithe figure carrying a sports bag. She moved through the crowd with the grace of a leopard. Like many Dutch people, Jacq was tall and had blue eyes.

'Sorry, Ell,' she apologised. 'I got caught up in my combat class. It was so cool. Have you been waiting long?'

Jacq's face was fresh from the chill outside. Even on a summer's day a sharp breeze could be blowing through Amsterdam. The city Jacq would never tire of. So full of character and history. The streets were lined on both sides with attached houses four stories high. Many of those centuries old. Cars and trams between them and pushbikes were many. People from all over the world lived in Amsterdam. The most cosmopolitan city of The Netherlands. Or Holland, as many preferred to call Jacq's country.

'Been waiting long? Not really, only forever!'

Ellie tried her angry face. It usually made Jacq laugh, but not today.

Crashing down on a chair Jacq grunted, 'I've got something to tell you.' Her tone of voice drew her friend's attention sharply. This was not the usual Jacq.

'It's really awful,' Jacq said. 'And I knew it might happen one day, but never gave it much thought. Till yesterday, that is. My life will be ruined!'

She began to massage her forehead. A reaction to stress. Her blonde hair was tied up in a ponytail because of karate lessons. Though she fought it, tears prickled in her eyes. She briskly wiped them away. Ellie had never seen Jacq in tears. During the few troubled times they had faced together as friends, she had always kept her vision dry. What was going on here? Overcoming her surprise, Ellie leaned forward consolingly.

'What on earth's the matter?'

Jacq with a tight voice explained from behind her hands. 'They are sending me to *Cryslis*! A place has come available, and I have to go.'

Ellie was quite stunned at this news. '*Cryslis*?' she exclaimed. She had never heard Jacq talk of it.

'Yes, the *Cryslis* Academy.' Jacq spat the words out in disgust. Her anger was showing. 'It's where my parents met before they got married.'

Jacq knew the story well. The possibility of her ever receiving a similar education had been mentioned. But at sixteen years of age, *Cryslis* was not something she had given much thought to. That had been a bad mistake. Her brother Anton, now postgraduate in Quantum Physics in the USA, studied there years ago. Jacq hardly remembered for she was so much younger. As siblings they were unalike. Anton seemed to have enjoyed his stay at the academy. Now her time had come to learn about Crylis. Unavoidably so. She was enrolled into an exclusive education. That help you reach the top of your profession, mostly in the sciences and commerce. Exclusive alright! Also, it was a somewhat secretive place. Elusive was another word for it. Most people would have never heard of *Cryslis*. Like Anton, Jacq had an aptitude for math and the sciences. But it was not where her heart lay. She was not interested in a left-brained way of life.

'Where is it, this academy?' asked Ellie.

Jacq dropped her hands onto the table, her face a little red. Not a perfect face but beautiful and very photogenic.

'*Cryslis* academies are the world over at selected places,' she grumbled while staring straight ahead. 'The European Academy is on Jersey Island.'

Ellie had never seen Jacq so dejected or brusque. She gave her a squeeze on the arm.

'It probably won't be so bad, Jacq. At least Jersey is not that far from here, just off the French coast.'

'Yeah, and it will still suck! No question.'

Fighting words, those. Jacq knew she should tone it down. This sudden mess in her life was not Ellie's fault. 'Sorry, Ell,' she offered resting her eyes for a moment on her friend.

'When will you go?'

Ellie tried to keep the devastation out of her voice. She and Jacq were really close. Like sisters, who rather than fight actually liked each other. Ellie could not bear to think of Jacq leaving.

'I'll go next week. Can you believe it?'

Jacq began to search her sports bag for a tissue and ended up pulling out a towel to rub her face.

'They have been organising this for months!' she explained from behind the blue cotton. 'It's a wonderful opportunity to finish your schooling, Jacq, in such a prestigious place. Not everybody gets such a great opportunity.' She mimicked her parents with noticeable sarcasm. 'What croc! As if I care! I didn't have any say in the decision either and that's what annoys me most. They don't even consider that I might want something different for my life.'

Ellie didn't know what to say. She was thinking about how this unexpected future would affect her!

They sat in silence thinking of their separation. Then Jacq straightened. She stood up to clear her lungs with a deep breath. She stretched her arms above her head not caring about being noticed with interest by some young guys. Let them goggle, she thought. Sperm brains. This rotten news was getting her down overly much.

'There's no sense in this misery spoiling my life, Ell,' she concluded. 'I simply shall have to go. Not going will be worse than war. I would lose the battle anyway. At least, we still have a few days left for some fun. Let's plan it properly.'

If *Cryslis* was to be her future, Jacq would make sure to optimise her short time left in Amsterdam.

'Just like them to determine how I want to live my life,' she continued ruefully about her parents. Jacq was calming down a little. 'They are so into their lifestyle of money, and success, and having more patents to their name. As if! Surely there is more to life than that?'

Jacq remained standing and gave one guy a hard stare. To his credit he did not budge on showing interest.

Ellie left Jacq's comments unanswered. She felt an awful sadness now that the bad news was sinking in. Silently she considered her best friend, who had everything money could buy and never seemed much impressed by that. 'For how long will you be gone?'

'At least for two years, I think.' Jacq shook her head sharply. As if to chase away dark pressure. 'Ah, stuff it, Ell! Why can't my parents be normal?'

Ellie shrugged her shoulders. She thought Jacq's parents were pretty cool and normal enough, but then she was not Jacq. 'Forget it, Jacq,' Ellie decided, pushing back her chair. She had no intention of thinking about a life without her friend for one second longer. They always had good fun together and that should remain. 'Let's go and do a movie.'

'Yeah, let's ignore the calamity that is about to befall Jacq de Bruyn!'

With some finality Jacq waved one arm about as if exiting a stage. She wanted to become an actor. I'm well and truly entering the theatre of life now, she thought ruefully. Much earlier than expected. A sudden premonition told her that the play ahead was to be some show indeed. It surprised and briefly made her shiver. She shook the feeling off hooking her arm into Ellie's. Picking up the sports bag they sauntered off to the cinemas. Wonderful Amsterdam. The sense of actually belonging here. How Jacq would miss it!

CHAPTER 3

HE SAW HER STANDING at the railing of the boat looking out over the sea and felt an aching jolt of recognition. He had not expected to meet her soon again. Remembered those spontaneous kisses very well. Not that he had got much further than kissing. With her, a weekend's fun would not be long enough for that. Unlike some other girls he had known. He was not even sure whether a year would have been sufficient, though possibly.

She had arrived with her parents to visit his own. Immediately she seemed enthralled with Stockholm, where he lived. So they had spent a few days exploring his beautiful city. Walking extensively through the old narrow streets. Visiting a palace and relaxing at the wide waters of the cityscape. It had been great. Too soon she left for Amsterdam leaving him strangely at a loss. But here she was, on this ship. He decided to hang back and observe her unnoticed. It was what he often did with people. His pale blue intelligent eyes were now locked in.

Jacq was scanning the horizon. France disappeared behind her and nothing but slow motion of grey sea ahead. It was just a 15 miles journey to Jersey Island.

The ferry making good progress in calm waters on the Atlantic Ocean. Jacq's emotions were different, anything but calm. She felt a sensation in the back of her head that made her search the crowd behind. Then she continued to stare across the slow rhythmic waves with her face into the wind. Perhaps it would blow her frustration away.

Taking leave from Ellie had been a wrench. From her parents as well, though she still blamed them for disrupting her life. They had pledged all the help she needed. Setting out alone was a daunting task. She would just have to manage it. Jacq was confident she could, but that gave her no pleasure. Was someone looking at her? Again she turned towards the crowd, this time more attentively. Then, she noticed him.

Oh, please no, Jacq thought, not here! She had detected the Viking. Tall and blond and sure-footed. Ellie had named him thus after Jacq's visit to Sweden three months ago. It was Erik, she had discovered amongst the passengers.

Jacq rather liked him. He was clever with girls. It had taken steely determination to keep herself in check that gorgeous night in Stockholm. She had, as she knew she could. Still, having Erik on this boat, obviously *Cryslis* bound, was a further complication. He waved as if only just discovering Jacq. That was not right. Erik must have been observing her for a while. It was a little unnerving. Onward he came in all his handsome competence. She waved back briefly and forced a smile. Erik, the Viking.

Jacq knew of his father being connected with *Cryslis* like her own parents. She had overheard that one day. Now he was approaching as a friend and a potential problem. *Cryslis* would be so much different from a holiday weekend. More permanent and far less fun. Jacq's spirit sank a little deeper. Meeting up with him was okay. But the way it had been between them would be best forgotten. There was no need to cold-shoulder him though nor would she want that. The difficulties in her life were stacking up fast.

Erik seemed his energetic self. Naturally, he was pleased to see Jacq. His smile and eyes that searched her face showed excitement. That she was also headed for *Cryslis* he considered good news. Erik was astute enough to notice that the Jacq of today was not quite the girl he had kissed so fervently. He toned down his welcome. She would brighten up, he thought.

'Not happy,' Erik suggested. A statement rather than a question.

'How are you, Erik?' Jacq would not discuss her feelings, not even slightly.

'Fine.'

And why wouldn't he be? Enrolling at *Cryslis* had been the plan for years and he was looking forward to it. Erik felt it would help him learn exactly what was needed. How to run his father's company.

'Off to *Cryslis*,' Jacq said, sensing Erik had figured that. Obviously, he had no problems with joining the academy. They were different people. That may have been part of the attraction between them. At least, it had been in Stockholm. Jersey would be another matter. Simply being friends would be best. Hopefully that would work. On the upside, she now had a friend in that place up ahead.

They talked and Erik made Jacq laugh. When the ferry arrived at St Aubin's Bay a car was waiting with a uniformed chauffeur. They drove through lovely countryside of fields bordered by granite walls and hedgerows. A number of narrow lanes brought them to their destination. Beautifully situated near the coast and seemingly in isolation. But, on an island of only 45 square miles, solitude would be hard to find, Jacq figured.

The *Cryslis* Academy was more like a hotel than a school. Every student was allocated a small recently built apartment. There was a restaurant and facilities for all kinds of sports. The grounds of the Academy were nicely set out. As might have been expected, for *Cryslis* meant wealth and success. Its campus would reflect that in every way. Jacq, after shutting the front door of her new digs with a bang, threw herself on the bed in despair. She felt at dead-end street. A street she didn't wish to be in. But one she couldn't get out off.

May the whole place be bombed!

Ahmed arrived a day later. He had travelled in from England, a longer journey than from the continent. Once in his room, he never even considered his bed. There was too much frustrated energy in him to crash down. His comfortable apartment did not appease. As soon as his bags hit the carpet, he felt like picking them up and storm out. A totally useless impulse, for there was nowhere to go. Instead, he decided angrily to take a walk and check the place out.

Everything was provided for. There was a gym, a pool, sauna and spa. You could play tennis, sail boats and ride horses. There was plenty of scope for walking too. Ahmed did the latter, taking a long hike transforming his anger into energy. The feel of sea air was relaxing. He passed an inlet where a few sailing boats were moored, climbed up a hill away from the coast and discovered open country. It made him consider his options, how to best find recreation in this place of his confinement. The answer was not difficult. He would need to acquire a horse. It would not come close to racing a car. But definitely was the best sport for him here on this island. After an hour he made his way back to the academy and headed for the stables. There he noticed a tallish elegant girl with shoulder length blond hair. She was talking to a man who turned out to be the stable manager.

The manager seemed friendly and introduced himself as Mr. Adams. Ahmed gave his name and learned that the girl was called Jacq. She had been asking Ahmed's question, about the availability of a horse. They were told that two horses had come up for sale from two graduates now departed. The animals were in the stables and needed some exercise. Mr. Adams pointed them out. Jacq and Ahmed saddled the horses with the manager looking on. He found these young people to know their job. The girl obviously enjoyed it. The boy was more reserved, but competent. Jacq had instinctively been drawn to the brown gelding, the more powerful of the two. Ahmed was quite happy with the bay mare. It seemed friendlier and less temperamental. He was in no mood for fighting a horse when out riding. Also, he perceived that Jacq was the better rider and that suited him fine. On a horse he never felt competitive as he did in a race car.

They took to the green fields at a canter. The horses were enjoying the exercise as might be expected of quality animals. It was their first run for a while. From a canter they entered into a gallop and after a while brought the pace down to walking. Neither rider spoke, each busy with emotions that needed private space. Ahmed had no intention of disturbing the thoughts of this beautiful girl sitting erect on that powerful horse. As if at one with it. He liked his own horse more than expected and for the first time felt somewhat at ease with himself. Jacq decided that to remain silent altogether would be impolite, if not rude. This brooding and handsome Indian deserved some recognition.

'I'm sorry that I am not talkative,' she explained. 'It has not been easy leaving home.'

Ahmed was welcomed the comment noticing her Dutch accent. It was only slight. She was comfortable with his native tongue.

'Fine,' he responded. 'That makes two. We'll talk another time.'

'Thanks.'

Jacq spurred her horse on back to the stables. Its hind legs throwing up clots of dirt. Ahmed purposefully followed at a slower pace. It allowed him to enjoy the sight of horse and rider up ahead. He wondered about Jacq.

They told the stable manager that the horses were fine. Their parents would pay the bills.

The new intake of students, a group of seventeen, assembled in the main auditorium. They were seated facing a Principal immaculately dressed in a dark suit and silk tie. Erik had found a place next to Jacq. He appeared interested in the meeting. The Principal spoke a few words of welcome and encouragement. He appraised the new group to be in his care for two years.

One thing they all had in common: these students were clever. The Principal stood behind an expensive table and began to talk about the small dark crystal ornament at its centre. It was shaped like a pyramid, but with a 60 degrees triangle as its base. The same triangles formed the three sides. Ahmed had recognised it immediately and felt his gut contracting. He deeply disliked the thing.

'This is a *Cryslis*,' the Principal explained. 'It's a copy of the original which is very ancient. No one knows how old exactly. The original *Cryslis* rests in a temple. It spends a twenty years on each continent. In the space of one hundred years it travels the globe. Presently, the *Cryslis* is in the Temple of Australia.'

That was one country she wouldn't mind visiting, Jacq thought. She had seen a *Cryslis* before and detested the thing vehemently.

'The *Cryslis* you see here before me has spent one year exactly in the Temple next to the original. It has absorbed some of the original's glow. A new *Cryslis* Academy is never started, anywhere in the world, without such a *Cryslis* being available.'

Ahmed wondered whether his father's one had spent time in the Temple. Surely, he would not have accepted anything less.

'You may have parents with one at home,' the Principal continued. He looked at the *Cryslis* with some affection. 'You can see its perfect shape. It shines beautifully with deep significance but is quite small. Size, however, never limits the power of the idea it represents. It is a very simple idea: that success in any field is linear, one layer of achievement building on the other. As you reach the top of your profession, you will find fewer and fewer people as capable as you are. This reality reflects the shape of the *Cryslis* in that it becomes progressively smaller higher up. The top ends in a sharp point.'

Erik nodded his head in affirmation. He had few doubts about getting near that top, eventually.

The Principal spoke with enthusiasm. 'Though few can ever reach the ultimate, reach the very top, there is much to be gained at any of the higher levels. It will bring you success. Also influence, money and personal satisfaction.' He explained that over the years many graduates of *Cryslis* had found it to be so. Together, they were a powerful force in the world.

Ahmed knew of only one graduate, his father, and for him, it was true enough. Jacq thought of four: her brother and parents and Erik's father, all highly successful people. She felt increasingly disturbed by the information.

'Have a look at the stability of the *Cryslis*,' the Principal continued. 'It always rests firmly on one of its triangles, perfect in balance and harmony. It reflects its environment and absorbs it into itself simultaneously. Those who live out the philosophy of *Cryslis* do likewise. They are always positively self-focused. Take in the world around them and set it to their purposes. Learn to do that and you will achieve your goals. To the benefit of yourself and others. Many graduates of *Cryslis* are bringing a wealth of riches to their chosen fields and to the peoples of the world.'

Hurray for *Cryslis*, Jacq thought cynically. Hurray for all the rich and powerful, so much needed and to be thankful for. She looked sideways at Ahmed in the row in front. His dark Indian face was set in stone. Jacq wondered what was going through his mind. Could this talk get any worse?

'You are here to become such achievers.' It was an obvious statement. Their parents would not have enrolled them for any other reason. Erik's smile didn't escape Jacq. Ahmed moved in his seat uncomfortably.

'You all know, that the shortest way between two points is a straight line. A focused worldview is such a line. How you decide the world to be. Your focus knows where it is going and how to get there. Again, let's have a look at the *Cryslis*.'

The Principal appeared to restrain himself from picking it up for that was strictly forbidden. Instead he looked at the darkly shining ornament intently.

'It is formed by six straight lines each of equal length and importance. They represent the six insights central to *Cryslis* philosophy. To how prosperity and wealth are created. This philosophy is spreading fast these days. Modernisation around the world always needs a *Cryslis* attitude to succeed. More and more countries now subscribe to that insight.'

Ahmed's thoughts had begun to wander. He was seriously questioning his ability to last the distance. The kind of indoctrination here would be difficult to take without adverse reactions. Not that the Principal meant any harm. He was obviously convinced of the wisdom he espoused. Ahmed wondered who else found it difficult. Jacq, perhaps, but that was just a guess.

The Principal pressed a key on his laptop and the *Cryslis* appeared on a large 3D screen. 'I will introduce you to our six fundamental beliefs,' he said.

Those were illustrated with some pictures of the cosmos. That cosmos indicates that these ideas are bigger than life, Jacq concluded scornfully.

CRYSLIS FUNDAMENTAL BELIEFS

- *Wealth is good.*

Without money nothing is accomplished.

- *Power is necessary.*

Without power there is no order.

- *Knowledge is science.*

Real knowledge comes from scientific enquiry.

- *Focus is central.*

Sufficient focus achieves great goals.

- *Failure is temporary*.

Failure is possible but need not last.

- *Success is Self*.

For success take yourself seriously.

The Principal next showed the guiding principle in one sentence.

Success is a functional dynamic to the top.

Jacq had a serious headache by now. If anything, she needed fresh air, some pain killers and a rest. Ahmed had studied the pictures of the universe. Much more interesting.

The mare enjoyed the freedom it was allowed. Ahmed had decided to let it find its way. The horse knew the grounds better than he. He smelled the sea mingled with the skin odour of his mount. A heady mix and just what was needed after this lecture. Fortunately, the academy was not in a city. Just imagine, *Cryslis* and the intensity that. Ahmed preferred open spaces with fresh air. Taking up riding had been good, better than expected. He was new to the horse but they seemed to get on well. She was a fine animal with more character than first thought. Ahmed put her into a canter at the bottom of a valley. The horse snorting with pleasure. It wasn't car racing, but good fun.

Up on the ridge another horse suddenly appeared in full gallop. Its rider was completely at ease urging her steed on. The brown high-spirited animal powered along. The sound of hoofs coming through the air over quite a distance. Ahmed gently reined in and sat looking at this display of horse and rider. It was Jacq, her blond hair blowing in the wind, free as freedom can be. It was a beautiful sight. Would have been so anywhere. Here in the hills of Jersey Island, it took Ahmed's breath away. Who is this girl? he wondered once again. His mare gave a whinny in recognition of her hard running friend in the distance.

Jacq had been encouraging the gelding with soft words clearly spoken. The horse had not been spurred on this hard for a long time, if ever. He took to it with all his might. Muscles were rippling at every point of his giant body. There was froth at the bit and the shine of sweat heavily on his coat. He would run for this rider whatever it took. Jacq knew him to be delighted. In her imagination the steady drumbeat of his gallop pulverised *Cryslis* into the sodden rocky ground. Hearing the mare Jacq pulled up and headed down into the valley where Ahmed sat quietly in the saddle. In passing Jacq shouted, 'Great, isn't it?' Those words seemed to drift in the air. Ahmed was unsure what she meant for her voice had an edge. Great, riding these horses? Or was it a sarcastic comment about *Cryslis*? Perhaps both. He hoped to find out one day.

***

An expensive jet landed on a private airstrip in the Australian desert. It adjusted to a hefty side wind. Once taxied in and coming to a standstill a single man disembarked. He was casually dressed suitable to an outback environment. The Director of Education stood waiting near the steps. He walked the man to a comfortable SUV. This flying visit occurred a few times per year and was announced only the day before arrival. The visiting man would spend some hours in the Temple. Then have a brief chat before flying out again. The Director hated those talks. No matter they only lasted a few minutes. Always the man seemed to look right through him. He was the senior figure of the Protectorate. Only once, at his appointment, had the Director met its three members. An experience he preferred to forget. All had been friendly, but with an authority of only the very rich.

During the short drive to the Temple the visitor remained silent. The rich man, as the Director called him privately, carried a mood of meditation. He would not be spoken to without his consent. During his visit it was essential to have complete silence at the Temple, no workmen or rangers in sight.

A text message asked for the Director a few hours later. The man was just inside the Temple entrance. There was no need for business talk. That was covered via the internet.

'You're troubled,' the man said.

It was no surprise to the Director that somehow he knew.

'You're correct. If anything strange happens, let me know immediately.'

After a faint nod of the head he walked back to his plane and soon was way up in the sky. It left the Director in a foul mood. He had been spoken to dismissively. Never mind his doctoral qualifications from the world's best universities. Or his experience in high management. He had been left with a few words that were of no help at all. Yes, you will know when something happens, he decided. But only once I have dealt with it.

CHAPTER 4

STUDENTS from all over Europe study at the *Cryslis* Academy. Lectures were in English on many topics with *Cryslis* philosophy subtly imbedded in each. The unit of study that lent itself particularly well to it was called Modern Worldviews. A study day began with assembly time reiterating what *Cryslis* believed in. In addition to a fixed curriculum students could select a few topics that were of personal interest. Students who disliked the narrow perspectives taken would find it extra difficult. The possibility of indoctrination was significant. *Cryslis* called this an excellent and effective education.

Jacq had settled into the routine and got to know a number of students better. None felt about their stay like she did. With the exception perhaps of Ahmed, but he never spoke of it. In fact, he had said very little on anything, thus far. Rather the quiet type, Jacq thought. Not that he would be empty headed. She knew that still waters might run deep. There would be more to him than met the eye. Jacq had noticed the way he looked at her on occasions. She knew not quite what to make of it. But then, she was always being looked at. It was the price you paid when attractive.

There would be no complaints from her on that score. She had to admit feeling a little empowered by that kind of attention. Fortunately, she was comfortable in her skin. In no need of responding unless she wanted to. Once, Jacq had talked it over with Ellie. They had decided it best to be on guard. The whole attraction thing was a trap. If looks were what gave you identity, you lived on a slippery slope. Becoming engrossed in your appearance and the effect it had on guys. Jacq didn't consider that her problem. Actually, right now, her problem was Erik.

She was on her way to the little harbour to mull matters over. Why the boats, she couldn't say. She had started on the path to the small inlet spontaneously. Erik, she concluded, was not to blame. But there was that subtle pressure between them. Jacq preferred it undiscussed. It just grated on her, having to deal with the Viking. She had enough emotional hassles with *Cryslis*. One day Erik would make his move, and why not? Their time together in Stockholm, just months ago, could not be wiped away. Jacq had no desire to hurt Erik, or to become involved again. The rules at the academy offered her no protection. *Cryslis*, as she had been told at assembly, was not against special friendships. Nice concept. There were boundaries in place for matters not get unwisely complicated. That meant, stupidly messy, Jacq had understood. The

Principal knew that a good number of couples over the years had met each other for the first time at the academy. As if Jacq didn't know. She herself was born of such a situation. Resolving the Erik problem might mean cold-shouldering him a little, Jacq reflected. It would create further difficulties. What would life be like with an angry Erik? No, she needed to be friendly, but firm. How their situation could last for two whole years without blowing up, she cared not to imagine. Before that thought began to depress her completely, Jacq arrived at the small harbour. She saw a dark figure sitting on a rock gazing out over the sea. She walked up quietly from behind. It was Ahmed.

'Sailing away, are you?' Jacq said tongue in cheek.

Ahmed turned his head. Recognising Jacq, he continued staring at the horizon.

'Thinking about it,' he admitted. If he could, he would sail away without hesitation. But it would not solve a thing. At home he had felt alone, but with plenty opportunity for distraction. Here he was alone with nowhere to go. Returning home would mean disaster. His parents in total disbelief. He knew that if he left *Cryslis*, his life would never again be carefree. Always, he had pursued most of what he desired. Allowed as long as his school results were first class. And his activities did not interfere with his parents' plans and lifestyle.

Jacq dumped herself on a rock nearby and stared out over the sea as well. They sat in silence together.

'It's that bad, is it?' she probed softly.

'Yep.'

This young Indian was a man of few words. Jacq had wondered about him and *Cryslis*. Sitting on a rock seemed a good time to find out. Perhaps she wasn't the only one at loggerheads with the whole affair.

'What happened?' she asked.

At first there was no response.

'Sorry,' Jacq apologised. Probably Ahmed wished to be left alone with his thoughts.

She began to get up, which shook him out of his dark reflections. He had never really spoken with Jacq at length. Hoped that one day he might. Something about her struck a chord and it was not just her looks. He knew a number of beautiful girls quite well at home and in India. Jacq seemed different.

Ahmed looked at her and smiled ruefully. His eyes were smouldering. 'I'm being rude,' he offered. 'Sorry. It's just that, I'm angry.' That was more of a confession than he would have made to most people.

Jacq nodded and remained silent. If pressed she would admit that she was actually sort of perpetually angry herself these days. She had kept it concealed below consciousness. Rather than noticeable anger she tended to experience a deep discontent. About lots of things, that she felt were generally unfair. Not to her personally, for she had nothing to complain about. Apart from this stupid academy. Her discontent was a broader issue, which she would have difficulty in explaining.

'The Principal invited me into his office. For a word of encouragement,' Ahmed said disgustedly. A subtle dressing down had been closer to the truth. That was how it had felt and the reason for him sitting on this rock.

'How come?' Jacq's attention was arrested.

'I glued a picture of a Porsche into the frame that shows the *Cryslis*,' he explained.

In every room a *Cryslis* picture hangs on the wall. Ahmed resented it and covered it over.

'That, together with my low marks in Modern Worldviews, got me the request for a chat.'

The staff might have reported on his lack of enthusiasm for the academy overall as well.

'Oh my god!' said Jacq, her eyes widening.

'I've been instructed to have special time with the Mentor,' Ahmed continued glumly.

The Mentor had been introduced at assembly as the person students should approach when finding things difficult. He was the school counsellor. A well-qualified psychologist in fact, who taught human sciences. The psychology of success and deal-making were two of the topics he lectured on.

'How did they find out?'

'The cleaner, I suppose,' Ahmed suggested. No one else had been in his room.

'I've stuck my friend Ellie over the *Cryslis*,' Jacq said alarmed. 'What did you tell the Principal?'

'Not much. He wasn't unfriendly and did most of the talking. It was all very subtle. I can't say any malice was intended, but he made his point. The *Cryslis* must never be covered over, not even its picture. He would also know I'm not happy here. Thus, the Mentor.'

'I will be up for the Mentor as well,' Jacq said with apprehension. She had not tried to adjust successfully either. 'At least that makes two of us. You'll have company.'

Ahmed raised his eyebrows in concern. But it was good news. In his struggles he was not altogether alone.

Jacq had found her answer. Ahmed must be feeling like her about being here. How much of a help that would be, remained to be seen.

An assigned time with the Mentor came about as Jacq had foreseen. The Principal invited her for a talk in his spacious office. There were small sculptures in various places. A man of culture was projected throughout the room.

'Jacq,' he had started in a friendly tone, 'please, make yourself comfortable. I just thought we ought to have a chat.'

Jacq nodded her head.

'I'm not sure that you have adjusted to our academy in ways that will benefit you most. Some students find it difficult to settle in. Perhaps we can help.'

They were sitting in easy chairs. The Principal smartly dressed as always. Jacq avoided looking at him. She kept her eyes at shoe level and said nothing. His shoes were handmade and boring.

'Many students, who did not settle in well at first, came to enjoy their time here,' the Principal continued encouragingly. 'They began to appreciate their studies better as well.'

That would refer to her poor attitude to Modern Worldviews, Jacq concluded.

'Perhaps it will help if you talked it over with someone who understands.'

Jacq nodded her head. She had decided not to make waves, at least not yet. Not that a choice was given her, about accepting the help on offer.

'I will have a talk with the Mentor, a nice man. I'm sure he can help resolve whatever is bothering you.'

'Thank you,' Jacq said, sensing a response was needed. How convincingly it sounded, she cared little about.

'My pleasure. I am always busy, of course. But my door is open to students at any time.' The Principal smiled warmly. He wasn't unkind. Just sold out on

Cryslis and had been for many years.

The interview ended. When they were standing the Principal made his final comment. 'It's excellent to have good friends.'

Jacq had wondered when the subject of Ellie would be raised.

'I wonder though whether you could find another frame for the photo you placed over the *Cryslis*?'

Jacq mumbled an apology. She would get a nice glass photo holder for Ellie. Had already taken the photo out. How could she ever have united her best friend with that piece of crystal anyway? The very thought now disgusted her.

Outside, Jacq found Ahmed waiting away from the main building. It was a gesture of support. Interest in how the interview went and how she was coping. Jacq liked it. She felt vulnerable. At *Cryslis* the cards were well and truly stacked against her.

Ahmed saw her furrowed brow and kept silent. Waiting for Jacq to speak. And so she did, without prompting. For a while words flowed freely as she vented her disgust, fuelled by impotency. Her anger left little to the imagination. She was fed up with the place. What it stood for and how she was being coerced into compliance. She had no idea what to fucking do about it but to grit her teeth. Two years here, she just didn't care to imagine it. May the whole place be bombed!

'I'm sorry,' she said, in the end running out of steam. 'I shouldn't bother you with this. It's not your problem.'

But it was. Jacq recognise that as soon as she spoke those words. Ahmed found himself in exactly the same position. She felt calmer now after giving free rein to her unhappiness. Some of the words she had uttered, surprised her. So what? It showed how deeply frustrated she was.

Being angry released in her a wonderful energy, Ahmed concluded. It was good to hear some coarse language. He would have used it too. He noticed Erik coming towards them and kept silent. Holding on to the memory of a furious Jacq. Erik had no skin in this. Any mention of meeting the Principal needed to end immediately.

'Here's Erik,' he said, with a sideways movement of his head.

Jacq turned around slowly and waited, trying to appear calm. Involuntarily, she took a deep breath.

Erik had no idea of her discomfort.

'I was thinking you might come along sailing,' he suggested somewhat gruffly. Annoyed at finding her with Ahmed. He had classified this Indian as a Musso. His discriminative word for Muslim. Not knowing that in fact Ahmed was a Hindu, at least his parents were. They took an easy approach to their religion. Being of a royal line in India they were considered specially blessed and merited anyway. Ahmed was named after his grandfather, whose parents had connections with Islam. Thus the Arabic nature of his first name.

'Not today.' Jacq was not in the mood for sailing.

'But you like sailing.'

'Sailing, yes,' Jacq said. She left the rest open to question. That was unfair. But Erik on a mission, right now – she wasn't game. All she wanted, was to be left alone.

'Come on, don't be like that.' Erik began to show his frustration. 'Perhaps Ahmed will come also.' He looked sideways at the dark Indian willing him not to accept. Erik was edgy. What on earth was making him defensive with Jacq? He hated being on the defensive, in anything. Particularly with girls.

'No thanks,' Ahmed responded archly. He felt uneasy with this young Swede. Intuitively he knew there was animosity between them.

'I am quite able to look after myself, if I want to,' Jacq retorted. 'I don't need Ahmed to keep the wolves at bay.'

This was crazy. With her combat skills she could handle Erik. But that idea was nuts, even thinking it. Erik was not nasty. Just a nuisance, particularly now. Jacq turned abruptly and walked off leaving the two guys standing. Ahmed simply looked at Erik without a word. The Swede stormed away in the opposite direction. Ahmed shrugged his shoulders.

The Mentor agreed to meeting with Jacq and Ahmed together rather than individually. It would relax them he had quietly decided and made for an excellent start. The arrangement might have to be changed in future for his research needed individual time with them as well.

The *Cryslis* Academy attracted only the very best of educators. The Mentor belonged to that echelon of achievers who are destined for success in their chosen field. The Academy was a perfect scenario for him. He had a three year contract and saw this time as an important stepping-stone. A handsome man in his early thirties, unencumbered by a wife and family, he found in *Cryslis* advantages in pursuing his academic writing. Even though the facilities for recreation were extensive and excellent, he left every fortnight for a weekend away to France. Just to keep my sanity, he told himself. His present interest was in young people. Their willingness to become seedbeds for ideas. *Cryslis* was perfect for that kind of investigation. Not that Ahmed or Jacq would ever know of this research. Neither would the staff at *Cryslis*. He never spoke of it on campus. The teachers themselves fell within his observations. He would publish those findings after his contract ended for not all was complementary. An article on youth might come sooner.

The Mentor looked at his two visitors keenly. He

concluded that maybe he had found what he was hoping for. Two students comfortably seated in his apartment, who strongly disagreed with *Cryslis*. They just need adjustment being away from home, the Principal had briefed him. But the Mentor sensed there was more to it.

Once they were settled, with cool drinks on the coffee table, he asked Ahmed and Jacq to tell about themselves. They were sitting side by side. Jacq nor Ahmed cared to disclose much. The conversation remained slow and superficial. If the Mentor became none the wiser that afternoon. Neither did they learn much about each other. There is no hurry, the Mentor decided. He did not press and stirred their emotions. Not this time.

Ahmed was looking at a model ultralight aircraft on the coffee table. The Mentor decided to disclose about himself. It was common counselling practice. He explained that his hobby was flying ultralights. Actually, he owned one. Ahmed nodded his head affirmatively without commenting. He considered the little plane as no more than wings and a lawnmower engine. Not his type of sport.

'Tell me about your parents,' the Mentor asked, aware that youth problems often originated from that relationship.

Jacq and Ahmed both gave a positive account of family circumstances, which their host did not fully accept. Further answers would be left for later. It was obvious that these two students had no dislike of their parents and that could be used as a stepping-stone towards adjustment at *Cryslis*.

'So, you have been well cared for,' he concluded. 'You have received a lot from your parents.'

Jacq and Ahmed could not deny that, nor would.

'But you don't wish to be like them?'

Few young people would. How deep that feeling sat with these two, again, was a matter for another time.

'No,' Jacq admitted.

Ahmed remained silent. He was well aware how this discussion was being guided and would gladly have walked away.

'Nobody here at *Cryslis* for a moment suggests that you shouldn't be your own person,' the Mentor continued. 'That is exactly what we desire for you. It is just that it is best achieved by the training at this academy. Your parents recognise that. I am sure they themselves would rather have you home. Perhaps, in response to their concern about your future, you might give your education here a positive try?'

Just what I thought, Jacq concluded. There is no escaping. This man is too clever not to be seemingly supportive. Friendly while being manipulative in the process. He was not interested in them as real people. His task was to make them conform. Intuitively she felt that strongly. Somewhere there was an agenda. She was in way over her head and worried.

After some insignificant pleasantries Ahmed and Jacq took their leave. With a next appointment a week later. They walked to their rooms in a sombre mood. The future looked bleak. The word survival was at the forefront of their thinking. The caring environment at *Cryslis* had a dark edge.

Ahmed decided to work a punching bag in the gym. He hammered himself into a mighty sweat close to exhaustion. One of the older boys asked if he could box. 'Yes,' grunted Ahmed as he swung his arms into the bag. Not right now though. A sparring partner, unless quite capable, might get badly hurt in Ahmed's present state of mind. He lacked the composure for a controlled fight.

A picture of Rugger flashed before his eyes. How long before he would see him again? It was true that over the years his contact with Rugger had been more significant than with his father. Ahmed was hurt about that. He hit the punching bag with his head in frustration before walking off to the showers.

Jacq felt in need of a friend. Nobody came to mind, though the girls here were friendly. There was no chemistry that could lead to real friendship. Not like with Ellie.

She considered whether to contact Ellie. Share her

problems. Jacq was reluctant to use her laptop for it used *Cryslis* internet facilities. Her messages might be intercepted. Whether that was so, she didn't know. Even her phone signal probably was relayed via the *Cryslis* communications tower. She had to be careful. Was it paranoia? Possibly. Jacq grabbed some tablets to ward off a headache and crashed down on her bed.

CHAPTER 5

EARLY ONE EVENING Jacq decided to spend time with her horse before visiting Mr Adams. The stable was warm, quiet and welcoming. The fine animal heaved its head and pressed his nose into her shoulder.

They had come to an understanding, Jacq and the horse. It had not taken long. He would not play tricks and she would give him the freedom he so desperately needed. To a point, that was. You couldn't reason that through with the gelding, but somehow he seemed to know. Jacq had named him Dappervoet. A Dutch name difficult to translate. It involved courage and the light, high stepping of the horse's natural gait.

'How are you, boy?' Jacq asked softly combing her fingers through his mane. She rubbed his nose with affection. 'Much better than I am, I bet.'

Dappervoet was about the only creature at the academy she felt safe talking. The horse shook its noble head as if resisting something. It had detected the sadness of his owner. 'We'll ride tomorrow,' Jacq promised him. 'You'll help me feel better.'

The only positive she could find at *Cryslis*, was this animal friend. She might ask her parents if they could ship him home after her stay here. That was a decision for later. It could wait.

The beauty and strength of the horse and the stable smell nearly brought Jacq to tears. She fought them back. Why were people and their forceful ideas so hard to deal with? Why couldn't things be simply beautiful? Like being here with Dappervoet? Jacq was convinced that the idea of finding true significance with a horse would never occur to anyone at *Cryslis*. They might admit to the possibility. But they would never really understand. Jacq took a deep breath and composed herself. It was time for her appointment with the stable manager.

Mr. Adams lived in a cottage adjacent to the stables. On Jacq knocking, he opened the door immediately. Ahmed had already arrived. Both the mare and the gelding needed to be shod. They had come to discuss new shoes for their horses.

The room was nice with a lot of exposed timber. Mr. Adams obviously had wider interests than caring for horses judging by all the books. One wall featured floor to ceiling shelves. Jacq and Ahmed sat quietly looking around while their host disappeared into the kitchen.

'The farrier is coming in a week's time,' he called out to them. 'I'll look after it, but you are welcome to see how it's done. I'll let you know when. Perhaps it will fit in with your study program.'

There was no reply to this suggestion as neither

Jacq nor Ahmed felt at ease calling back.

Mr. Adams was fit and healthy in his mid-fifties. Ahmed thought he could easily be director in one of his father's companies. He had that kind of presence. But then he also seemed suited to the care of animals. He was a fatherly figure. Ahmed and Jacq liked him. That he was perceptive became clear by the comment he made once three cups of steaming coffee had been placed on the low table between them.

'You two don't seem too happy here.' It was half a question, half a statement.

Jacq and Ahmed were taken aback. They looked at him carefully.

He smiled in response. 'You can trust me.' He took a sip of his coffee.

'I'm here for a particular reason and not part of the staff that keeps an eye on students.' An edge to his voice made the statement acceptable. He seemed annoyed at something.

Jacq had become very careful about anything related to her dislike of *Cryslis*. It showed on her face. Her outburst after visiting the Principal would be the final expression of her true feelings about the place. In future only Dappervoet was ever to hear any of it. As her situation could not be resolved anyway, why talk about it.

Ahmed felt less constrained. He began to slowly open up. With silent encouragement of Mr. Adams.

Obviously, he had not spoken to his horse, Jacq thought with wry amusement. Finding her sense of humour still intact was a positive.

'*Cryslis* boxes me in,' Ahmed said in the end. 'It's oppressive.'

'Like brainwashing,' Jacq added. It was her only contribution.

'It can do that,' Mr. Adams agreed. 'It probably tries to. That would be a problem to students who don't like a science only approach to life. If you have a mind that is not infatuated with goal setting and competencies. All designed to bring wealth and world domination.'

Ahmed and Jacq were speechless. They looked at Mr. Adams in disbelief. It was the first time anyone spoken out against the *Cryslis* philosophy.

The stable manager just smiled and shrugged his shoulders. 'I told you. I'm here for a reason. *Cryslis* is a poor substitute for the real thing.'

'What do you mean?' Ahmed had found his voice again.

'It will explain that later perhaps. All I would say now is that the *Cryslis* represents a very old story and not the most worthy part of it.'

Before they could ask further questions, Mr. Adams began to rummage in the top drawer of his desk and pulled out two sheets. He handed one each to Ahmed and Jacq.

'It's *The Myth of Shalomat*,' he explained. 'Please read it carefully and do come back in two days, in the evening. I must stress the utmost secrecy. If this gets out, I lose my job immediately. You dislike *Cryslis* and so do I. Perhaps we can solve that problem.'

Jacq and Ahmed accepted the handout. I should give it right back, Jacq thought. But she didn't, for some reason. They took their leave astounded at what they had just heard. Neither of them felt to talk about it. In silence they walked to their apartments. How weird was that? Jacq mused. Not at all sure she liked this new development. Ahmed had no thoughts left, really. Confusion reigned. Safely in their rooms both were taken aback when reading the myth from Mr. Adams. It spoke of *Cryslis*.

***

The Myth of Shalomat

In a cosmic realm the gods *Sophius* and *Igod*, were playing ball with two small spheres, one golden and the other dark crystal. They used ancient movements of gracious harmony. It was never clear whether the gods were playing the spheres or whether the spheres were playing the gods. It was a celestial game of intricate patterns and unpredictability. *Igod*, the darker god, secretly became annoyed. The spheres dictated him and envied their power. This discontent grew into a smouldering rage. Though it would take sinister courage to break this game of balance, and with dire consequences, it was what he planned.

The crystal sphere is the more beautiful, *Igod* felt. Its dark lustre intrigued him without end. One day he caught the glittering blur as it swerved past. It felt cool and smooth. Gripping the ball firmly he managed to hold it still. It needed all his spiritual strength. *Igod* shaped a small flat area onto the round crystal surface. The sphere had lost its perfection and movement. *Igod* began to shape a different form, not round but still perfect. The crystal sphere was ground down into a triangular pyramid with each of the four planes a 60 degrees triangle. It had power still but its dark beauty became a menacing force. *Igod* named his creation the *Cryslis*.

This initiative disturbed the whole cosmic realm. A destabilising influence had entered the spiritual world. The leading gods gathered to find a solution. They decided to take the *Cryslis* from *Igod* and throw it onto planet Earth. In future Earthlings would have to deal with its dark power. When the golden sphere named *Shalo* was found drifting in aimless futility, it also became destined for that planet. Neither *Cryslis* nor *Shalo* was very large, easily fitting into a human hand.

However, as the gods well knew, the size of an object was no measure to the force of its power. The spiritual would never be limited by the material.

The dark influences of *Cryslis* created an imbalance on Earth. But it needed not to last. Earthlings could fix the problem. The *Cryslis* would lose power. A riddle had to be solved on the day that the three planets of *Xrisis* fully aligned. And on that day only.

The Riddle of Shalomat

When triangle becomes circle and ripples are created from a symbol of halves will balance be restored through chaos.

Only the leading gods knew the secret of this riddle and the timing of the fateful day. For *Xrisis* was an obscure star in the cosmic realm.

Igod rejoiced that his power on Earth would be greatly increased. He had no idea what the riddle meant. It mattered little so long as it remained unfulfilled. There was just one problem. *Sophius,* the other god who had played the game, was deeply disturbed. He became fully dedicated to reining the power of *Cryslis* in.

***

It was Saturday, when Jacq took Dappervoet for a ride in the chill of the early morning. She had a wonderful time. The air was calm and crisp with a wisp of mist over the fields. The world was waking up to a new freshness, a new world. But the old would return soon. Her time with the horse, alone and free, was invigorating. It made Jacq happy. Inspiring energy surging through her bones. Dappervoet seemed to sense it. He was now well into a full-out gallop. The gelding never needed prompting. The sheer power of riding overwhelmed Jacq that morning. This is what to be born of the earth feels like, Jacq thought. To be truly real. Her spirit yearned for authenticity, for connectedness to a deeper significance.

She was in a good mood when making her way back for a shower. Nearly home, she bumped into Erik, who had been waiting.

'How about a sail, Jacq?' he asked. 'I need a crew.'

Erik the Viking looked so genuine and expectant that she had not the heart to say no. She agreed to meet him later. It promised to be a good day for boating, calm and mild. Sailing would not be an effort, Jacq decided. When handling the sails required little attention, there would be time for Erik to suggest other things. Not what she was looking for right now. She admonished herself. What was the harm in a bit of flirting?

In the event, her time with Erik turned out a pleasure. The wind stiffened and the boat gracefully climbed the waves. Erik was a first-class sailor. At a young age, he had joined a number of ocean races on his father's yacht. Sailing had been in his family's blood for generations. Once set on course they talked about home and the academy. Jacq never let on about her true feelings for *Cryslis*. She mostly let Erik do the talking and he seemed in need of it. He was not irritated by what *Cryslis* stood for. Erik was positive about all that. But it could still be a lonely time. Jacq was a good listener and felt sympathy for this friend. So handsome and so different from her. The sea brought out the very best in him, like with herself on Dappervoet.

When back on land they happened to stand close together. Eric kissed her briefly on the lips. It seemed right, and Jacq let him. She responded just a little. Their relationship could go beyond a good friendship, if that. A good friend is what she needed on this island, but without complications. Expecting Erik to fit that role was unfair. She could not blame him for wanting more than she was willing to give. Not here on this island she would give it. Not to anyone here.

After dinner that day, Ahmed approached her about *The Myth of Shalomat*. He seemed in a dark mood. Jacq began to detect another male problem. She was right. Ahmed had been trying to find her when someone told him Jacq was out sailing with Erik. That should not have annoyed him, but it did. Jacq was free to do as she saw fit. But the idea of her on a boat with Erik grated, even hours later. He tried hard not to be glum once catching her. Never having mastered the skill of hiding his moods, he failed dismally.

Ahmed's bearing flicked a switch in Jacq. It was all too much. After the first really good day at this academy, forgetting all her frustrations, she was now facing a downer with the brooding Indian she hardly knew. Give me a break, she thought. She told Ahmed in no uncertain words that she was not interested in that myth. She was not interested in anything right now beyond some peace and quiet - definitely not in his bad temper. She left him standing. Ahmed kicked himself for his sullenness that took hold too often. Definitely, *Cryslis* was making that much worse.

I've had enough of males and this whole *Cryslis* business, Jacq muttered to herself angrily. She got to her room and flopped onto the bed, tired and fed up. She decided to phone Ellie. Who cared if anyone spying at *Cryslis* was listening in. She pressed Ellie's contact number.

'Hi Ell!'

'Jacq, where have you been?' Ellie was pleased to have Jacq on the line. She had not heard from her for over a week.

Jacq apologised. *Cryslis* was to blame. Too much

on her mind to work through. 'How's Amsterdam?' she asked. That question brought the feeling of homesickness into sharp focus.

'Not at all the same without you,' Ellie replied despondently. 'But you know that.'

Ellie was great to talk to. Obviously, she missed Jacq, and it hurt. But she tried to hide it most of the time. Their conversations never became heavy. Jacq began to tell of her day. Having guy problems always made for an animated discussion. Ellie herself was trying to keep one at bay right now, someone Jacq knew. 'Don't even think about it,' she told her friend. 'He's trouble.'

Her own difficulties with Erik, and now Ahmed seemingly as well, were talked about at length. Ellie remembered the Viking. His presence at the academy, its unexpected surprise, had come up previously. And now there was Ahmed. Ellie was intrigued. Jacq was obviously annoyed. But she didn't sound as forcefully negative as with some guys in Amsterdam. Ellie asked for a picture of Ahmed. Jacq scoffed at the idea. Didn't have one.

'How's Dappervoet?' Ellie decided to change the conversation.

'Great! I love him,' Then Jacq added: 'The only male here that doesn't give me troubles. He's been neutered!'

Ellie cracked up laughing. That was the Jacq of

old. All had not been lost. They wished each other well and promised to get in touch again soon. Jacq felt better for having had a chat and really missed Ellie. Turning onto her stomach she pulled the pillow over her head and thought of home. No more shopping with mum for a while. That always had been fun besides being lucrative. Unfortunately, her father and mother, who loved her dearly, had no feeling for the arts. They were clever enough to distinguish excellent from second rate, but that was their limit. It never deeply grabbed them. Even if they could understand it and appreciated the need Jacq felt about acting, from their point of view it should still involve *Cryslis*. It was the best path toward success. Jacq groaned in utter frustration with a pain in her soul she could not put into words.

Most of the following day she spent in bed suffering from stomach cramps. When she got up to pour a drink from the fridge, she found a note pushed under her door. From Ahmed, and it was an apology. It surprised her, though she wondered why. Generally blokes never sent notes. He must have felt properly bad. It said no more than sorry. Still, that was enough. An old Beatle song about lonely people and where they all came from trundled through her to mind. Was it always going to be this hard? Jacq surely hoped not. She crawled back under her comfy blankets.

***

At midnight the Director received a call on his secure line. That could only mean one thing. With his head spinning from a quart bottle of whiskey he became instantly alert. It was essential to keep his voice steady and clear. He heard no 'hello', there never was. Just information and instructions.

'It has become clear now,' the crisp voice said. 'You will remember *Shalomat*. The three planets of *Xrisis* are soon to align. I don't know when, but step up security.'

The Director understood the ramifications for he knew of *Shalomat*. His whiskey brain mulled it over. He tried to overcome his annoyance about how he was treated. These calls always gave the idea of him being dispensable. It irked him greatly.

What was he supposed to do? Fight shadows? Beefing up security was easy. Or not really, for it was already tight enough. And where was the danger anyway. The riddle was a mystery, complicated and unlikely to be solved. *Cryslis* had never really been challenged ever. Nobody seemed to know where that little golden sphere called *Shalo* was. Its presence might just be an illusion. Though it was true that the *Crislis* had actually been found on Earth. Whether that discovery had been pure luck or by some mysterious design was open to debate. That the power of *Cryslis* could be overthrown now it had spread around the world, he very much doubted. Riddle or not. He could not ignore the unrest in his spirit though. Perhaps that had to do with how the rich man treated him. It definitely was getting worse. Or were those unknown events he was to guard against getting him down? The Director poured out a fresh three fingers and took a large gulp of whiskey. His job, that had looked so promising, was turning into a mess.

CHAPTER 6

IN THE EVENING DARKNESS Jacq slid down and doubled over on an outside bench. She was holding her stomach with her arms, felt sick and cramped up. She should have stayed in bed and would have. If she had known about this evening with Mr. Adams. How it turned out.

Ahmed stood nearby completely at a loss. He had no idea what to do.

'Just leave me,' Jacq mumbled. 'I'll be okay.'

Don't ever say the word *Shalomat*, she thought. For that's why she felt so gutted. The ridiculous and infuriating nonsense of it all. Or perhaps it made sense. She couldn't care to consider that idea right now. Not that Ahmed would discuss it, here in the dark. He was too stunned and disturbed himself.

They had visited Mr. Adams as arranged. Jacq did not cancel though it had been tempting. They were made to feel welcome, once again. Ahmed had already arrived and looked a little awkward when she entered the room. Her fiery outburst roamed still through his mind. Jacq's warm smile soon set him at ease. He was taken with this gritty girl and returned her smile. After a few pleasantries and chatting about care of the horses, Mr. Adams changed the conversation.

'If you race a car,' he said, 'and would like to go with optimum speed around the track, there is only one way. You will have to follow the preferred racing line. It ensures the most effective racing.'

Ahmed's attention was immediately drawn. What did this man know? Or was it pure coincidence? He had told no-one here of his favourite sport. It felt strange.

'It is the most insular way of getting around. You are highly concentrated and won't notice the first thing about the scenery. That is not your purpose.'

Neither Ahmed nor Jacq responded, waiting for what was to come.

'Have you read that story, the myth of *Shalomat*?' Mr. Adams asked.

They both nodded. It was an intriguing story, though far-fetched.

'You might say that *Cryslis* takes a racing approach towards life. Be linear, self-focused and achieve your goals through purpose and training. Make sure you use up-to-date technology. And have your car tuned to perfection. Then, you can be very fast and superior. It's rather admirable, really.'

Ahmed thought about his Porsche with a pang of regret. That sensation of the thrust of power in his back. He could almost feel it for real! But where was this talk leading?

'When this insular idea about human existence dictates the best way forward for everyone, that's when the trouble begins.' Mr. Adams sipped his tea and took his time. That summed up *Cryslis* pretty well, Jacq thought.

The conversation continued.

'This approach to life and knowledge is very effective in its limited way. It is also attractive for it offers wealth and success to those who follow it. A large part of the world now applies *Cryslis* thinking. Soon it will have subdued almost everything. Much to the detriment of other fruitful ways in which to enjoy life.' Mr. Adams let those words sink in. Both Ahmed and Jacq had narrowed their eyes and were on guard.

'Once entrenched in society as the way forward, *Cryslis* philosophy discourages all further enquiry. About what it might mean to be human. People feel they have no need of it. Even if they are attracted to non-practical ideas, the more artistic side of life, it is in an ego-centric way. All centres on what *they* might achieve. In doing so, humanity is losing an important part of its soul.'

'Can you explain that?' Ahmed asked carefully.

'I will. A detailed understanding of the problem requires a lot of discussion but the basics are not that difficult.' Mr. Adams collected his thoughts. 'Perhaps we should get back to car racing for a moment.'

'The road guides you through scenery but you

don't see it much. The experience of speed brings enjoyment to your soul but only of a certain kind. Take a pushbike and that road will be so different. Your soul will be fed differently as well. A pushbike may be slow. But very rewarding in its own way.'

'*Cryslis* doesn't believe in pushbikes,' Jacq said, briefly thinking of her own in Amsterdam.

'Exactly,' said Mr. Adams. 'And if society mostly prefers racing around and enjoys it, life will become one-dimensional and shallow. For instance. You will never be a good actor, if you never ride a pushbike.'

That jolted Jacq. Was it a coincidence or what? This actor comment.

'There is a place for racing,' Ahmed mumbled to himself. He disliked pushbikes. His remark wasn't meant to be noticed, but Mr. Adams took it up.

'The principles of *Cryslis* in themselves are not wrong. In fact, they can do a lot of good. When they become an end in themselves problems will arise. Or when used for negative purposes, like the domination of others.'

Like sending me here, to *Cryslis*. Jacq regretted the thought immediately, but that was how it felt. Mr. Adams got up on his feet and disappeared into the kitchen.

Jacq wished for the meeting to end. This conversation was heavy going. She shouldn't have come. All that

Cryslis stuff, and what for? She was apprehensive and briefly glanced at Ahmed. He raised his eyebrows. Shrugged his shoulders.

'You don't look well,' he said. 'I didn't see you around today.'

Jacq nodded her head. 'Yeah, thanks. I'm okay. Feeling better after a day in bed.'

Ahmed was the first person for a long time, apart from Ellie, to show interest in how she was. And he seemed sincere.

'I'm okay. Fine,' Jacq lied. She felt vulnerable.

'I will make one more observation and then we can close. Well almost,' Mr. Adams said while placing fresh drinks before them. 'Thanks for hearing me out.'

Neither Ahmed nor Jacq responded.

'Where will a mostly mechanical approach to life and success lead us unless challenged? What about qualities like common sense and intuition? About imagination, for instance? All very important. Good use has been made of these legitimate ways of gaining knowledge for thousands of years. In a mostly *Cryslis* dominated society there will be plenty entertainment. But little real feel for the arts. With religion downgraded to a sideshow. Cultures will be decimated around the world. With nature exploited solely for the purposes of wealth. Lip service will be given to preventing such matters. With just enough positive action to keep the concerned troops pacified.'

Mr. Adams had just summed up what Jacq and Ahmed instinctively felt to be their problem with the world.

'Now, this is what you must understand.' Mr. Adams paused and looked at his guests. They seemed to relate to his comments, though it confused them. What he was to say next would add to it.

'The point is,' he emphasised, 'there are cosmic reasons behind all this!'

The silence was deafening. Cosmic reasons, what on earth was this man talking about?

'Surely, it can't be *Shalomat*?' Ahmed suggested hesitantly. He had wondered about this talk and that myth. After all, it was the reason for their visit.

'It's just a myth,' Jacq grunted. A nice story but dubious. Admittedly, *Cryslis* got its name from it.

'There is always truth about human life imbedded in any myth,' Mr. Adams said. 'That's what makes it a myth. It reflects reality in some way.'

'You mean this myth is sort of for real?' Ahmed asked incredulously. 'The *Cryslis* is opposed by Shalo?' At least, that's how the myth ended. But so what? It was just an interesting story.

A very perceptive comment, Mr. Adams thought and was pleased.

'Oh no,' muttered Jacq as if in pain. She had a crazy notion about this discussion. Didn't like it one bit. She now sat bent over with both arms across her stomach.

Ahmed looked at her alarmed.

Mr. Adams ignored her protestation.

'You're right,' he replied to Ahmed's question. 'This myth is for real, very much so. It is more real and active than a myth usually would be. *Shalomat* is working itself out in detail. You can sense that once you get to the original *Cryslis*.'

'In the Temple, you mean?' Jacq straightened up. This really was getting weird. A truly cosmic *Cryslis*.

'Yes. There you will experience the original *Cryslis* and its power. But the scope of what's at stake reaches far beyond the Temple.'

Mr. Adams went on to explain that the power of *Shalo* needed to be better expressed in the world. Otherwise, people would be destined to a very poor psycho-spiritual life. *Shalo*'s counterpunch was soon to come. On the day that the three planets of *Xrisis* align perfectly. As foretold in the myth. Nothing, however, was guaranteed.

Jacq and Ahmed were completely speechless. Why this information? Jacq wondered so less than Ahmed. She was becoming seriously cheesed off and also concerned. Mr. Adams seemed to find the whole situation rather non-exceptional.

He continued his explanation. The secrets of *Shalomat* must be unlocked. The Riddle is the key. On the Day of the Planets it must be fulfilled. That should happen. But it required people. Human are to solve the riddle's mystery. The right people, of course.

God help me, Jacq thought. Surely, it was a joke.

Mr. Adams concluded his explanation.

'*Cryslis* insists that success is a functional dynamic to the top. *Shalo* is very different. It has no simple core statement of belief. It is not linear, has no sharp edges or points. It doesn't cut and divide, and create a rat-race. Rather, it brings harmony and wellbeing to people and societies. In its fullness it will unite art, language, the sciences and spirituality. It can unite cultures too.'

It was a passionate statement. A heavy silence pervaded the room. Mr. Adams looked away from the two young people before him and at his hands. He was a kind man, who knew his task. He liked these two and preferred not to think of what might be ahead.

Mr. Adams reminded him of a preacher man, Ahmed thought. 'You sound as if there is a force at work here greater than human nature,' he said. 'Like in the myth.'

'Absolutely. I know there are forces at work here beyond merely human nature and ingenuity.'

In confused disbelief, Ahmed had no idea what to make of that.

'Who are you?' Jacq wished to know and asked it none too friendly.

'I represent *Sophius*.' The response was firmly

spoken without a hint of an apology.

Ahmed was astounded but had not yet cottoned on like Jacq. Mentally, she was now trying to escape from this room. Faintly heard the horses in the stable. The only one to trust at this weird academy is Dappervoet, she thought.

'The world is in the power of *Cryslis* and that must change,' Mr. Adams reiterated. 'It is possible for the Day of the Riddle is near.'

'How?' Jacq found courage to ask this dreaded question for she knew the answer.

It hit Ahmed in the chest like a swift punch from Rugger.

'You two can change it, if you want to. Solve the Riddle,' Mr. Adams suggested.

Ahmed was stunned. 'No way,' he retorted. He jumped up from his chair in alarm. This was crazy stuff.

Jacq just sat motionless, clenching her jaws till it hurt. She felt completely arrested. There was no clear reason for it, but in her spirit she had been cornered. That was how it felt. By a cosmic dynamic perhaps, if you believed in that kind of thing.

'How?' she managed to ask for a second time hardly being able to speak.

'That will be revealed progressively,' Mr. Adams responded kindly. He noticed that Jacq looked angry and exhausted. It was unsurprising. 'The first step is for you to get to the Temple of *Cryslis* in Australia.'

'But you have to be invited for that trip. Do very well in *Cryslis* philosophy,' Ahmed objected.

Mr. Adams shrugged his shoulders. 'Get invited then,' he suggested, with a smile and total seriousness. 'You're both more than capable of that.'

'So, it's up to us,' Jacq said. 'And we can refuse?'

No answer, simply a next shrug of the shoulders.

'It is just nuts,' Ahmed objected forcefully, now deeply disturbed as well.

They left the stables silently walking together, until Jacq collapsed on that bench.

CHAPTER 7

THE TEMPLE DINNER was an illustrious event. Only staff and students leaving for the *Cryslis* Temple in Australia were invited. Jacq and Ahmed had applied themselves and made the grade, though with difficulty at times. Working undercover put an edge on life. That was how they both felt. They were at the dinner under false pretences. Hopefully for a good cause. It all seemed quite unreal. Ever since deciding to take on *Shalomat*, nothing had happened in giving them an idea that this mission actually existed. All they had done was to hide their aversion to *Cryslis* principles. Act as if they were true believers. It had been a strain and better be worth it, Jacq thought. She was seated next to Erik at the expensively dressed table.

After their meeting with the Mr. Adams, about four months ago, they had not known what to do. The whole situation was surreal. They had let the dust settle. After a few days normality returned. Ahmed was sceptical but intrigued. Against her wish Jacq felt intuitively that the challenge should not be ignored. Never mind it being farfetched. But they were both thoroughly confused. It drew them together a few times in discussion. Jacq noticed Erik was becoming jealous. She took pains to see it avoided. With the staff they made sure not to draw attention to themselves by behaving secretively.

Ahmed and Jacq were out horse riding for a good final talk. She felt better by then, not so tense. After that fateful evening Jacq had spent another day in bed. Had no energy to face people let alone lectures. A myriad of emotions had surged through her soul. The seeming inevitability of it all was the most disturbing. The idea of having to rescue the world from *Cryslis*, it seemed utterly ridiculous. Finally, her emotions had run out of force like a wave upon a beach. She fell into a deep sleep. Matters improved from then on. Now a week later, they sat on an old log well away from the campus. To have their decisive discussion. The horses were tied to a fence.

'We must make up our minds, once and for all,' Ahmed decided. 'Or the matter will never be resolved.'

Jacq couldn't agree more. 'It's really quite simple,' she said.

'You mean we do, or don't, go to Australia?'

'Yes, there's that. Who knows what will happen once we are there. That is, if we do go!'

Jacq felt a great deal would happen. She wasn't at all sure she liked that idea.

'So, what do you suggest?' Being at *Cryslis* with quite a different motive from the ordinary appealed to

Ahmed. So much better than his present situation. He would get some of his own back.

'I've actually always wanted to go to Australia,' Jacq admitted, side-tracking the issue for a moment.

'So have I. But not really in this way.'

'Okay,' Jacq firmly concluded. 'I am no saviour of the world. But it seems in a mess and is getting no better. It is very sad. We have to decide whether to take up the challenge of that riddle. Even if we don't know what it involves. The motivation that makes us commit is quite simple. Do we hate *Cryslis* enough? Will we try and do something about it? If we want to, then we must accept Mr. Adams' story. However strange it is. See whether we can make a difference. Somehow. Even if we don't like the circumstances we may find ourselves in.'

'I hate the place,' Ahmed grunted with a passion.

'So do I,' Jacq agreed.

These last few days she had begun to sense an intangible dark purpose behind the business of *Cryslis*. She doubted even the staff at the academy were aware of it. Perhaps it was just her imagination.

'All we have to do right now is making the grade and to be invited to Australia,' she said. 'I can manage that, if I wanted to.'

'So can I,' Ahmed had to admit. 'It might mean selling part of my soul though.'

'That's two souls then for the price of one,' Jacq

agreed. 'No, that is nonsense. Just keep our souls out of it,'

Jacq had no intention of being brainwashed. It need not happen. *Cryslis* principles were not that difficult to master. At home she had lived with them for years. The whole thing was part of human nature anyhow. It just was the part she was less enchanted with.

Ahmed sensed that the matter had been decided and he was right. 'Anyway,' he suggested, 'we can always opt out if need be. Also, we won't be in any danger, here at this academy. Nobody knows what we are about, except Mr. Adams.'

'Sure. But I don't intend opting out,' Jacq retorted. 'Otherwise I won't start.'

'Okay, if ever there comes a point of giving up, it will be by mutual agreement. Having a real talk about it first,' Ahmed said.

Jacq could see the wisdom of that.

'Do we now have to cut ourselves and mix blood?' she asked with a smile.

Ahmed extended his hand and she shook it. He had a solid grip and held on for a few seconds. It may well be the most important handshake ever given her, Jacq thought wryly. A premonition conveyed exactly that. Ahmed let go reluctantly and walked off to his horse. He would have gladly grabbed the whole of her in a firm embrace.

From that day on their grades improved. They worked hard and handed up their assignments on time. Soon sessions with the Mentor stopped. It quite surprised him. Psychologically speaking, it was unexpected unless there were hidden factors in play. But he couldn't deny their progress. The Principal was delighted. He felt vindicated in his assessment that given time they would adjust and settle down. Ahmed's anger began to subside, while Jacq kept her personal feelings mostly at bay. Not much else changed but for Ahmed and Jacq no longer kicking against the pricks. Mr. Adams never mentioned that strange evening again. When they told him of their decision he was pleased. All he asked was to make sure to visit him just before flying off to Australia. Should they qualify.

In the end, the invitation to visit the Temple of *Cryslis* had come to both of them. Their parents were so proud, they would have paid for the journey twice over. Jacq and Ahmed had achieved stage one of their mission. Going on an overseas adventure that was a mystery.   Not much had changed between them. Except that Ahmed had not ever been moody with Jacq again.

The dinner, as expected at *Cryslis*, was tops. Everyone was enjoying the fabulous food in anticipation of a journey to the Australian desert. The Temple of *Cryslis* was situated near Alice Springs at the centre of that continent. The students would stay at Alice for two weeks and fly home via Frankfurt. For another two weeks of holidays with their parents. There were twelve student and two staff. The woman in charge of Business Studies and the Mentor. He was group leader. He secretly hoped to fly an ultralight above the red sands of the outback.

The Principal tapped his crystal wineglass with a dessertspoon. Nothing loud, but quietness quickly settled.

'This,' he said, 'is a very special occasion that only happens every two years.' He looked around proud of making that announcement.

'You, who are invited to the Temple of *Cryslis*, are fortunate indeed. Of course, you have very much earned the invitation and are to be commended for that. Well done.'

'Hear, hear,' a staff member exclaimed and clapped the students.

'I remember my own journey to the Temple well,' the Principal continued. 'Quite some years ago now. Not in Australia but in South America. The biggest spiders I have ever seen.'

The comment brought some laughter, which was acknowledged with a smile. 'Rather an experience that visit,' the Principal admitted. He took a sip from a glass of water. Perfectly done in full composure. He obviously enjoyed making speeches.

'As you know, at our Academy we have a *Cryslis* that has been near the original for exactly one year. It is here just behind me. Very beautiful and enchanting. It emanates a kind of power that is difficult to define. Let me tell you though that this power here is only a faint representation of the original *Cryslis*. Once you have seen and experienced that, you will not quickly forget.'

The Principal stopped and savoured the memory.

'So, make the most of this opportunity. You are not on a study trip, though there may be a lecture or two at the office near the Temple. Mostly, you will be on holidays and deservedly so. You might consider your journey in part a pilgrimage. Although there is nothing remotely religious about your visit. At *Cryslis* we believe in the power inherent in all people. Power to investigate, to understand and to succeed. It is not some sort of supernatural quest. Power is simply energy round about us and in us. The original *Cryslis* radiates this reality more noticeably than anything I have ever come across.'

The Principal cleared his throat and paused. He had come to the end of his speech but for an award to confer.

'Always, when a group like yours is invited to the Temple there is an award in recognition of excellent scholarship and attitude.'

The students sharpened their attention. No one had ever said anything about an award.

'This is a surprise, I know. It's meant to be. We would not want you to have consciously worked for it. It belongs to the student who spontaneously achieved it.' There was a real expectancy in the room now. Who would be that student?

'It is now my pleasure,' the Principal announced, stopping briefly to heighten the tension, 'to bestow this award upon ....' He glanced quickly over every student's face: 'Upon Erik.'

A surprised Erik got up from his seat to loud applause. His grin said everything. Well done, Jacq thought. Glad it wasn't her. Imagine getting that while being undercover. It would make her feel even more hypocritical than the usual. That was bad enough. Ahmed clapped because he had to. Made some appreciative noises, not caring for any of it.

When Erik made his way back to the table Jacq was genuinely happy for him. He showed her his award with some intimacy. Erik was pleased and why not? Jacq's smile, while looking absolutely stunning, made him feel a sting of regret. How could he ever bring back those days in Stockholm? When Jacq had so freely flung her arms around him.

The dinner continued. Everyone seemed to have a good time.

'Let's go,' Ahmed urged Jacq while the guests were breaking up. 'We need to say farewell to our horses and

Mr. Adams.' Ahmed saw that Erik had been cornered by a staff member. He couldn't seek Jacq's attention. Jacq noticed the same. She would have liked to spend more time congratulating him, but Ahmed had a point. They needed to get to the stables. Their transport would arrive tomorrow morning early. She couldn't leave without a goodbye to Dappervoet.

Quickly Jacq and Ahmed slipped away to the stables. Jacq would miss her horse even though she was to be back in four weeks. At least, that was the plan. A second sense seemed to tell her otherwise. Ahmed also felt his mare deserved a farewell. It was a good horse. She had made life at the campus much more bearable.

While they were taking leave of their horses, Mr. Adams joined them. He didn't say much besides warmly wishing them well. He assured them that their animals would be well looked after. Not that Jacq and Ahmed had ever doubted it. Then he handed them a little notebook and a key. 'Take that wherever you go,' he urged them. 'Make sure you don't lose it. They are central to the success of your mission. Don't forget to look in the notebook regularly.'

Ahmed and Jacq were a little taken aback. They had only recently discussed the possibility that their *Shalomat* adventure might be mostly imaginary. That what they were involved in was no more than a hoax. They didn't really believe that. But to what extent was the challenge actually real? Life had continued in its normal way. The whole thing was confusing. If all came to naught, at least they were going to Australia. Now that Mr. Adams was handing them these two items, their *Shalomat* mission came sharply back into focus. There was obviously a plan. Even if they were not privy to it.

Apprehension showed on their faces. Mr. Adams smiled with encouragement. 'Don't ever doubt,' were his final words. 'Don't ever, ever doubt.' He said them with absolute surety and it clearly held a warning.

The notebook was only little. It easily fitted into the pocket of their jeans together with the key. On the way back to their rooms Jacq suggested they open it and have a look. Ahmed did, wondering what they were to find. On the first page it read:

When triangle becomes circle, and ripples are created from a symbol of halves, will balance be restored through chaos.

***

The Director was utterly frustrated. The threat he was fighting was like a fog. Without shape or direction. He had increased the security around the Temple months ago. The Rangers were warned to be extra watchful for anything extra ordinary. He knew they were slacking off now and could hardly blame them. Every day all seemed completely normal. So what about that Riddle and the Day of the Planets? When would that day be? He was told it was near and nothing else. A great help, that was. The rich man, who recently had paid another short visit, had no idea either. Look out for the unusual, he had been told again. Could an instruction be any vaguer?

An internet search produced not one mention of the star *Xrisis*, let alone its planets. With trillions of stars in the cosmos and most of those invisible to even the finest instruments, that was no surprise. *Xrisis* might not even exists. But the Director doubted that. Somehow he sensed the thread to be directed against the actual *Cryslis* itself. Hiding the ornament for protection was neither possible nor necessary. Only a fool would touch it. Its surface burned like napalm. When the *Cryslis* was to be transported to the next continent, after twenty years, they simply closed the marble sides of the box it resided in. Presently, its base was firmly anchored down. Surely, the *Cryslis* was safe enough.

So where to look for the enemy? What was to happen? Again, he checked the list of future arrivals at the Temple and could find nothing even slightly disturbing. There were some students due from Jersey Island. All of them high achievers sold out on *Cryslis* philosophy. It had qualified them for their visit. The Director filled his lungs deeply and exhaled as if blowing out steam. When you gave a man a job, give him something to work with. He had no idea how to proceed. This was shaping into a possibly major stuff-up.

CHAPTER 8

THE LONG FLIGHT was uneventful. Once well in over Australia Ahmed saw the red earth of the interior spreading out as far as the eye could see. It seemed a desolate place of distinct beauty. The sky at sunrise reflected wonderful colours of red, pale blue and a greenish tint. Later on he was to recognise this stunning beauty in paintings by Australian artists. Already, from high up in the stratosphere, this land began to enchant him.

A few rows further forward Erik and Jacq sat together. Jacq too was peering out of the window. She moved back so that Erik could view the panorama below. Her feelings were drawn to this country she had never set foot in. The attraction was coming from deep within without particular reason. Being from Holland, where millions of people spread themselves across relatively few square miles, the uninhabited space below held a real fascination. As if somehow it would allow for an extension of spirit she would never find at home. This feeling was partly spoiled by a sense of foreboding.

Ahmed felt the little notebook and key inside his pocket pressing against his leg. What could be the purpose of these two objects? It was a mystery waiting to be revealed. He wondered once again what they had got themselves into. As far as he was concerned, it was great that it involved Jacq and Australia. These thoughts were interrupted by the seatbelt sign coming on. They were starting a long descent into Adelaide curving in over the sea. It was early morning.

Adelaide was a one-night stay. Tomorrow they would fly to Alice Springs, the only town in the central Australia. At Adelaide Airport custom officials used sniffer dogs. After a long flight the students were weary and impatient to get into the sunshine. Once under the clear blue sky excitement soon expelled their weariness. They waited for the courtesy bus to take them into the Adelaide CBD, a short drive away.

On Jersey Island, they had pored over the Lonely Planet guide and learned that Adelaide was not that large, about a million people. It had an international airport because of the sheer size of Australia where significant population centres were far apart and mostly on the coast. Though Adelaide, in South Australia, was situated on the south of the continent, its sea front and beaches faced west. The city spread along on the east side of a large bay and was known for its spectacular sunsets over the water.

They were unlikely to see one of those from their hotel though. It was away from the coast and close to the central railway station, casino and city mall. Jacq wouldn't mind some shopping, but it could wait. Ahmed knew that his phone had international roaming but needed to make sure about GPS and connectivity in such a large continent.

After settling in and a welcome shower, the students discussed how to best spend the day might. They were eager to visit a beach. The hotel advised to take the tram to Glenelg. It offered beach volleyball, lots of eateries, and also shopping on Jetty Road. Going shopping excited neither Erik nor Ahmed. But the beach and food would suit them fine.

It took a half hour ride on a modern tram through residential areas. Looking through the tinted windows Jacq recognised some European flora amongst mostly Australian trees and bushes. There was little in the way of high-rise buildings, at least by European standards, until arriving in Glenelg. Many homes had, what seemed to her, sizeable yards.

Glenelg was small, mostly one long shopping street, but the beach stretched along the coast for miles. A pleasant place on a warm day. After their lunch, taken on wooden benches and tables in the main square, the Mentor decided the group should split up into pairs. Meet again at the jetty later. Jacq preferred Erik for company rather than Ahmed. She would have liked to avoid either, but that was not possible. Erik's presence seemed less complicated.

Without shared secrets about myths and riddles. Ahmed snuck away alone and found a shop where he could ask about his phone.

Adelaide is home to a large ship building complex where Swedish designed submarines were once constructed for the Australian Navy. Friends of Erik's family worked there in a maintenance project. They had arranged to pick him up for dinner. The other students decided to visit a cinema nearby. A movie would be welcome entertainment.

Jacq had enjoyed the day. She was keen for more fun than just the cinema after her long isolation on Jersey. Adelaide certainly was not Amsterdam. But there were enough people about in the streets. She sensed things were happening. City energy with its liveliness and music. Also sex, she imagined. On her way back to the hotel Jacq was a long way from falling asleep. She was restless, not ready to end the day, and pulled Ahmed aside. 'Do you want to sneak out again?' Anything for an extra dose of city, she thought.

Ahmed needed no persuading. He would happily stay up all night in the company of Jacq. The day taking a turn for the better. Obviously, Erik was out of the picture. Jacq had avoided Ahmed in Glenelg and though he understood why, it had grated. In the cinema they had sat together, which mattered little. Jacq's body language was all wrong. She badly needed her own space. The suggestion now to slip out for some nightlife was a surprise. They agreed to leave separately, through the restaurant door of the hotel rather than the lobby. They would meet on the corner nearby. The Mentor had set a curfew for the evening. He might have asked reception to keep an eye out for his pupils. It seemed unlikely, but why take a chance.

Whether because of the different time zone, or the considerable stress of the last few months, Jacq was feeling decidedly blue. She was eager for quality human contact. It was difficult to put explain. She had wondered about Ahmed lately and wished to know him better. After all, they were partners in a task that could be very difficult. They soon found a busy venue where they could sit at the back. Just in case the Mentor had planned himself a night on the town and walked by. Jacq ordered a lime soda. Ahmed an iced coffee.

'I wonder where all this *Cryslis* stuff is going,' Ahmed said. They were seated across each other.

'Same. Who knows?' Jacq sipped her drink. This was not at all what she had in mind. 'Let's drop that for now,' she suggested, with a faint edge to her voice.

Ahmed looked up and got the message. 'How's Erik,' he asked much to his surprise. He regretted the question immediately.

'Okay. Lonely, I think. I didn't know you cared.'

It was true enough, he didn't.

'You're never lonely, I suppose?' Jacq challenged.

Ahmed was taken aback. He would never have discussed his loneliness with anyone, but it was Jacq asking. 'Why would you be interested?' he countered.

Jacq considered the intelligent handsome face before her. The dark eyes that now had a hooded expression. Ahmed looked in need of some opening up, she concluded with female intuition. Males could be altogether too defensive.

'I just am,' she said simply. 'Interested.'

Ahmed disliked the question but sensed Jacq was genuine. To date no-one had ever asked him about his loneliness. His parents left such topics well alone. As an only child, with no real friends, he had learned to keep significant feelings to himself. Rugger was not one for the emotional stuff either. Now this question from Jacq. The one person who could ask him and he might answer truthfully. He looked at his drink and admitted that yes, he could feel lonely.

'Tell me about it?'

'Why do you want to know?'

'Just tell me.'

Perhaps she was on ground best left untouched. But Jacq didn't care. She needed to know. Something inside her urged the question. It might be a desire to escape the superficiality of the many months at *Cryslis*. It might be the need for a deep-and-meaningful with another person. If male, so much the better right now. She would not mind a bit of baiting actually. Raising this question gave her a sense of womanhood. Right in her gut, and she liked it. She needed it.

After a while Jacq wonder whether Ahmed was opting out. Then he began to speak. It took effort at first, but with Jacq as a good listener, talking became easier. Yes, he was lonely, he told her. He figured that many people were quite lonely, so why complain? It was one of those feelings that you have to manage somehow. Difficult, for it kept nagging at you deep inside. People didn't like you talking about loneliness. They had no answer. Ahmed still had hope for better though.

'Perhaps one day it may change,' he said, looking into his empty glass. Unsure how he felt about unveiling his deeper emotions. The telling had not been that hard. He just wasn't used to doing it.

'When you meet someone?'

'Sorry?'

'It will be resolved when you meet someone.' Jacq looked at him keenly. 'That's what you mean?'

'Perhaps.' Ahmed was not so naïve as to think that meeting someone special would automatically solve the problem of loneliness.

'What about perhaps? You mean love doesn't work?' Jacq detected a hesitation with Ahmed about what a significant relationship might achieve. Her own hopes were stronger than that.

'Yes, perhaps. I don't know much about love,' Ahmed said defensively. He gazed away momentarily. 'I haven't been there.'

'Neither have I,' Jacq admitted.

For a while they sat in silence. Jacq emotionally restless. She missed Ellie and felt alone at a significant level. She needed to talk.

'You are not asking me the same question?' she said softly. She was aware that Ahmed was a stranger to intimate conversations. Not woman-smart either.

'You probably give me the same answer,' he countered, annoyed at missing his cue. He should have asked about Jacq's loneliness in turn.

'That's not the point, is it?'

Jacq was looking intently at him. Should she stop talking about this? But Ahmed would gladly hear her story. That much she knew.

'I'm sorry,' he offered. 'I should have asked.'

It was time for another drink. Jacq pushed her chair back and went to order at the counter.

'You're right,' Jacq admitted when she returned. 'My story is very similar.' She took a sip of her soda. 'I have girlfriends I can talk to. One in particular, my best friend Ellie. But she's miles away now.'

Jacq explained about her family in Amsterdam. About her feelings of being left to her own devices.

Her parents worked long hours. Ahmed understood that only too well. 'Ell's a real help,' she said and smiled. Not that Ahmed was ever likely to meet her.

This talking was therapeutic to Jacq. She took her time. Amsterdam seemed very far away now. The city needed to be brought back to life in her mind. She spoke about her desire for acting and parents who could not understand. Yes, she had boyfriend once. It ended up quite meaningless. Her weekend with Erik, she left unmentioned.

Ahmed was sitting quietly. He gave Jacq his full attention. She seemed to be talking mostly to herself, not to him. She was animated, but clearly in a blue mood, expressing a kind of longing and sadness. He was fascinated and began to sense what it would be like having a real friend to discuss things with. Someone like Ellie, but in his case called Jacq. The thought of having a girl as an intimate friend was a new to him and slightly unnerving. Most likely, Jacq was just blue right now. He shouldn't read too much into it. Ahmed was aware of his usual male bravado to be totally inappropriate as a response to this girl who stirred him like no other. He had much to learn on the feeling side of life. He wondered why Jacq was showing him that. Ahmed sensed it was more than her need to talk of home that brought this conversation on. But he found it puzzling.

'Why are you telling me all this?' he asked. Jacq

had finished her story.

She looked at him with a faint smile and shook her head.

'Wrong question?' Ahmed ventured, with a pang of discouragement.

'Wrong question.'

Jacq had no idea why she had told him that much about herself. She appreciated Ahmed. More so now she knew him better. He was lonely, considerate and so wonderfully male and handsome. Would she be able to get behind his emotional defences? Judging by tonight, she thought she might.

'I feel dumb,' Ahmed said, getting annoyed about being shown up.

'No, you're not.'

She should stop playing games, Jacq decided. Ahmed had done well.

'I'm sorry,' she said warmly. 'I didn't know much about you and I'm interested. You're good company. You don't know a great deal about girls though. Beyond what they look like, and some more I suppose.'

She appraised him teasingly.

Ahmed gave a rueful smile and felt he was growing up fast. It was true enough. What really did he know about girls beyond their physicality?

Get a hold Jacq, she admonished herself. It was unkind to show Ahmed up like that. Before she could rectify the matter he came with a suggestion.

'You can teach me,' he said softly, looking at her with speculation. 'About girls.'

She rather liked the question and grinned. It was a clever response that confused her. His words, so quietly spoken, evoked unexpected emotions.

'I could,' she admitted.

She let this comment hang mid-air, before ending the conversation.

'Come on. It's time to get back.'

The street scene was busy. Not many under drinking age like themselves were about. Jacq was lost in thought. Side by side they turned into a narrow passage that led to their hotel. It was quiet there and shaded from city lights. Ahmed stopped near a darkened alcove. Jacq, a few steps on, turned back slowly to face him up close.

'Why are you stopping?' Her blue eyes revealed that she knew full well.

'Teach me, now,' Ahmed suggested. There was a hint of a challenge in his voice.

Oh, my god, Jacq thought. But she had been asking for it, that much she knew. 'What if I do?'

'Just for tonight.' Ahmed felt insecure and he feared that it showed. He would never be a natural seducer.

'Just for tonight,' Jacq agreed softly and pushed him gently into the alcove.

She raised her lips and felt Ahmed's arms slide around her back and down. He clearly wasn't new to this. There was urgency in their kissing at first and she took the ride without hesitation. Right now nothing else mattered. Life needed it.

'Oh, nice,' a leering voice cut through from behind. 'Can I have a go now?'

Two blokes had approached unnoticed. They looked intoxicated and in search of mischief.

After the initial surprise, Jacq kept her arms firmly around Ahmed restraining him. She whispered into his ear. 'Don't be a hero, don't move. Run, when I run.'

The force of her instruction arrested Ahmed's initial reaction. He was mentally rehearsing his boxing skills. Jacq slowly turned around stepping out of Ahmed's arms towards the two assailants and stood very still. Surprise was of the essence.

'Not bad,' one of them said looking Jacq over unashamedly. This was a stunning girl. He grinned at the two little lovers cornered with their back against a wall. Ahmed they could handle. This promised some chick wrestling.

Suddenly, with lightning speed, the guy collected a kick to the ribs at heart level that made him choke for breath. Then Jacq, turning to his companion gave him a perfectly placed foot between the legs. Both actions happened within seconds. They buckled over in agony.

'Run,' Jacq shouted to Ahmed, who stood rooted

in surprise. He could see that there was hardly any need for running but for the first few steps. Still, he followed Jacq at a pace. Out of the passage and towards the hotel. Soon they were alone, slowed down into walking and caught their breath.

'Where did you learn that?' Ahmed was impressed.

Jacq stopped still.

'Never mind where.' She was flushed from an adrenalin rush and breathing hard. It was the fight that had caused it, not the kissing. At least that's what she told herself.

'Let's forget this evening.'

Ahmed understood immediately. 'Not likely.'

'Yes, absolutely,' Jacq insisted.

The altercation with the two drunks made her realise that their involvement with *Cryslis* could not handle a romance. It would be too messy. The kiss had stirred deep emotions, rather surprisingly. But they were committed to a mission that might demand more than they cared to imagine. 'No more necking,' she said. 'No more.'

Ahmed began to experience the start of a deep anger. With the vagaries of life, the *Cryslis* mess and rotten luck.

'Don't be angry, please,' Jacq said anticipating his reaction. 'It's not you. I have not one regret about this evening, not one. But being under cover, whatever that means, and whatever *Cryslis* may throw at us, it needs a friendship without romantic complications. I can't feel safe any other way.'

This statement about safety was true enough. Jacq felt it the moment she spoke. A shiver ran down her spine.

Ahmed noticed that shiver. 'Quit?' he asked.

'I don't want to quit, no way. I hate this *Cryslis*. It needs beating – anything that it will take.'

Jacq looked at Ahmed, all eyes and desperation. His heart was melting. She was absolutely beautiful in the light of a street in Adelaide. High colour accentuated her face. He found it difficult to speak.

'Just friends,' he agreed gruffly. It crossed his mind that if he really cared for Jacq, he owed her that. Though he loathed the idea of merely friendship. Like Jacq, he hated *Cryslis* with a passion, definitely now. He was determined to help destroy it.

Jacq remained silent. She was thankful that Ahmed understood. She could imagine how he must be feeling. A great sadness washed over her. A sadness caused by more than just her personal problems. The feeling seemed to connect with the deep undercurrents of human suffering. The pain of life and good things not finding fruition.

Ahmed followed slowly. They entered the hotel without incident. Obviously had not been missed. Quietly they found their rooms.

CHAPTER 9

THE GROUP OF STUDENTS had discussed the size of Australia while still at Jersey. But nothing could have prepared them for the reality, once they actually faced it. The awe-inspiring dimensions of this continent, and its emptiness, compared with no other country any of them had ever visited. It was difficult for Europeans from densely populated areas to comprehend how far a person could travel between destinations without meeting either towns or villages. That was particularly so in the outback where the group from *Cryslis* was headed. The Temple was near Alice Springs, a tourist town at the centre of Australia. Looking out of the window when flying in gave them an idea of the isolation. During the days ahead, they would come to experience it for themselves.

Alice Springs was nestled in the MacDonnell Ranges. It had a long pioneering history. Good hotels, smart restaurants and even a casino were on offer. An endless stream of visitors travelled through. That slowed down at the height of summer, when the weather was very hot and possibly humid.

Europeans settled in there in 1872 manning a repeater station for the Overland Telegraph Line from Darwin to Adelaide. It covered a distance of a few thousands of miles. Alice Springs was located about midway and became an obvious point of support. In Darwin, closest to Indonesia, the telegraph line connected with Asia and Europe.

The students arrived in autumn when Alice Springs was buzzing with people from all over the world. From the airport they were driven into town in two large four-wheel drive vehicles. They would travel on to *Cryslis* later.

Jacq, while ambling through the main street, overheard two young backpackers speaking Dutch. She recognised German and also French. There were Asian visitors also forever taking pictures. It was all quite cosmopolitan. She could imagine herself back in a European city. Alice Springs though came not even close to that. In fact, it was quite small. Just two long main avenues and a few surrounding suburbs. Jacq could pick out the Australians in the crowd, and not just by their accent. It was as if living here long enough gave you a certain bearing in life. Fairly laid-back at a steady pace. It was noticeable and she found it attractive. She passed restaurants, pubs and shops. Central malls are similar the world over, she though. Major stores were always represented. She recognised some she had seen in Adelaide. What was particular to Alice Springs though was the number of places selling Aboriginal art. The town included a sizeable Aboriginal community, the original Australians being about in large numbers.

Ahmed, also wandering around the mall, was struck by the dishevelled appearance of some of these people. They were much darker skinned than he. It reminded of the untouchables in India. Clearly, for all its riches, Australia had significant problems with its indigenous population.

Ahmed liked Aboriginal art for it exuded spirit life. In one shop, engrossed with looking at a large canvas, he found himself standing next to Jacq. He had not planned meeting her that way. Rather, they were trying to stay apart within the group as much as possible. For safety reasons and to avoid animosity from Erik. Jacq seemed impressed. Ahmed looked at her sideways, but she remained oblivious to him. Fully taken up in the array of colours and patterns before her.

At breakfast in Adelaide she had asked Ahmed not to make matters more complicated than they already were. He had grunted in reply. And don't become moody on me, she had warned him. That was fair enough. He would do his best. Had nodded in agreement while keeping his eyes on his muesli. With last night still fresh in his mind, and a night's sleep of tossing and turning, staying positive needed all the energy he could muster. The attraction of Alice Springs helped a lot. It would not be their last visit to this town, they had been told.

On their way back to the cars Ahmed found a cash withdrawal facility. He and Jacq had decided earlier to draw out maximum money once again, just in case. He was following through on that. Secret agent Ahmed, he thought ruefully. He took his money from the slot. Under cover, and without the faintest idea of what was next.

The journey to *Cryslis* took a bitumen road that soon turned into well-maintained dirt. The dust blowing behind the two vehicles was heavy in the air. The car following the lead vehicle pulled the luggage trailer. It kept well back staying clear of the thick cloud ahead, allowing it to blow out. The students were looking intently at the unfamiliar landscape. Many low bushes were spread about in a vast expanse of red sand. The occasional gumtree stood tall. Everything was dusty. The vegetation had that grey-green look of hardy drought resistant flora. Alice Springs was situated in the Red Centre of Australia. The name Red Centre made perfect sense. Red sand everywhere. Travelling east from Alice for many miles the famous Simpson Desert could be entered. It had over one thousand parallel hills of red sand.

Eventually a compound appeared in the distance when coming over a rise. It was built in the outback style of Australia with deep verandas offering shade on every side. Dotted about were a significant number of buildings. This had to be *Cryslis*. Ahmed noticed a communications tower reaching up high into the blue sky. It might seem isolated, but that tower would keep the compound in touch with the whole world via satellite.

The cars drew up at modern guesthouses. Walls were a mixture of coloured panels, corrugated sheeting and some timber. Also glass and stainless steel. It all shone brightly. The students piled out of the vehicles marvelling at the size of their holiday place. Everyone was given a private room bordering on a common recreational area. At *Crylis* only the best would do. There were eating facilities with the option of sitting inside or on the veranda. Also a conference room. One student asked about the other structures around. Ahmed was pleased to hear about tennis courts, a large shaded pool, a gym, volleyball and basketball courts and also stables. This last piece of information lifted Jacq's spirit. It would be awesome to ride through the landscape here. She asked where the stables were. As horses attracted flies, and there were enough of those about already, the stables had been built near the maintenance area well away from the main complex.

The office building was separate from the guest quarters, along with a few homes. Most personnel travelled in from town, but some staff lived on site. That included the Director. The whole complex looked efficient, quite clean considering its exposure to the sandy desert winds, and endearing. It was a fantastic spot. As the students began to grab their baggage, Ahmed noticed the arrival of a pickup driven by two men in uniform. It had the word Security written on its doors. Clearly, everything necessary to guarantee a smooth operation was attended to at *Cryslis*.

Later that afternoon the Director welcomed them in the conference room. He sounded American, Jacq thought, or Canadian perhaps. The man was solidly built, highly intelligent and attractive. But instinctively she dislikes him. He was putting on an act for just another group of visitors, sort of déjà vu. Their group was one of a number to arrive each year from around the world. Perhaps she was being unfair. Maybe he was simply too busy to give them his undivided attention. Jacq wondered if anyone else noticed him just going through the motions.

'Congratulations to you all,' he began. 'You have earned this holiday and have done well.'

Ahmed saw a man who reminded him of his father. His father though would be much more warm-hearted. Perhaps it was the efficiency factor that stood out in both men.

'There are no rules here at *Cryslis*,' the Director continued. 'Apart from you behaving yourself and keeping the set times for meals. You will find the cooks excellent.'

His secretary brought him a glass of water while he continued his welcome. She was nice-looking.

'I don't need to explain the importance of *Cryslis* to our world. If you weren't convinced of that, you wouldn't have earned the privilege of being here at the Temple. Much of your time will be spent relaxing. Plus a few excursions. One with our Rangers into the desert around here.'

The security people, Ahmed surmised.

'You will make a trip to Kings Canyon and to Uluru. Also known as Ayers Rock. You would have seen pictures of this Australian symbol somewhere.'

The word symbol reminded Jacq of the riddle they were supposed to unravel. It spoke of a symbol of two halves. Involuntarily she cringed. Now actually being here, at this efficient and obviously influential place, she couldn't come close to imagining how with Ahmed she might challenge the power of *Cryslis* successfully. The whole deal, without an actual plan either, seemed ridiculous.

'Surely,' the Director continued with his well-modulated voice. 'The highlight of your stay will be a visit to the Temple with the *Cryslis*. The original is ancient. Nobody knows exactly where it came from. It is connected to a cosmic force. You will notice that for yourself.'

There was no reference to the myth of *Shalomat*. Both Jacq and Ahmed figured the Director to be familiar with that story. Still, their academy had never mentioned it. Perhaps didn't know the myth. The top leadership must have kept that information secret.

'The Temple is about a mile away.' The Director pointed to outdoors. 'It's behind that rise you can see looking north. You are not expected to go near it. Not just you, that goes for everyone at *Cryslis*. The temple is only visited at full moon. That will be tomorrow. I will give you the details then. In the meantime, enjoy your stay.'

He departed, followed by his shapely secretary.

It was an hour before dinner. Ahmed decided on a workout in the gym. To his delight it had a punching ball, which he found most effective for letting off his frustration. He gave it an almighty battering practising his boxing skills. He was alone.

By the time one of the locals entered Ahmed felt exhausted, but happier. The energy of good health was rushing through his veins. Once in the shower, washing off plentiful sweat, he concluded once again that Jacq was right. He should keep his cool. About her friendship with Erik. Jacq had known Erik before joining the academy and they were just friends. Perhaps that may have been different in the past. But not so now. Jacq had not been playing games with him yesterday, Ahmed felt. She had wanted to kiss as much as he.

Like Jacq, he was apprehensive about the future. With this *Cryslis* mission great carefulness was needed. He had long decided that they were being drawn into this quest almost by stealth. Though that didn't quite seem the right word. But there was a power in play he had no idea about and no control over. Rugger had often impressed upon him what separated the men from the boys in a fight. Ahmed had been tested on it more than once. It is self-control, had been the instruction. Also staying alert to danger, particularly when it hurts. Use your emotions to fire you on, Rugger would say, but keep control, stay cool. That was pertinent advice right now and Ahmed would follow through with it. Jacq deserved better than him acting like a spoiled brat. He had to be bigger than that.

The next day was free of official engagements for the students to catch their breaths. The air was hot and dry. Heavy storms could hit Alice Springs creating large floods, but none were expected for a while. Jacq and Ahmed decided that when the sun was less fierce, they would try out the horses. Taste the open country.

And they did. They experienced an abundance of space. It took any desire for conversation away from Jacq. They rode on in silence. On Australian Stock horses known for their mobility and endurance. The animals obviously knew their way about.

Jacq and Ahmed had received a small map with

some markers and were told to keep an eye on the landscape. If they became lost, just give the horses free rein and they would easily find their way home. They had asked about restrictions on riding out and were told that there were none. Apart from making sure to take water for themselves as well as the horses. And to stay within a certain radius of the complex. Don't ride beyond the markers on the map. Also, look out for snakes. A horse might detect one before its rider. Do not force the animal when it behaves unexpectedly.

During their ride they noticed a *Cryslis* security vehicle on the horizon and imagined a Ranger was checking them out with binoculars. A sharp flash of reflected sunlight projected from the car. Perhaps he was just making sure they could handle the horses. Even in the desert, solitude was not guaranteed.

It was a good ride. Invigorating but tiring, and full of impressions. Back at the compound they decided on a swim. Jacq found Erik at the pool and instead of taking a dip followed him to the restaurant chatting amicably about nothing much. She sensed that Erik was testing her on how she felt about riding with Ahmed. She just played easy but tired. It was quite normal for Erik to seek her company. I will simply have to live with it, Jacq concluded, once again. She would not ruffle any feathers unnecessarily.

Ahmed was left to swim on his own. The lanes, half the size of an Olympic pool, were shaded by large white sails strung from metal posts. After forty laps of freestyle at speed, he was quite exhausted and knew the heat had been taken out of him in more ways than one.

That evening, at half past nine, the students began to assemble in the conference room. It was full moon and a visit to the Temple could be made. There was a feeling of anticipation amongst all, except for Jacq and Ahmed. They were apprehensive but careful to hide it. Stay up-beat and keep smiling, Jacq told herself more than once.

'Seeing the original *Cryslis* is a unique experience,' the Director began. 'You may be wondering whether I am exaggerating. Well, you will find out.' Over the years he had noticed how deeply it affected people.

'The protocol for the visit is quite simple. Don't talk, remain silent all the way, and follow the guidance given by hand signals of those in charge. There will be no problem knowing what to do. Basically, you will just stand in a circle and focus your attention solely on the *Cryslis*. I suggest you really make that effort. You will not regret it. When you hear the sound of a crystal bell, you will file out as you have come in. At no stage during the visit should anyone speak, not during the walk to the Temple, and not on the way back either. Seeing the *Cryslis* takes away any desire for talking anyway. Afterwards, you will probably just want to go to your rooms. As you know, the *Cryslis* travels all the five continents and stays in each for twenty years. In every continent the Temple is placed at a certain point on the world's psychic grid. There is no need to enlarge on that, but it has its effects. Now, this is important. The *Cryslis* should never be touched by a human hand, not that I expect you to try. It will instantly burn you very badly. Years ago in Africa someone ignored that advice and had some fingers amputated. There are a few photos of that hanging in the main hall. The person concerned didn't actually live very long and died in mysterious circumstances. Perhaps that was a coincidence.'

The way it was said showed the Director having little faith in coincidences. Ahmed remembered those photos not knowing what they were about. Now he knew. Psychic grids, burning fingers, and a mysterious death. He felt the soft tentacles of fear begin to crawl around his chest.

'You will see the *Cryslis* placed in a black marble box, with all its sides flattened out. They fold together when the *Cryslis* is to be moved between continents. Placed around the original *Cryslis* are three others of an expensive crystal but unlike the original. We have no idea what the original is made of. The three copies are intended for new academies we are planning or the offices of particular graduates. They will remain in the Temple for exactly one year to absorb a little of *Cryslis* lustre and power. You would have learned about that at your academy on Jersey Island. It was established hundreds of years ago, well before my time.'

The students knew of their college being that old. Its facilities had been upgraded and looked anything but dated. Apart from a number of old stone feature walls. Previous buildings would have been bulldozed to make room for a brand new era. Sentimentality had no value at *Cryslis*, Jack thought.

'We will now walk to the Temple together with our permanent residents. I would ask for complete silence and a relaxed pace.'

The Director calmly stepped ahead indicating that the group should follow.

They filed out in pairs, Jacq and Ahmed walking side by side. The group was about thirty people. Erik happened to be next to their woman group leader. The full moon shone brightly in a calm and cloudless night. Its light threw moon shadows and faded the stars. Gorgeous that, thought Jacq. If only they weren't headed for the Temple. Still, in spite of everything, she was intrigued.

As the Temple came into view Jacq recognised the building. They had seen part of it in the distance when horse riding. It had the same shape as the *Cryslis*.

The Temple was made of burnished stainless steel and darkened glass. It loomed majestically in the moonlight. They all walked silently not a sound was to be heard. The top of the Temple, normally closed, was wide open to the moon sky. No one uttered a word. Ahmed, heavy in thought, noticed his fear to be gone. Instead, he felt strangely peaceful here in this desert beside Jacq. He forced himself not to look sideways. Ahead was the reason for their visit to Australia, where they needed to be, according to Mr. Adams. At the entrance Jacq was guided to the left and Ahmed to the right. As they walked on silently the group formed a circle around the original *Cryslis*. It rested in an open folded marble box, slightly above eye level, on a circular piece of glass. That glass sat on a mat black pillar from which three arms extended at a lower level. The arms supported three other *Cryslis* which were not anywhere near as illustrious. It was obvious where the power dwelled.

The original *Cryslis* projected a forceful aura of light and energy. Intensified by the moon shining in through the roof. Both beautiful and enchanting, it was from Jacq's perspective weird and menacing.

Ahmed glanced at her, standing right across from him in the circle. She looked even more beautiful now than that night in Adelaide. It was not smart to look for long. He quickly directed his gaze towards the *Cryslis* sensing to be observed. But by whom? Ahmed began to focus on the small dark crystal ornament. Not an ordinary ornament, for sure. Gazing at it he came under its spell. Felt challenged deep inside. The wealth of his parents and his life of luxury flashed though his mind. He couldn't take his eyes off the *Cryslis* now, even if he wanted to. Can anything so enchanting be really that bad, he wondered?

Jacq had her own emotions. She looked at the *Cryslis* horrified. She too could not turn her eyes away. The power and shape of the ornament repulsed her. She had never found it particularly attractive, but now began to perceive a deeper significance. Jacq yearned for a reality more rounded than this efficient, sharp-lined, ruthless piece of crystal, so small and yet so powerful. Her heart cried out for *Shalo*, which much surprised her. The idea had never crossed her mind. Their mission began to impress its significance at deeper levels. In her soul Jacq was almost choking. Her feelings were cutting in raw. Tears began to well up in her eyes, spilling out onto her face. She wanted to run away screaming from this awful place. But knew to keep up an appearance of calm, not drawing attention to herself. It was almost impossible to stay that self-controlled. Jacq managed it only just. With every fibre in her body highly agitated. Let this time here be short was her silent plea.

The Director kept a close eye. Responses to the *Cryslis* might disclose a lot about people. He needed to be alert for the unforeseen. Particularly with the Day of the Riddle now supposedly near. Not that he expected anything untoward tonight. He noticed Ahmed glance at Jacq and understood its meaning. Not for the first time did young love visit the Temple. To Ahmed's credit, he quickly focused back on the *Cryslis* and became enchanted. All was normal there. Jacq's tears he wondered about. Perhaps the girl was confronting some deep grief. He kept his eye on her for moment. Under some sort of stress, he decided, but nothing out of the ordinary. The *Cryslis* was bringing emotional healing. It had happened before.

After a while the crystal bell rang three times and the group filed out. Walking back as they had come, each person lost in thought. A visit to the Temple had to be brief. It was psycho-spiritually very demanding. No one spoke. Ahmed was thoroughly confused. As if he desperately needed to escape from something. Jacq felt totally spent. But had no wish to be alone right now. They ended up on the terrace near the tennis courts. Under the light of the moon, each in need of company. Erik was nowhere to be seen. Jacq had noticed how he was in a world of his own. Feelings quite different from hers, of that she could be sure. He would stay away and his absence suited her fine.

'How do you feel?' she asked Ahmed with a thick voice. They sat side by side in the bright night. It offered a different enchantment from the *Cryslis*. But that remained unnoticed.

Ahmed was coming to grips with the Temple visit. He looked at her with concern. Jacq sounded gutted.

'What's wrong?'

'Do you have that little book on you? I would like to have a look.'

Without asking why, Ahmed took it out of his pocket. He preferred keeping the document close. They had opened the book a number of times trying to figure out the Riddle. Not even an inkling of an idea had arisen. Ahmed handed her the little book without a word. Perhaps she had an idea about that Riddle. Her face looked drawn. Something was badly askew.

Jacq opened the notebook having no idea why she had asked for it. This night was unnerving her. She shivered at seeing the first page. Unbelievable! She couldn't believe her eyes. But there it was, written clearly and coming out of nowhere: Well done, don't despair!

Without a word she handed the book to Ahmed, the open page clearly visible in the moonlight. She began to weep softly putting her head in her hands. It sounded like a deep and private grief. Ahmed looked in disbelief, first at Jacq and then the little book. Again, as on that bench at the academy months ago, he had absolutely no idea what to do. He just stared at the miraculous sentence. It blew his mind.

***

It was nothing, the Director concluded. Nothing strange had happened. All was normal. If only he could be sure. He stayed behind in the Temple to mull it over. The moonlight had shifted to another angle and the *Cryslis* glittered less brightly. But not with diminished power. Give me an idea of what is going on, he solicited silently. Enough of this uncertainty. He had never before asked the Cryslis for help. Just drawn strength in its presence. Asking wasn't right, he sensed. He simply had to wait for the problem to present itself. Then deal with it.

Walking back the Director admitted how badly this business was affecting him. His usual confidence was beginning to wane. He felt drained, every day now. Not that anyone must notice, absolutely not. He decided to visit his secretary and not his office. She would be able to release him of some of his stress.

CHAPTER 10

THE TWO LARGE four-wheel drive vehicles were on their way to Kings Canyon. The students travelled through the MacDonnell Ranges for over an hour to Hermannsburg. A Lutheran Mission outpost from 1877. The old whitewashed buildings of quarried stone, flattened kerosene tins and corrugated iron had been restored. It included a small church. There was a sizeable local store. The missionaries had left long ago handing ownership over to the local Aboriginal community. Apart from these historic buildings much of the settlement looked neglected. Some of it looks trashed, Ahmed thought. Like in the slums of India.

The group from *Cryslis* spent time walking about and visited the local gallery of Aboriginal art. Since Alice Springs, Ahmed and Jacq had been powerfully attracted to its wonderful and colourful patterns on canvas and bark. They could easily have lingered longer than planned. Erik seemed more interested in the skill of the missionary builders. From Hermannsburg, the road to Kings Canyon was graded dirt. The weather was excellent with a clear, hard blue sky that outlined the mountain range sharply. It promised to be warm without humidity. A dry heat that smelled of dust. Typical of the Australian outback.

For Ahmed, the day after the Temple visit had been one of catching his breath. The best way to regain his composure was sleep, food and exercise, he decided. Jacq's despair, and that crazy little book, had affected him badly.

Jacq had told the Mentor of feeling sick, some virus she thought, nothing bad. It might be best if she spent time resting. She preferred not to participate in activities that day. Mostly games of tennis and some swimming.

Ahmed had welcomed the sport. It was just what he needed to clear his head. Rugger had taught him about the benefits of exercise when something was bothering you. It changes your metabolism, he had explained. People reach for alcohol or drugs when they feel troubled. But a hard workout is a far better response. Ahmed had found plenty of opportunity in his short life to put that into practice. He knew that easily rising anger was his problem. It needed keeping a close eye on it. Rugger had been frank about that in no uncertain terms. Channel it into positive action, had been his advice. Anger can be a motivator, if you prevent it from becoming destructive. If you are forever angry, you've got a problem. Fortunately, that was not Ahmed. He just flared up easily. Mostly in his mind, without showing it much. The sordid mess he was finding himself in now, with Jacq clearly troubled, stirred his emotions beyond a simple flare-up. He felt a deep, furious anger and let it smoulder. But he knew these feelings needed changing. Organised sport for the day had been welcome. He belted the life out of tennis balls and lost his games. In swimming, he purposely forgot all about technique bashing through the water with a mighty splash. Not a great swim, but very therapeutic. He began to feel better. His anger melting away slowly and a sense of vigour returned.

Later on, Ahmed decided to practise his boxing in the gym. A number of staff members, with the help of a young fitness coach, were sweating through an aerobics training session. It didn't stop Ahmed from putting the gloves on hammering away in a corner. First at the ball and then the punching bag. He worked through his shadow boxing moves with quick feet.

James, the instructor, ended his time with the staff. He saw that Ahmed was obviously a boxer and asked about some sparring. It was a while since James had the opportunity to box. This young Indian seemed fluid and skilful enough to make it an even bout, he thought. Well, almost.

Ahmed was pleased. The last time he had boxed with a partner other than Rugger was in England. They put on the headgear, bit into their mouth-guards, and had a great time. Ahmed probing beyond the long reach of James. James trying to connect with the young Indian who moved like lightning. They both landed punches with impact. Neither would hurt the other badly. With a punch correctly placed and all his weight behind it, Ahmed knew that he could do damage. That James presented a danger to him was without question. At one point, Ahmed had to hold back a little, not hitting the Australian too hard. James acted likewise, when Ahmed's defences were badly breached.

Afterwards, Ahmed felt better than he had for a long time. He was also very tired. His legs were like jelly. Consequently, he hurt himself by miss-stepping on the veranda. He twisted his ankle and grimaced with pain.

James could not help but smile. Down for the count after all, he thought with amusement. He liked this kid. Better get some ice from the freezer in the gym.

With a bag of ice on his ankle, James left Ahmed sitting on the steps. He had supplied a bandage for when the swelling subsided. Ahmed sat on the steps for a while soaking in the pain that seemed to identify with how he felt altogether. He found he could still walk though gingerly. It was not a serious strain. For the next few days he just needed to be careful. Inexplicably, the gently nagging pain brought him some solace. Perhaps it harmonised with how he felt. In their discussion about loneliness Ahmed had told Jacq that he didn't know what being in love was like. That now had changed. Jacq's tears had showed him how much he cared.

There was nothing he could do to help. Jacq had drifted off into a world of her own, clearly needing space. Ahmed knew that she would find her way back. She had indicated that much.

The group arrived at the Kings Canyon Resort and moved into luxury cabins for a night. It was real outback Australia. The kind of environment they had driven through for the last few hours. A primordial landscape that kept serving up new surprises. It was dressed in the wild grandeur of unspoiled nature that millions of years bring. Jacq was in awe of it.

Ahmed and Erik made certain to avoid sharing a cabin. Instead, Erik found himself with the Mentor, which gave Ahmed some unexpressed delight. Not once had the Swede made an effort to be more than barely civil to him. Remembering Jacq's embrace in Adelaide, Ahmed tried not to gloat. He was realistic enough to know that there was every possibility of losing Jacq, like Erik had. If honest about it, he could well understand the Swede's frustration Jacq was acting cooler towards him these days. Ahmed knew little about their relationship before *Cryslis*. But guessed that it had been beyond a simple hello. She might have kissed Erik as urgently as she had him. Perhaps more had happened, but that he doubted. Whatever occurred in Stockholm, it was no longer current. He was sure of that.

The Kings Canyon itself, originally called Watarrka by the local Aboriginal owners, was a short distance away from the resort. The group arrived by car to attempt the Kings Canyon Walk. It should take about three hours. Promised breathtaking views from high up the sheer rock wall that glowed red in the sun. Only their tour guides, who were experts in the Australian bush, knew that they would have to climb 500 steps. With more to follow. Finding that out suited Jacq perfectly for she had a plan of her own. Once at the steps, she told her teacher of Business Studies why she was not up to climbing. She was beginning to feel unwell again and needed to sit down. When she felt a bit better, she would make her way to the vehicles where Ahmed was with his bad ankle. He would keep her company.

It was a sensible suggestion and Jacq was left behind. She watched the group stepping away. The guides had stressed the importance slow climbing. Too much haste early on and they would run out of energy. Not reach the top. The conservation of strength was always important in a hot climate. The temperature was okay right now. Had it been a really hot day, the climb would have been called off. Every member in the group carried a small rucksack with water and energy food and was advised to use it. Dehydration was serious in the bush. You had to drink regularly before you got thirsty, but not too much. That would not be her problem, Jacq thought. She found a rock to sit on in the shade. Still, she would keep her fluid levels up.

Jacq let her eyes wander over a bushland lined by towering walls. It was typically Australian. Ghost gums, with their stark white trunks stood silhouetted against a russet-coloured backdrop. Beneath a sky amazingly blue. The scrubby vegetation included native mint bushes, spinifex and a variety of grasses. In the clear light, with a clarity to be found only in certain countries around the world, the bush looked dry, deserted, but stunning. Sharp shadow lines of the rock face fell across the uneven slope. Jacq heaved a sigh of pleasure. This honest scenery made her feel better. There was stillness about, only interrupted by the soft buzzing of insects. She moved her foot away from a line of ants and relaxed. It felt great.

Jacq was surfacing from her emotional withdrawal. The last two days had been deep waters. After the Temple visit, she had fallen into a dreamless sleep. At least, no dreams were remembered. She must have been too exhausted. The encounter with the *Cryslis* had left her with enough impressions for a month of dreaming. That she knew for certain. No nightmares to fight with to date though, fortunately. Tiredness from travelling had taken their toll. She had slept like a log that night to wake up in a strangely subdued mood. As if not quite in touch with anything. Not even her own self. She seemed to be living in a mild mental mist that day.

In need of personal space, away from Ahmed and Erik. Not ever had Jacq felt like this before. She drifted in a calm fog without sharp edges and didn't dislike the feeling. When her grandmother died unexpectedly some years ago, Jacq had crashed badly. In bed for a full day her feelings had been acute and painful. Now, in response to the trauma induced by the *Cryslis*, she seemed beyond any pain or grief. Was just dwelling in a haze.

She called in sick and possibly was. Something in her soul that she didn't understand. Could not if she tried. Nothing depressive. Her mood was not dark like that. She just felt subdued, as if all her energy was needed deep inside of her. Detached from people and her own thoughts. She had got through yesterday feeling half dead and strangely at ease. Her strength had left her and yet, all seemed okay.

The warm air in the canyon was soothing and the stillness acted like a balm seeping into her. She reflected that life would be richer if her emotions had space to work themselves out. Without her always needing to understand what was happening. Life had many undercurrents that simply required an embrace rather than analysis. That was the foundation of true art, she thought, including acting. She sighed.

Her emotional mist had a healing dynamic, it seemed. Now coming out of that fog she felt so opposite to that time in the Temple. That experience appeared a stepping stone. Really strange. She felt more the person she would want to be than ever before. Definitely different. How that was possible, Jacq didn't know. Perhaps *Shalo* had something to do with it. According to the myth, that sphere was on earth like the *Cryslis*. Perhaps her mental fog had come from *Shalo*. Who could tell? But the power of *Shalo* was real enough. How else could she explain that mystery sentence in the little notebook?

She heard voices coming her way. Closer by, she recognised German. She should walk back to the cars where Ahmed was hanging out alone. Be strong with your decision about romance, she told herself. Even if it was going to be difficult.

That night, under the open sky in the peacefulness of the bush, Jacq looked at the stars. The sky was alive with a myriad of lights, shining like a celestial city. The Milky Way emitted a distinct haze across the dark. Never had she seen anything like it. It was a night for poets and mystics. For everything that was beyond the controls of humanity. She would never fathom the depth of nature in all its splendour. It made her feel ever so small. And thankful for this magnificence in the desert of Australia.

The group travelled on to Uluru after a good night's sleep. Their evening dinner had included emu, camel and kangaroo dishes. You could buy kangaroo meat in city stores Jacq had found in Adelaide. At King's Canyon, she enjoyed the taste of it. The soaked and marinated meat was placed on high heat briefly. It seared the steak and left the inside raw and tender. Ahmed ventured ordering emu.

Uluru came in view from a long distance away. The huge rock was a monolith, one very large singular unit of stone. Of deep spiritual significance to its owners, the Aboriginal people. Western explorers, when faced with it, had named the stone Ayer's Rock. Its official name reverted back to Uluru and the rock was declared a World Heritage site.

The two *Cryslis* vehicles arrived early afternoon. After checking in the students were free to wander. Surrounded by desert the conveniences were city-like. A supermarket, restaurants, cafes, a post office and police station. There was an airstrip and a hospital.

Uluru was famous for its colour changing dramatically at dusk and dawn. Before sundown the students were driven up close to witness its splendour in the dying sunlight. The huge rock flared up while the sun set. Jacq found the sight unforgettable. She noticed how the colour kept changing. Glowing red like a log in a fire and then darker. Uluru, resting immovably in the grassy desert, dominated everything around. It took her breath away.

Her companions seemed oblivious to how really awesome the sight was. Their chatter irritated Jacq. She walked away, glad not to be followed. Not in the least religious, she would yet describe the event as deeply spiritual. Others, it seemed, found it no more than interesting.

Ahmed noticed Jacq moving on and wondered whether to tag along. He decided against it. She still was withdrawn. Hopefully, that would soon change. He too was annoyed with all the talk and sauntered off in the opposite direction. Uluru was affecting him. The immutable rock spoke of a different world. Human effort appeared feeble against this lasting testimony of nature so rooted in its own certainty. These feelings made a strong impression on Ahmed. Subconsciously deep and very real.

Sunset was the other time of the day when the magic of the rock could be seen glowing. With a clear sky at dawn, it would happen again. On the opposite side against the eastern sun. Another moment of pure beauty. Jacq and two others loved to see the explosion of colour once more early next morning. The rest of the students, including Ahmed, stayed in bed. Again Uluru's changing and the feel of the outback, mesmerised Jacq. What kind of a world was this? Totally stunning! A number of kangaroos hopped about in the still morning air. Jacq drank in the quiet of the bush in gulps. As if having been parched for weeks. She felt herself becoming fully alive again. The mist in her soul had cleared up. It promised to be a great day.

The rock could be climbed in the morning, when the temperature was not yet hot. The Aboriginal owners wished for the rock to be left alone. It was mentioned at the Information Centre. Yesterday the students had enjoyed music from the didgeridoo there. The appeal was ignored by many tourist who were spiritually insensitive. Like the group from *Cryslis*. It felt no compunction either. It would be foreign to the *Cryslis* attitude to abscond from achieving such a statement of dominance as conquering the Australian icon with your feet. The climb, holding onto a chain for much of the way, looked easy. But surefootedness and a basic fitness levels were required. Sometimes people needed rescuing. Falls and heart attacks were not uncommon. Ahmed with his strained ankle was excused. Jacq simply wasn't up to it yet. A perfect way of opting out of this obligation. She might have refused and create the kind of attention she could do without. It would have dented her image as a believer in Crylis philosophy. Ahmed remembered how the rock had affected him at sundown. Climbing it felt like sacrilege. Also, he preferred not to insult people close to his own colour of skin.

'Why don't we take a walk over that hill?' Ahmed's ankle could manage that and he was keen to get away from buildings.

Soon they met an Aboriginal woman, her face very dark and creased with the wrinkles of age. She sat cross-legged in the sand and was painting a canvas. In the dots style her culture is famous for. Surprised, they quietly approached.

Jacq was reminded of how she had been moved by an Aboriginal painting in the shop in Alice Springs and another two days ago at Hermannsburg. She and Ahmed watched with fascination as the lady added dots to the canvas by dipping a small stick into a cup of paint. The piece looked almost finished. Eventually, she looked up and smiled.

'You think I'm painting,' she said, putting the little stick down slowly. That, indeed, was what Jacq and Ahmed thought. Then she asked, 'Where you from?'

With so many people from all over the world visiting Uluru it was a reasonable question. From Holland and England, they told her. All the while gazing at the enchanting canvas. The woman nodded her head, she had heard of those countries.

From a brochure Ahmed and Jacq had learned that the colourful patterns, circles, and lines, that seem so natural, could only be created from deep within the being of the artist. It calls on generations of people having the same cultural experiences. These then are painted out abstractly by those with that ability.

'No, not painting.' The old Aboriginal shook her head. 'Telling story.' Patting the dirt next to her she motioned her two visitors to sit down.

'Story of my people,' she said pointing to the canvas. 'Long time. Many stories.'

It doesn't look like a story thought Ahmed. Just dots on canvas, beautifully coloured and arranged. Still, he readily accepted the explanation.

'You know story?'

There was a profound stillness about this painter. The way she went about her work. She was unhurried and needed no quick answers to her questions. Neither Ahmed nor Jacq were quick to respond.

'What kind of story?' Jacq asked after a while. She understood the economy of the communication. The fewer words said, the better. She liked the idea.

'Story,' the old woman repeated. She waved a hand across the desert suggesting there were plenty of stories to be found. There would be. But not by two young people from Europe.

Jacq began to sense the implications of this communication. Her home country was crowed, full of people with little space. And no stories that would in any way fit this vast land. Holland didn't have many stories of nature and space. At least not that she knew of. She considered how to answer this impressive Aboriginal artist. What story could she possibly tell?

One to do justice to the open desert? Then she had an idea. Perhaps she did have a story.

'One story,' she offered, simply.

'You tell.'

The woman settled herself. The telling of a story must be treasured. She gazed motionlessly across the land ignoring her visitors.

Jacq took her time in starting. There was no hurry. There shouldn't be. The only adequate story she was knew was the myth of *Shalomat*. It fitted in these wide-open spaces at Uluru much better than on the sheets of paper given them by Mr. Adams. She tried to remember the myth and stood up.

Jacq began to speak drawing on her acting skills. She savoured every word. Made her body talk. Her feelings in the Temple and the days that followed, coloured her narration. She became one with the mythical event of *Shalomat* sensing its tragedy. The gods *Sophius* and *Igod*. The wholeness of *Shalo*, against the limitations of *Cryslis*. The displeasure of the godly realm. Deeper shades of meaning were revealed to her that she was unable to verbalise but projected in her voice. Never before had she told a story in this way. The desert seemed to release her in the telling and was urging her on. She felt beyond civilization and part of a far more primal world. If asked afterwards Jacq would admit, that she could not be sure whether she had been telling the myth, or that the myth had told itself through her.

With the last word thrown into the open air above the desert, three human creatures were sitting silently in a large universe. Ahmed was amazed and dumbfounded. No way would he be the one to speak and break the spell.

Timing it perfectly, the Aboriginal painter said, 'Good story.' She nodded her head and seemed to return from another world. 'Yes.' There was a deep satisfaction in her voice. She looked at Jacq with speculation and understanding. 'My people, many stories,' she said.

There was no response. Jacq had no desire for talking. She stared out toward the horizon. Coming back from a realm that until now had been completely foreign to her.

'Your story, I feel,' the old woman told Jacq. She patted her chest. 'Good story, always you feel.' She looked at Ahmed wondering whether he understood. Jacq obviously did.

'Not my mind?' offered Ahmed. Gesturing to his head as if the lady was unfamiliar with that word. It was a spontaneous reaction. To language simplicity and the importance of gestures.

'No, not head.' She shook her head firmly. 'Inside.' She placed a hand over her stomach.

Ahmed sensed this aging artist knew exactly why they were having this conversation. One she had initiated. It was strange.

'You feel, then you know,' she told them nodding her head with conviction.

'You think, then you know,' Jacq joined in, still gazing out over the desert. 'The motto of our modern world.'

The woman looked at her with a twinkle in her eyes.

'No, no,' she smiled. 'Not enough,' and waved her hands about. She looked carefully at Jacq. Her intelligent face posing some kind of mild challenge.

Jacq understood the unspoken question. There are other ways of gaining knowledge than through the intellect alone. Go and find them, seemed to be the message given her today. Jacq could only agree.

'What shall I do?' she asked. It seemed the right response.

'You feel!' was the reply. 'You feel.'

The lady kept observing Jacq till she was satisfied. Next, she picked up her painting stick without haste and considered where to place a dot on her canvas. Without taking her eyes off that task she added, 'No *Cryslis.*'

The old Aboriginal understood the implications of the story Jacq had thrown about into the Australian outback perfectly. It was time to move on. But for a final word.

'Seek sunrise,' the painter told them.

'What does she mean?' Ahmed asked Jacq as they walked back to the hotel.

'No idea.' Jacq preferred not to talk. She had a lot to think about. 'It may be important though,' she admitted. Still, it could wait. She would study acting, absolutely. It was a certainty No matter what her parents thought of it.

They entered the lobby before the others returned from their climb – sweaty, tired and excited. They had conquered. Travelling back to *Cryslis* was a four hour drive. Along the way they visited the twelve meteorite craters at Henbury, fragments from a huge meteor break-up 4700 years ago. Jacq felt her normal energy to have returned. She was trying to ignore the feeling that something was about to happen that would change everything.

CHAPTER 11

THE NEXT DAY they spent doing little. Apart from a short drive to aboriginal rock art that pictured the spiritual beliefs and customs of indigenous people. Ahmed's ankle no longer needed a bandage. But he kept it on. Jacq felt her normal self again. If normal meant that she was alert, tired and apprehensive. She wished to get away from *Cryslis* and suggested a day's horse riding tomorrow. Ahmed was only too happy. Erik hated horses and that left him neatly out of the picture.

An extended ride needed permission from the Mentor. They told him that their map was a very good one. They would be careful not to tire the horses and make sure to carry sufficient water. The idea was to explore the foot of the mountain range.

The Mentor was in a good mood. He had found an ultralight in Alice Springs and was just about to take it into the sky. He knew of their skill with horses. He gave his permission presuming that they would not be given the livelier animals in the corral. Enjoy the ride, he told them.

Leaving the Mentor, Ahmed saw a black Porsche Carrera exiting the Director's garage. It gave him a sharp pang of desire and regret. What would he have given to get his hands on the steering wheel of that car right now!

It promised a cooler day, though still warm. Jacq and Ahmed rode off. The Mentor's perception about the quality of their horses had been correct. Both animals seemed docile, much to Ahmed's annoyance. It didn't bother Jacq. Being out in the open, and crawling back from an emotional time, was more important right now. Today she would forget about *Shalomat*. The Riddle, which they had tried to make sense of many times, kept its secrets. However much they opposed *Cryslis*, there was nothing to lead them forward. The miraculous notebook remained silent. It was time to take a break. At least, Jacq would try. Forget about the whole affair.

Ahmed's concern wasn't *Cryslis*. Sitting in the saddle riding through the rocky grassland his thoughts were on Jacq. Perhaps he could get a little closer to her today. He had begun to wonder whether their kissing in Adelaide was a momentary fling. Though Jacq never gave that impression. He looked at her riding slightly ahead, at the natural way in which she united with a horse. Ahmed felt an ache. It stung in ways completely foreign to him.

They followed the foot of the mountains. The horses stepping with confidence and at ease. Ahmed and Jacq chatted about Australia and the outback. After riding for a while, they heard a sound that seemed out of place. Very dull at first but gaining in strength as they rode on. Forceful hammer blows were coming from behind a curve in the rock face. It was so unexpected that they stopped and looked at each other. As they followed the curve a simple dwelling appeared. It had an open extension attached at the back, or perhaps it was the front. The place was built with local rock, weatherboard and corrugated iron. It looked more like a workshop than a home. An old car lay rusting to one side discarded. The whole site was a kind of rambling shambles, Jacq thought.

An older man was applying blows to a chisel onto granite. He was obviously a sculptor. The area around was covered with artefacts. Jacq and Ahmed reined in their horses and sat observing the scene. It took at least a minute before they were noticed. The man looked up from his chiselling. He pointed to a water trough for the horses not saying a word. Surprised to find this place in the middle of nowhere, Jacq and Ahmed dismounted. Using a long-handled manual pump water soon filled the trough and the horses began to drink. Then they introduced themselves.

'Sit down a while,' the sculptor suggested walking to plastic chairs on a shady veranda. He wiped his brow. Moved his fingers through a full head of grey hair. The man seemed friendly and glad to see them. 'I hardly ever get visitors,' he said. Not that such lack of company seemed to bother him. 'Just call me, Petrus.'

He went to a small outside fridge and extracted a bottle of water. Ahmed could hear the soft purr of a generator somewhere away from the house.

'You have come,' Petrus said, giving them a glass of cold water with lemon.

'Yes,' said Ahmed. Not knowing what was meant by that comment.

'From *Cryslis.*'

Ahmed nodded. Jacq became alert. Something was going on here, but what?

'Recognise the horses,' said Petrus.

He was silent for a moment and thought it simply had to be. No point delaying.

'I gather you have heard of *Shalomat*?' he said.

Completely stunned by this unexpected mention of the myth, here in the middle of nowhere, Ahmed nor Jacq responded. This talk was taking a disturbing turn. They sat stock-still.

'The Day of the Riddle is near,' Petrus continued giving them a speculative look.

Ahmed and Jacq remained silent. Apprehension showed on their faces. When Petrus delayed following on from his mention of the Riddle, Ahmed finally found his voice.

'Who are you?'

'A friend of Mr. Adams.'

'He sent you over here?' Ahmed thought that unlikely. It was obvious Petrus had lived in this shack for years.

'No,' said Petrus shaking his head. 'He didn't.'

'What do you know about the Day of the Riddle?' Jacq had now become perturbed. Again, things were getting weird, like finding those words in the little notebook.

'It's the day when the three planets of *Xrisis* align. You would know.' Petrus looked at them, at their puzzlement and anxiety.

'When will that happen?' Ahmed asked, glancing at Jacq. She had begun shuffling her feet and didn't want to know.

Ahmed was curious. 'Do you know when?'

'I don't know exactly yet, but I may know soon.'

This ambiguous comment tipped the balance for Jacq. Her nerves were raw. She had been living on edge for days. The total mystery about what they were supposed to achieve and the way Petrus was talking. That they were undercover and exposed to danger. It all became too much. The past months had left them both feeling mentally abused and emotionally drained. Now another surprise full of complications. Jacq let fly.

'I have no idea who you are!' she shouted at Petrus getting up forcefully from her chair and tipping it over. 'Ahmed and I don't know what we're meant to be doing. It's a rollercoaster ride of confusion. We can't be for one another what we'd like to be. We tried to find some peace today so we could have a good time and we end up talking to you!' She desperately tried not to cry from anger. 'You speak about the Planets and the Day of that Riddle, just like that, and we're just supposed to act as if nothing strange is happening. Just some more rotten stuff we don't understand, some more confusion and pressure. I'm out.' Jacq was furious with frustration and ran back to the horses.

Petrus left his seat with a speed that belied his age and rushed after her. Ahmed was hot on his heals ready to defend Jacq, if needed. But Petrus only grabbed the horse's bridle so Jacq couldn't ride off. She got into the saddle and looked down at him, eyes ablaze. What she saw was an old man's friendly face, tears rolling down his cheeks. He looked up at her not saying a word. It jolted Jacq away from her anger. She felt a little chastened by this look of apology. Ahmed, also angry, and glad that Jacq had vented frustration for both of them, stood motionless. Jacq said nothing. Did nothing but lift her gaze toward the mountains. Their red surface pitted from centuries of corrosion. Her heart was racing.

'Please come and sit down again,' Petrus finally managed to say. 'That was unforgivable of me.' He let go of the bridle and walked back to the shade and the chairs.

Ahmed didn't move. Jacq's comment about their relationship was engraved in his mind. Also, that she wanted out. 'What do you want to do?' he asked.

'What do you want to do?' Jacq's was now weary. With all the tiredness she had felt before coming back. She kept the horse still.

For a while they just stayed there together waving the flies away from their faces.

'Come on,' Ahmed said encouragingly and slowly began to walk back to old man Petrus. He tried to imagine what it would feel like if *Cryslis* remained unchallenged. A thought too much to bear. Quitting might be the easy way out, but was it really? He would never forgive himself. They were in too deep now. Well over their heads, and coping, if only just. His fighting spirit began to assert itself.

Jacq had no desire to move at all. Just sitting on the horse for an hour would be fine. She watched Ahmed as he walked away with his easy step and agile back. Her heart decided to follow him. On autopilot she got out of the saddle.

Petrus had poured each of them a fresh glass of water and began to talk.

'I have been alone far too long,' he explained. 'Lost touch with how hard it is to be young. How difficult your circumstances at *Cryslis* must be. I'm sorry. What I told you about the Day of the Riddle is true. I am assigned to give you information. But I should have been more careful with my introduction. Sorry to have caused such an upset.'

That seemed a genuine apology. Jacq's emotions were settling down. She began to wonder what they were about to discover.

'I have been waiting for you. Two young people to undo the hideous one-sided power of *Cryslis*. To restore balance in our world. Only people with the future still fully ahead could ever succeed. Your age fits that category.'

Petrus sipped his water and collected his thoughts. 'When you became so angry, the unreasonableness of it all struck me hard. What is and might be expected of you. There is nothing I can do about that. All the same, the task ahead can be achieved.' He looked at Jacq and was heartened that she seemed to have regained some of her composure.

'The Day of the Riddle is indeed near. I don't know exactly when, but I will be told by *Sophius* at the appointed time. First, two young people need to present themselves. I believe you two to be those. We shall soon know for sure.'

'How?' asked Ahmed.

Jacq sat as if hewn in stone, staring ahead with a drawn face. Not a word of Petrus' talk was escaping her. She wondered how *Sophius* might convey a message about the planets. Perhaps Petrus was a mystic of some sort. It wouldn't surprise her.

Petrus explained. 'The right young people will be able to find the sphere of *Shalo*. No-one else can.'

'It is here? Do you know where it is?' Ahmed asked incredulously.

'I am the Keeper of *Shalo*. The sphere is on earth as is the *Cryslis*. I can tell you where to look, but could never discover it. Only you two can, if you are, who I think you are. *Shalo* will emit light in the dark for those who are destined to find it.

'So you're saying that we can see *Shalo*, but you can't?' Ahmed was not sure he understood.

'In daylight I could see it, but not in the darkness where it is hidden.'

'But if we don't find the sphere, can't see it either, we will be free of our obligation?' Ahmed reasoned.

'We'll find it,' said Jacq. She remembered her telling of *Shalomat* at Uluru. How she had identified with that small golden sphere. They would find it alright. She was certain.

Petrus looked at them both. Satisfied with what he perceived. 'I think you're right. I never thought to see the day.'

'Where do we look?' Ahmed asked.

'You take the horses a mile west along the foot of the mountain.' Petrus pointed onwards from where they had come. 'You will find three trees and a large boulder with a few bushes against it. Get close to those bushes and you will discover you can squeeze past and get behind the boulder. The horses as well, no problem. You will find a path that dips and turns and leads through a canyon. You would never imagine it to be there. Eventually, you will need to leave your horses at a narrow gap. Take the last few hundred meters on foot towards a cave and a billabong – a waterhole. The sphere of *Shalo* is somewhere in that waterhole. The journey shouldn't take you more than forty minutes.'

The directions were simple enough. They should find that waterhole easily.

'Just remember,' Petrus concluded, 'those who find *Shalo* can touch *Cryslis* unharmed.' He made sure that Jacq and Ahmed understood this final comment well.

Without a word Jacq stood up and walked to her horse. Ahmed looked at the old man, also without comment, and followed her. No sooner were they in the saddle and they heard Petrus take up hammer and chisel again. He hit the rock with careful blows. Harder than before.

They rode to the rock-face in silence. Each deep in thought, keeping an eye out for those trees. Ahmed stopped after a while and Jacq turned her horse to face him. She sensed something was up.

'Do you want to quit?' he questioned. They had not actually discussed that, really. 'I feel that we must be sure, both of us, if we go on.'

Jacq shook her head. She had considered it.

'It may get nasty,' Ahmed pressed on. 'Finding the sphere won't be the end of it.'

He looked away from Jacq over the head of his horse and seemed annoyed. Jacq's comment about their relationship was playing through his mind. That he was being deprived of it.

Jacq was certain that finding the sphere would not be the end of it. For a moment she considered her Indian friend. He sat so erect and stiff on that horse, looking like a prince of the Punjab. 'And you feel that I'm difficult company right now,' she suggested with feminine intuition.

Ahmed kept avoiding her eyes. Said nothing. She had got it right, Jacq concluded. Told herself to be careful. Accept what was grating at him. To take it seriously, even if it took her effort.

'No. I don't want to quit,' she said eventually and with conviction. 'I don't want to be a hassle to you either.' She could hardly expect Ahmed not to wrestle with their constrained relationship. 'I think, I know how you're feeling. I need your support. But I can't guarantee you anything. It's all way too hard. I feel a complete shambles.' Tears were again welling up in her eyes.

The horses were placid animals. Jacq and Ahmed could sit at ease. Jacq was determined to look at him straight and not hide her emotions. She needed his help badly. He was the only person she could turn to.

Shame came creeping up on Ahmed. Already he regretted raising the issue of their relationship. Jacq, he realised, was perceptive. He decided on having it out in the open about how he felt. Here sitting on a horse in outback Australia.

'I feel, as if my heart is in two,' he said with some difficulty, looking down at his hands. They held the reins loosely. He pushed on. 'I can handle it, if you tell me that you care.'

Jacq didn't respond immediately. She wondered how she could ever find the balance in showing her true feelings. Between what was growing in her heart for Ahmed, and the detachment their mission needed. In desperation she just looked at him with tears now flowing freely. She didn't feel like speaking. Words would simply get stuck in her throat.

'I'm sorry,' Ahmed mumbled. 'It's not your fault.'

They were so much thrown about by everything, that he was not sure of their special friendship lasting the distance. Would it crash under pressure? Would Jacq drift away from him? It was all too muddled up, the whole sorry mess. How they felt about each other. The troubles they faced. He could not kiss Jacq again for she wouldn't let him. The closest they ever got was talking. Ahmed badly needed more, even if it was just a little.

Jacq found her voice. 'I need you to help me,' she said wiping the tears away with her fingers. 'I cannot leave *Cryslis* unchallenged. However much I dread what is ahead. I cannot walk away. I blew up at Petrus because of the way we are exposed to things. Not because I'm not sold out on our mission.'

'It's okay,' Ahmed offered. 'Just forget it.' His question about whether to go on had not been the real issue. As Jacq had so correctly perceived. He now preferred this conversation finished. Start riding.

Jacq had no intention of forgetting. Ahmed had expressed how he was feeling. It was quite a step for him. He wished to know whether she cared. Right now she didn't know what to say about that sensibly. Of course she cared. She would be as considerate as possible in the days ahead. Romantic involvement had to remain excluded though. If ever they were to succeed against *Cryslis*. There was no other way.

Ahmed raised his two hands in apology. Palms outward at chest height. Jacq had asked for his support, and she could count on him. He decided not to mention the matter of the feelings between them again. Until their task was over with. Hopefully, this *Cryslis* saga would soon end.

Jacq brought her horse a step closer. She put two fingers to her lips, reached out, and touched Ahmed's mouth. He felt her fingertips lingering, with gentle pressure. As if reluctant to take her hand away. He tasted the salt of tears. Her face he had a little smile. He saw pain in her blue eyes, but also warmth. Slowly Jacq shook her head, conveying that just now getting close was a no-go. But there was promise of good times. They were both hurting. That was clear.

His question about her really caring had been unnecessary. Of course she did! He should not have doubted. Ahmed rebuked himself while forcing a smile in return and nodded.

Jacq was grateful. She understood, Ahmed would allow her space. A sudden urge to lean over and grab him, she forced away. Jacq groaned inaudibly. Why does it all have to be so complicated? She briefly shut her eyes and controlled her emotions. They sat astride their horses close together. Bright sunlight made the outback glitter. Then Jacq pulled the reins, turned, and began heading for the boulder.

Petrus' instructions were easy to follow. The ground became increasingly rocky as they approached the three trees. They found the path behind the boulder. As said, it ran via a canyon to the cave and waterhole. The horses were left behind where the path narrowed. In plenty of shade. The final stretch they walked in file. Ahmed took the lead. Protected from the sun by the rock-face the air was surprisingly cool. The place they were to find was isolated and beautiful. A cave with a sandy floor on the edge of a pool that was not large, but probably deep. Rock walls rose up around. Staring into the pool bending over they could see their faces. It was impossible to see further. The still, glassy water was a mirror. *Shalo* was not going to be found just by looking in.

'We need to jump in,' Ahmed concluded.

Jacq began to strip herself of shoes and jeans. Ahmed did likewise. They slid into the water bracing themselves for a chill. It was not bad. Cold, but not freezing. A welcome refreshment after a hot ride. Their movement stirred up a host of particles spoiling under water visibility. No bottom was felt below their feet.

Ahmed came up for air. He held on to rocks at the edge. 'Let's both stay very still for a minute,' he suggested gulping breath. 'Then we gently slide under, and slowly look around.'

Once the water was clearer they submerged once more. Came up gasping, again having found nothing. Ahmed broke surface just after Jacq.

'Two bodies create too much movement,' Jacq concluded. Breathing heavily she climbed out of the water. She would sit on the edge for a moment. Her wet t-shirt and panties were clinging like a skin. They would dry soon enough, Jacq felt. Ahmed couldn't take his eyes off. The wet cotton against the contours of her body.

'You do it,' Jacq said grinning. She knew full well the reason for his fascination. 'I'll sit on a rock over there in the sun.'

As she stood up, Ahmed saw her against the blue sky. Long legs dripping with water. The imprint of her nipples. For a moment he forgot all about *Shalo*.

'Go on then,' Jacq urged him, mischievously.

On his third dive Ahmed noticed a dim glow. In the dark rock wall about a meter below the surface. It definitely was not natural. With difficulty he moved a large stone aside and kicked up to the surface for air. Down again and on a small ledge he found the sphere of *Shalo*. In the murky light it looked golden. Rather small, a little larger than the *Cryslis*. Apprehensively, he took careful hold of it. It was very smooth, not at all heavy. It fitted into his hand.

When Ahmed broke the surface with lungs bursting for oxygen, he held his find up high above his head in triumph. It had been discovered. After who knows how many years in hiding, the sphere of *Shalo* was out in the open! Ahmed thumped the air from sheer exhilaration.

Jacq quickly moved over and took *Shalo* from him. It felt smooth and cool. Touching it released a positive sensation. She noticed that right away, even though it made little sense. Jacq too was excited that they had found the golden sphere of *Shalomat*. It was unbelievable. She had wondered about the *Cryslis*. Whether it was simply a piece of crystal shaped years ago by a clever jeweller. Her experience in the Temple had exposed her to its power. But that could be more because of placement on the psychic grid rather than an otherworldly origin. Finding *Shalo* today erased any doubts that *Shalomat* was real. No need to question its cosmic dimensions. However incredible and strange. They had made an amazing discovery. The sphere consisted of material Jacq didn't recognise. Gold, but with a deeper glow than gold. She noticed its light weight. It could easily be carried along.

Ahmed had got dressed. He accepted *Shalo* back and pocketed the sphere. Jacq's T-shirt had dried.

Time was passing. They could not linger. Should get to open country with some haste. The horses were found where they had been left. Jacq and Ahmed rode as quickly as possible to the boulder and dismounted. Ahmed peered from behind the huge rock to check whether the Rangers might be about. The coast was clear. They moved onto the wide and level dusty plain without being seen. No time to visit Petrus. Neither of them felt like doing so anyway.

Nearing the *Cryslis* compound they noticed the Rangers in the distance. Perhaps they were on the lookout for them. But the white pickup never slowed or changed direction. Jacq and Ahmed felt seriously undercover. Against their will, imagination played its tricks. Surely no one could possibly know about their find. But that brought them little comfort. All the way to the stables and while unsaddling the horses, they forced themselves to relax. Pretending to have an ordinary time.

***

The Director was thinking it over. Something made him uneasy about that Indian boy and the blond girl from Holland. Nothing specific. He could not put his finger on it. But they needed keeping an eye on.

He had invited the Mentor for a talk. Learned that after a shaky start, the two youth had become fine students. This raised the Director's suspicions. Was the Mentor, being a psychologist, surprised about this change of attitude? Actually, yes, was the response. But there had been no indication since, that they were anything but sincere. In answer to the question of Jacq and Ahmed's present whereabouts the Director was told that permission had been given for a day's horse riding. It not being prohibited, he could hardly object. But suggested horse riding to be off the agenda in future. He did not give a reason.

Next he had instructed the Rangers by satellite phone to find out where those kids were riding. Just to make sure they had not come to any harm. They should be either back by now, or at least close. The Rangers soon reported that the two were on their way home. All seemed well.

The Director remained troubled. Something was afoot. But how could two kids on a couple of horses possibly mean trouble for *Cryslis*? Surely, there was nothing to tell the rich man.

CHAPTER 12

AFTER BREAKFAST the next morning Ahmed was waiting for Jacq to discuss what to do. Surely, *Shalo* had not been found without reason. He had slit a tennis ball and pushed the sphere inside. They were meeting at the corner of one of the outer buildings, out of sight from the main areas. Not that Ahmed expected an idea about the Riddle. They were getting used to not knowing what was going on. Discovering the next move in surprising ways. It irked him, but nothing could be done about it. Ahmed now carried *Shalo* in his right pocket, the small notebook and key in the other.

'Where is the sphere?' Jacq asked as soon as she joined him.

Ahmed showed her the tennis ball.

'Have you looked in the notebook?'

He had this morning to no avail. Nothing had been added to the writing. All it said was, 'Well done, don't despair!' It summed up their situation nicely, but was of little help.

'Can I have a look?'

Ahmed extracted the little book from his pocket. Jacq took it not really knowing why. She had quite accepted his comment about there being no changes. She opened it anyway. Immediately, her eyes were riveted onto the page. Fear crept over her face. Without a word she handed the book back to Ahmed. He was looking at her in alarm. As well he might. For a new instruction had appeared. It read: Take the *Cryslis* to Petrus.

They were totally stunned. As so often in their crazy quest. Something like this was to be expected, perhaps. Those in possession of *Shalo* would be able to touch the *Cryslis* unharmed, Petrus has said. Still, the idea of having to steal the thing had never crossed their minds. They were dumb-founded and in shock.

At that precise moment the Mentor arrived looking for them. They had not noticed his approach. He quickly discerned that something was wrong. The reason for the shock on their faces would be in that little notebook. Ahmed began to put it back into his pocket. The Mentor stretched out his hand. There was no way but to surrender it. Horrified and with obvious reluctance he obliged. This meant the end of everything.

The Mentor had a look. All he found were empty pages. Puzzled, he asked them what the problem was. Why were they looking so disturbed? Jacq and Ahmed remained speechless. The Mentor didn't comment on the notebook. Apparently, he couldn't read what was inside. Ahmed received the book back.

'You are both acting strangely. Anything the

matter?' The Mentor raised his eyebrows.

They just shrugged their shoulders. He was aware that young people could act strangely for all kinds of reasons and let it be. Instead, he gave his message. Horse riding would be out for today. Probably for a few days. He looked at their blank faces as they nodded.

'It's time for you to mingle more with the rest of the group. This morning we are holding a doubles tennis competition. I expect you both to participate.' With that comment he turned and walked off.

Their heartbeats took a while in slowing down enough for conversation to continue.

'We need to talk,' Ahmed suggested. Stating the obvious.

'Not here.' Jacq thought it better to find a less secluded spot. They should not raise suspicion. 'Let's go to the barbecue area. Put a smile on our faces.'

There was no one at the barbecue when they sat down at a table.

'This whole thing's crazy,' Ahmed said. 'But then, perhaps it is not.'

He had done some thinking during their brief stroll. They were on a wild goose chase, but somehow on target. Their progress was being orchestrated step by step. From elsewhere in strange but effective ways. The sphere in his pocket was proof of that. It would not be believed if you told anyone about *Shalo*. But it was very real. They possessed a notebook only they could read. And now they had to steal the *Cryslis*. As if that was not super dangerous!

'Yes,' agreed Jacq, lost in thought. 'It's crazy.'

It would catapult their mission completely into the open with grave consequences. But she felt there was another hurdle to overcome. Not just the stealing of the *Cryslis*. If only she could put her finger on it.

'I'm being used,' Ahmed exclaimed with some anger.

Jacq felt the same. 'We seem to have been chosen to be used.'

Actually, that was her problem. It had reared its head yesterday when they were with Petrus. Again now, with this latest instruction. It seemed to totally disregard their safety.

'Like in war,' Ahmed suggested. 'As a soldier you do as you are told.'

'Sort of.' Jacq hated the very thought of war.

'You either accept it, or you make sure to get delisted.' Ahmed continued on with the gist of his thoughts. He felt to be following a line of reasoning that could be helpful. 'It's also like boxing.'

'Boxing?'

'Yes. Don't start a fight. unless you want to win. Why take a battering for nothing? Also, getting hurt is no excuse for opting out. Only a knock-out punch should stop you.' Rugger had told him that once.

Recalling one of his own fights as a young man.

'Sounds like *Cryslis* philosophy,' Jacq retorted.

'Yes,' Ahmed agreed. 'Perhaps *Cryslis* isn't all bad.'

'This is different though,' Jacq objected. '*Cryslis* is self-serving.' Their quest surely was not.

'Hand-to-hand combat, do you ever half commit?' Ahmed asked thinking of Jacq's karate.

'No, it wouldn't work. You'd get badly hurt.'

Ahmed said no more.

'So, what are we going to do?' she wondered tentatively.

'As we're told,' he suggested. 'Yesterday we both decided not to quit. Revisiting that issue with every instruction is of no use. However weird or difficult it may seem. So far, somehow, we have been doing okay. Let's trust in whatever is behind all this. We really have no option.' Ahmed just couldn't see it any other way. It would never work in any other way.

'Trust,' Jacq mumbled. Then added, 'don't ever doubt.'

'Sorry?'

'That's what Mr. Adams told us. Don't ever, ever doubt.' Her words hung in the air.

So he had, Ahmed remembered. 'Fine by me.' This discussion was resolving a major issue for him. They had place trust in what was asked of them. That it would be possible. Use all their wits to make it happen. It wasn't that bad, really. The surprises and recklessness of their adventure had its attractions. 'Let's do it,' he decided for them both. 'Let's take the *Cryslis* to Petrus.'

It was time to move on. With still lots to talk about. Jacq suggested that Ahmed come to her room. No-one would expect him to be there. It should be possible to sneak in unseen. 'I'll change for tennis first,' she told him. 'Come in ten minutes.'

Ahmed didn't object. He had never been in Jacq's room.

They decided to steal the *Cryslis* on horseback. Grab it. Make a dash for it. Riding was forbidden but the Mentor might not have informed the stables. The best time for this move was later today. Pretending to take a short ride before dinner. They would carry money, their credit cards and passports. Also a change of clothes. A small rucksack could easily hold that much. Both Ahmed and Jacq figured that once Petrus had the *Cryslis*, he would know what to do and look after things. Surely, they would not be back at this campus.

The tennis doubles was a welcome distraction. Jacq nor Ahmed was focused. But they played well enough to avert attention. The task ahead kept nagging at them. For Jacq the game was hard. She had made sure to be paired with Erik. If she spent time with him all morning, he wouldn't hassle her later. She told Erik that Ahmed was a bit of a bore, but good company for riding. They would briefly go out later. She would catch up with Erik that evening. Left the nature of it to his imagination. Jacq had to ensure the Viking would not be looking for her that afternoon. She disliked spinning lies about Ahmed and catching up with Erik. Once again, she felt compromised by the demands of secrecy and guile placed upon her. Still, she had been undercover for months by now. She should get used to it. But it had not been necessary to deceive a friend so blatantly before.

The Mentor was quietly observing the morning. He decided that everything seemed normal. Jacq was spending time with Erik, as she often did. Ahmed was not looking at her. The Mentor had no idea what effort that took. Though understanding what Jacq was about, Ahmed hated it. That she managed to laugh quite naturally, while aware of what was ahead, amazed him. He needed top concentration to make a game of his tennis.

One of his opponents was the Mentor. It made focusing easier. The man irritated him which fuelled Ahmed's desire to win. That they still lost, was not his fault. Though his game had been average. His partner was a pleasant girl, but hardly athletic. Not like Jacq. With Erik, she won the day. No surprises there.

The Mentor was satisfied with his win and the success of the morning. He told Ahmed that he would again take to the sky in an ultralight. That afternoon. The pleasure of it showed in his face. He had no idea how this comment buoyed Ahmed. No Mentor close that afternoon. The man flew his lawnmower on the other side of Alice Springs. Ahmed put a tennis ball in his pocket. It would be cut for the original *Cryslis*.

The sun stood well past its zenith when Jacq and Ahmed arrived at the stables. The place was deserted. Rather than walking directly, they had made a detour. To stay out of view. They were unsure whether to take the docile horses from yesterday or two more spirited animals. The quiet ones would have to do. Then they could not be blamed for selecting the wrong animals would someone enter while they were saddling up. The calmer horses were less also likely to jeopardise their advance on the Temple. If all went wrong and they were chased by the Rangers, faster horses made no difference. Came someone asking right now, their story of taking a brief ride before dinner should be believable. Unless the Mentor's instruction against it was known. Then they might face disciplinary action. But their mission could remain a secret. Once the *Cryslis* was missing from the Temple, their cover would be well and truly blown.

Saddling the horses seemed to take ages. Jacq felt a knot in her stomach. Ahmed, also tense, sensed his adrenalin kicking in. They rode away quietly. It felt as if a thousand eyes were boring into their backs. All remained peaceful.

They directed the horses away from the Temple to travel in a wide arc. Their approach would be from the other side of the hill behind the building. Once well away from the *Cryslis* compound the horses were spurred on. No Rangers in sight. But that could change instantly.

The horses were tied up to small trees at the foot of the hill. The Temple could be reached via a gully. Everything was working out fine, thus far. Ahmed had offered to sneak towards the building alone. But Jacq didn't want to know about it. They would take this *Cryslis* together or not at all. She would be afraid, absolutely. But nothing would please her more than seeing that object disappear into a tennis ball.

The Temple door was unlocked. Who would dare to steal something that burned your hand off? That brought death? There was no need for security. Quietly they slipped into the cool and austere building. First Ahmed and then Jacq. The double-glazed tinted glass created an oasis in the desert. In a corner a sculpture with water flowing and surrounded by flowering plants was bubbling gently. It must have been switched off during their visit at full moon. All that had been noticeable then, was the stillness of the night. The Temple was utterly peaceful, but for their racing hearts.

As Ahmed carefully stepped closer to the original *Cryslis* in all its splendour, he stopped with a moment of hesitation. They had agreed for him to take the little pyramid. Even without moonlight the *Cryslis* was enchanting. Ahmed felt uncertain.

'What's wrong?' whispered Jacq.

'Nothing,' he whispered back. Slowly he reached out. He felt a resistance to his hand. The thought of burning himself crossed his mind.

'Hurry up,' said Jacq with urgency. Perhaps she should take this horrible thing without further ado.

Ahmed took courage and picked the *Cryslis* up. So small and yet so powerful. It felt cool with sharp points digging into his hand. He took the tennis ball out of his pocket.

'Let me do it,' Jacq said. 'Please!'

Ahmed handed her the ball and the *Cryslis*.

Jacq felt the same coolness and the sharp points. Grimly she pressed the dark crystal object into the tennis ball and out of sight. For a moment a dour smile played on her face. They had done it! It felt almost surreal. They had stolen the *Cryslis*. It was unbelievable! Quickly they made their way back to the horses and set off at a gallop. Nobody noticed.

***

Often the Director visited the Temple late afternoon.

In the middle of a busy day. He enjoyed the quiet space but less so lately. The Temple seemed to carry a mild accusation. As if he was coming up short in his job. Today he took a dune buggy to the sanctuary in haste. Something was amiss. Time alone with the *Cryslis* might ease his apprehension. Possibly. He entered the Temple with no inkling of what was ahead.

At first he was too stunned to have one sensible thought. About what was before him. He stood totally perplexed. Whatever troubles he had imagined, it never included the disaster he now faced. The *Cryslis* box was empty. Who could possibly have got away with this incredible theft? Fear gripped his heart. For he understood the enormity of the event. He became consumed by a massive anger. A cold furious power. It settled into him like a stone. The myth of *Shalomat* flashed through his mind. This theft was related to that ancient story. He remembered the warning of the rich man about the Planets aligning being near. Then there was that Riddle nobody understood. Cosmic dynamics were in play here. A stolen *Cryslis* made no sense otherwise. His life had been changed from a competent directorship into an enormous crisis. With eyes blazing he closed the box. The *Cryslis* had rested inside for centuries. This disappearance would remain a secret. No one should find out. Whatever it took, he would retrieve the *Cryslis* and return it to this Temple. Pity on those who dared stand in his way.

The Director suspected Jacq and Ahmed to be the culprits. It seemed ridiculous that those two could take on the might of *Cryslis*. But if there were cosmic powers involved, anything was possible. He locked the door of the Temple and rushed back to the guest buildings. He asked after the two students and learned from Erik about their horse riding. It was all the proof he needed. They had disobeyed his orders. Only stealing the *Cryslis* would have made that happen. He contacted the Rangers. Explained that Jacq and Ahmed had gone riding without permission. They needed to be brought back immediately. Probably they had passed behind the hill at the Temple. It was an inspired deduction. One of the Rangers telling him of a cloud of dust he had seen in that vicinity. They drove to the hill at speed and found the horse tracks. On the dusty and rocky ground the tracks could only be followed by driving slowly.

This disaster will be rectified, the Director felt. Soon the *Cryslis* would be recovered. No need for the rich man to know.

***

Jacq and Ahmed reached Petrus with their horses in a high sweat. As before, they found him chiselling at a large rock. He downed his tools quickly and got them water. They drank greedily. Though late afternoon, it was still hot.

'Here's the *Cryslis*,' Ahmed offered, wiping his mouth and taking a tennis ball out of his pocket.

'No, no,' Petrus responded. 'I can't touch that. You must take it on further.'

'To where?' Jacq was alarmed.

'Towards the sunrise. That is all I know. Really!'

Petrus was extra apologetic. He was not playing games. He had no idea what was to follow. Jacq remembered the Aboriginal painter saying the same. Seek the sunrise. Why was she only mildly surprised?

'Where. What sunrise?' asked Ahmed urgently.

Petrus didn't answer.

'Look,' he urged them, 'I don't know. But I have been told when the Planets will align. It's the day after tomorrow. The day after tomorrow. On that day, and that one only, the Riddle of *Shalomat* must be fulfilled. Later and all will be lost.' He stressed the point.

'And if we fail?' Jacq asked.

'Then *Cryslis* will dominate unchallenged and the moment of restoring balance in our world has forever been lost.'

'What must do?' Ahmed pressed on. 'We don't know.'

'Fulfil the Riddle of *Shalomat*.'

Before he could explain further Petrus noticed a dust cloud on the horizon. 'You must go,' he urged. 'The Rangers are coming.'

Jacq and Ahmed were struck with fear. Events were taking a serious turn. How much help was Petrus to be? None at all, it seemed.

'Can you drive a ute, a pickup?' he asked Ahmed.

'Yes,' he nodded. If he could race a Porsche, he surely could drive a pickup. Jacq looked surprised.

'Take that ute.' Petrus pointed to an old white car with a tray on the back. 'Drive to the hidden path. Park a little away from there and flatten a tire. Make it seem broken down. Take the two blankets that are in the back and stay in the cave tonight. The keys are in the ignition.'

The dust cloud was fast approaching. As they hurried towards the car, Petrus had a final instruction. 'About the sphere of *Shalo*,' he shouted after them. 'It must be returned from what it was taken.'

They couldn't ask what that meant. Knew full well no answer to be forthcoming anyway. The engine of the car fired immediately and Ahmed drove off as fast as he thought safe. Towards the hidden path. Jacq, in a state of shock, asked him where he had learned to drive so well. He grunted that at home he raced a Porsche. She raised her eyebrows wondering. They bounced along over the rocky terrain. Jacq hanging onto the open window with her hair flying all over her face. She was impressed with the driving. The wheels often slipping until the car found traction again. Braking to a stop, they flattened a tire. Grabbed their rucksack and the blankets and ran for it. After a mad scramble into the entrance of the path they disappeared. Clambering as fast as possible over an uneven rocky surface. Once well away from the boulder they slowed into a steady pace. It wasn't long till the billabong and cave suddenly appeared.

With the Rangers, Petrus confirmed that indeed two youths had galloped in. They had stolen his car. As the Rangers could see, he was giving their horses much needed attention. I don't think they will get far, Petrus told them. He pointed in the right direction confirming his innocence. The Rangers had seen the dust cloud thrown up by his old car anyway. They left and soon found the ute with a flat tire. But no sign of the students. The ground was solid rock and left no foot prints. Unless you were an Aboriginal tracker. A scan with binoculars revealed nothing. Somehow the youths had disappeared into thin air. The Director was told. He instructed the Rangers to get back to base and bring in Petrus. The old sculptor seemed unsurprised when taken hostage.

Petrus had noticed the *Cryslis* complex many times. But never cared to set foot in the place. The sight of the Temple in particular made him deeply cross. Staying well away from that sterile building had been the best medicine for his wrath. For decades he had lived in his isolated spot practising his art. Signing his life away to *Shalo*. It had not always been so. When young life had held many promises. Until that day someone visited him. He was told to be in line for a special task. He was to commit to the sphere of *Shalo*. Until The Day of the Riddle. That day might happen in his lifetime. He could have refused, and would have. But Therese, the love of his life, left him for another man. The solitude of the Australian outback appealed and was to become his refuge. Petrus was suited to the contemplative life. He enjoyed the empty space around him and had no regrets. Now he was facing his final task.

The Director asked the Rangers to wait outside his office. He looked carefully at Petrus and saw an old man in dusty clothes staring back at him without fear.

'Where are those kids?'

'Gone,' Petrus said and added with satisfaction: 'So is the *Cryslis*.'

That comment gave the Director a jolt. 'What do you know about that?' His anger was spilling over.

Petrus remained unperturbed. 'More than you,' he said calmly.

It infuriated the man behind his glamorous desk. Nobody had ever spoken to him like that. 'Who are you?' he snarled.

'I represent *Sophius*.' Petrus looked him straight in the eye. The gaze and the authority behind those words involuntarily made the Director shiver. The mention of

Sophius was a shock. This disaster took on a dimension he might have foreseen but didn't. *Sophius* and *Igod* were the two gods at loggerheads in *Shalomat*. They were the forces behind the reality of *Cryslis*. He believed that old geezer. For the first time, he was facing his opposition for real. It was unnerving but had possibilities.

'Where are those kids?' he asked softly but with menace.

Petrus no longer responded. His face had turned to stone dismissing any further contact.

The Rangers were called back in. Those kids, the Director said. I have no idea what he's done to them. God knows whether they are safe. Get it out of him. I don't care how.

And that would be just the start, the Director thought.

Petrus had taken a pill from his pocket unnoticed and swallowed it.

The Rangers had no qualms with an interrogation. They grabbed the old man roughly. He briefly stood his ground and then began to crumble. Petrus had fulfilled his task and was happy to depart this world. His last thoughts were a prayer for Jacq and Ahmed. This collapse did not perturb the Rangers at first. The old fellow must have fainted at the ordeal ahead. When they examined him closely, it became obvious that actually, he had died.

'He's dead,' one of them said, looking at their boss.

The Director was incensed at this dusty old man there on the spotless carpet of his office. His quarry had escaped him. Necessary information would now not be forthcoming. 'Take him back to his shack,' he ordered. 'Dump him. Then go and look for those kids again.'

Once regaining enough composure, the Director called for the Mentor. He explained that Jacq and Ahmed had disappeared, must have got lost. Against his instructions they had gone horse riding. The Director looked sharply at the Mentor suggesting he should have prevented that. Meekly the accused proposed that contacting their parents would be appropriate. That idea was rejected as premature. It was a problem, the Director agreed. He showed a caring face with difficulty. Surely, they would soon be found. The Rangers were looking for them already. If anyone were to contact the parents, it would be him. It could wait. Why worry those parents unnecessarily. The students could not have gone far. Even a night in the open, if that were to happen, should not harm them. They would have enough water.

The Director asked that at daybreak the Mentor should take to the sky in an ultralight. Scan the mountain range. In case Jacq and Ahmed had got lost in there. Unless they were soon found, of course. He had quietly decided to hire a helicopter from that tourist service in Alice that offered scenic flights. Have a look as well.

Before daybreak the Director received a call from the rich man. The Planets would align tomorrow. Be especially vigilant. Before he could respond the line was dead, as usual. The Director didn't call back. If the rich man would be curt, so could he. He would soon solve the problem anyway. But the call brought the urgency of his predicament into sharp focus. He had till tomorrow's end to prevent the Riddle from being solved. Whatever that meant.

CHAPTER 13

THERE WAS NOTHING TO DO in the cave but be as comfortable as possible. It meant shaping the sandy floor in a way that allowed for a headrest. The stress of the day had taken its toll. Ahmed and Jacq fell asleep on top of their blankets well before dark.

Jacq had sat on that rock near the pool for a while. The one from yesterday with Ahmed searching for *Shalo*. She would never have imagined being back this soon, on the run as a fugitive. She tried to collect her thoughts. It was hopeless, her mind in a muddle.

Ahmed crashed on top of his blanket soon after reaching the cave. He begun staring up at the wall. It showed the kind of rock art they had visited a few days ago. With their guides from *Cryslis*. For a while he tried to figure out what the drawings depicted. Some of it he could understand. Failing to stay awake his eyelids fell shut.

They woke up later thoroughly cold. Rugged up properly and felt their empty stomachs. No dinner that evening. It was doubtful they would have eaten much anyway because of stress. Through the night sleeping deeply Ahmed and Jacq remained oblivious to the cave. To the nocturnal activities of wildlife and possible danger.

Jacq opened her eyes to the sound of birds. A new day. She lay still, pulled the blanket around tightly and looked up at the rock paintings. They were beautiful in their simplicity. Jacq was not scared of this cave. Although in central Australia in the wild, she did not feel at all alone for some reason. It was as if a host of people belonged to this place where she was now finding shelter. People, who knew how best to survive in nature. It comforted her. There is much more to the world than meets the eye, Jacq knew.

The Rangers cut through her reflections. Any feeling of safety here was an illusion. The Australian outback could be a threat also. People got lost and they died. Even in modern days with all its possible communications. She had read that. But this morning, being surrounded by a dome of brownish rock and paintings from another era, Jacq felt secure.

After waking up Ahmed concerned himself with what to do next. He would be highly surprised if Petrus came to the rescue this morning. The only instruction given of any meaning was to seek the sunrise. The sun rises in the east, so that would be the direction to take. From Alice Springs you could either travel southeast back towards Adelaide or north to Darwin. He remembered that. Straight east was just desert. The southeast road they had travelled returning to Alice Springs from Uluru. Somehow they needed to find that road. If it wasn't east but at least it went eastward. Ahmed didn't feel like explaining that to Jacq just yet. He would wait a few minutes. She was gazing away at the rock face, lost in thoughts.

Their mission was in the open now. Ahmed was convinced the Director would chase them down to get the *Cryslis* back. Last night he had placed both tennis balls on a ledge in the wall. It had been uncomfortable sleeping with them in his pockets. Briefly, Ahmed considered the yellow balls just an arm's length away. He had drawn a triangle on the one containing the *Cryslis*. The tennis balls appeared so innocuous. In reality he was carrying dynamite around. Harmless to Jacq and himself, but lethal to anyone else. That the future shape of global culture depended on these two objects, was beyond his him. He couldn't even begin to get a grip on that. It was hard enough figuring out what to do next. How to succeed. Ahmed thought he heard a car in the distance, very faintly. Fear of the Rangers gripped his chest. It couldn't be them though. The sound came from the east rather than west. Perhaps there was a road in the vicinity. He observed Jacq for a while. The contours of her face. She was beautiful. Her blond hair tussled about, partly hidden by the blanket.

Aware of this attention Jack smiled and accepted his gaze without objection. A surprisingly decent sleep had refreshed her. Her blanket was still pulled tight against the morning chill. They would have to move on soon. But a little longer in the warmth should do no harm. It was daybreak, only just.

Ahmed got up and walked to the waterhole. He drenched his head with cold water. The crystal clear liquid stung. This place would have an Aboriginal name, for sure. He called it the pool of *Shalo*.

Back in the cave Ahmed conveyed his ideas about what to do. Jacq had figured for herself that east would be the way and agreed. He also mentioned about hearing a car. So there should be a road nearby, opposite to how they had come here. Retracing their steps through the canyon obviously was not an option. They should leave this idyllic place at the other side of the waterhole.

After hiding their blankets in the bushes they began to climb. Early morning wildlife was active. A rock wallaby hopped away without haste. Scrambling over large rocks they arrived at another waterhole. Much bigger and suitable for swimming. A clearly defined path was visible at the opposite bank. The quickest way would be through the water. But the sun remained hidden behind the mountains and it was quite cold. Being wet for long would be unwise. Also, the rucksack had to stay dry. Carefully they began to follow the edge of the large waterhole. It was slow going.

After much clambering they reached the path that

would bring them to a car park. A wide space with small trees and bushes. As they stood catching their breath, Jacq noticed an old Ford panelvan. In the distance under a gum tree. A station wagon with one bench up front and panelled sides. It had full height double doors at the back.

Suddenly, Ahmed looked up, alerted by a noise in the sky. Like a giant blowfly. It got steadily louder. With a shock he figured what it was. 'Come on,' he urged Jacq and grabbed her by the arm. Startled, Jacq followed his lead as he raced to a cluster of thick bushes. 'Dive,' he shouted. 'It's the Mentor!' Jacq was quick and they both scrambled out of sight just in time. The Director had ordered the Mentor in his ultralight to start looking for them. How well hidden they were, was unclear. The bushes provided shelter, but only just.

The Mentor flew as low as he dared between the mountains. He tore the silence of the bush apart. Unable to cover the ground around the waterhole in one sweep he turned the light plane and flew back over again. Ahmed and Jacq made themselves small. Hopefully, they would be hard to spot. Not knowing the real reason for their disappearance, the Mentor was expecting them to wave and beckon. They had got lost after all and liked to be found. But he felt uneasy. The situation didn't add up. But what could he do? Flying in the MacDonnell Ranges, with the valleys still in shadow, he was simply following orders. Keeping a close eye on the ground while navigating was difficult. But he would try and was enjoying himself anyway. The little plane hopped over a ridge and soon the stillness was restored. Only the sound of buzzing insects remained.

The back doors of the panelvan opened. A young man climbed out. He looked up at the sky after the retreating racket of the ultralight. He didn't notice Ahmed and Jacq. They remained hidden to make sure the Mentor had flown away. The man was searching in the back of his car when they approach. 'Leave the story to me,' Jacq whispered. She figured a girl would be more readily believed.

The man straightened hearing their footsteps. At first he just looked at them without a word. He was in his mid-twenties, with longish hair, tangled from a night's sleep. That ultralight had woken him much earlier than planned. Though only half awake he was not easily startled. Weighed them up with the ease of having seen it all before. Or most of it anyway.

'What's this?' he said. 'First that plane and now Adam and Eve.' He had a way with words and was grinning. He thought it rather funny.

'Ahmed and Jacq,' Jacq said stepping in closer. Trying to act matter of fact.

'Hi Jacq,' he said appraisingly. Then looked at Ahmed with interest. 'What are you running from?

From that plane?'

'From some real dumb idiots,' Jacq responded as convincingly as possible. 'They left us down here, last night. We got away from them. They invited us for a swim. It got personal.'

Jacq left what that meant to the imagination. The man seemed to have plenty.

'Not smart,' the guy responded and rubbed his chin. 'And Romeo here offered no protection?'

'Romeo stuck with me.' Jacq replied.

He nodded his head. This girl had pluck.

'We need help.'

'I'm sure you do.' He smiled. This conversation woke him up. Not a bad thing. 'And I'm Batman,' he suggested. 'Robin has just gone for a walk.'

'Superman,' Jacq offered, trying to humour him along.

'You're doing well.'

He grinned appreciatively, was nobody's fool and not unfriendly. Had an Australian liberal spirit. He liked these two kids so clearly tourists. They seemed in some kind of bother.

'I can't very well leave you here then, can I?' he concluded.

'Rather not,' Jacq agreed with some relief.

'You're from Alice?' he asked, turning to Ahmed this time.

'Yes, but we need to go east.' Jacq jumped in

before Ahmed could speak. It made the young man turn his attention back to her.

'Lost his voice, has he? Or yours sound better?'

Again he smiled. He was aware of Jacq's tactics.

'Sorry,' Jacq mumbled.

'Anyway, I'm on my way back to Alice soon for some busking.'

He was a musician then, Jacq thought. Sleeping in the back of his van. It made for a cheap bed.

'We need to go east,' Ahmed joined in. 'We can pay.'

The Musician gave Ahmed a speculative look.

'Coober Pedy is sort of east. A day's drive.' He thought of a friend there he had intended to visit soon and could bring that forward. 'It's more south than east, but the only bitumen road out.'

'How much?' Ahmed asked. Anything eastward would do. As they had decided at the waterhole. Getting away from Alice Springs.

'Four hundred.'

'Two hundred now. And two on arrival.' Ahmed wanted to make sure they would get to Coober Pedy.

Again a speculative look. 'How do I know, you have the money?'

It was said in a way of not being that concerned. He got pleasure out of this conversation. A kind of gentle tease.

'Four hundred now,' Jacq butted in. She did not

think to make matters more difficult than they were already. 'But we get going right away.'

She looked at the Musician, who nodded slowly. This girl was someone in a hurry. Jacq began to draw the money out of her back pocket.

'And no questions asked, hey?' he suggested. Their problems had nothing to do with him. People should be allowed to keep their hassles under wraps. He had been in strife a few times himself, defending his right to secrecy.

'Yes, no questions,' Jacq agreed gratefully.

Ahmed heard another noise in the sky far away. It was a clattering sound quite different from the ultralight. He understood it immediately. He grabbed Jacq's arm and said, 'Get in, fast. Come on!' He dived into the back of the van with Jacq following. She had also understood.

Momentarily, the Musician was startled. Then he calmly shut the doors on them. Ahmed ended up on his side with Jacq half on top. She noticed a familiar smell that took her back to Amsterdam. To the streets with the coffee shops. It was the smell of pot. She felt how Ahmed's right leg had ended up between both of hers and was pressing. He had a faint smile on his face finding humour in their situation. They were tangled up together in a van on a stranger's bed hiding from a helicopter. It was laughable, if it wasn't so serious. 'Teach me,' he whispered. Jacq had to smile. She remembered that evening in Adelaide. Looked into his eyes searching. Her blood was rushing and there was no stopping it. Oh, you gorgeous Injun, she thought. What the heck, I will teach you. Impulsively she grabbed his head with both hands. And she taught him in that van next to a guitar case.

The Musician stood staring up at the helicopter. It flew over twice checking him out. Stuff you mate, he thought. You won't find anything. He disliked the powerful statement that machine was making.

After some minutes the copter flew on and he opened the doors. 'Out you come,' he ordered. 'We'll have to sit all three on the front bench. You can sit next to me Jacq.' He looked at her with a mischievous grin. Too young, he concluded. Only just and a nice kid. She looked flustered and he wondered. But it was not his concern. 'Don't worry,' he assured her, 'I'm very safe, when I'm driving.' That comment seemed to humour him once more as he walked to the driver's door grinning.

It took half an hour to reach the highway out of Alice Springs. The van had seen better days, but was comfortable. Three on one bench worked fine. With Jacq moving close to Ahmed, who liked it. In Alice they stopped at a roadhouse for fuel. Jacq bought health bars and chocolate plus two bottles of water. Ahmed stayed with the car keeping an eye out. Unsure why, but it felt better that way. The Musician noticed their fugitive behaviour and never asked. It wasn't his problem. Soon they were back on the road with the sun appearing ahead in all its splendour and ferocity. A clear and hot day was ahead.

Ahmed was annoyed with their speed. Six cylinders pushed them along smoothly. But they could go a lot faster and drove well below the speed limit. Coober Pedy would be a long time coming.

The Musician slotted in a CD of Tool. Not Jacq's sound, or noise perhaps. She failed to recognise it. Ahmed liked the heavy beat and pulsing sound behind the distinctive voice of the singer. It reflected how he was feeling. Rough and heavy with concern about what might be ahead. No one spoke as the Musician drove his van along the first-class highway.

Cruising along in the middle of nowhere a black Porsche overtook them fast. It disappeared around a large hill. Ahmed was alarmed easily recognising the car.

'Stop,' he shouted. 'Please stop now, we need to get out.'

The Musician was slow to react. Surprises hardly ever triggered him much.

'Look, just stop. Please!'

Jacq, fully alert now looked at Ahmed with alarm. The Musician braked and pulled over onto the red-earthed embankment without a word.

'Come on,' Ahmed urged Jacq.

Grabbing the rucksack he jumped out of the car and ran to a large boulder at the side of the road. Jacq, still confused, followed close behind. They dropped flat on the ground, out of sight. Hidden by the large rock and vegetation at the edge of an embankment that sloped down.

The Musician shrugged his shoulders. Getting out also he walked leisurely towards a bush away from his passengers to have a pee. A few seconds later a car approached from the opposite direction. It was the Porsche. After passing it made a u-turn and parked behind the van just ahead of the boulder. Two Rangers got out. They left the engine running, were not going to be long. Hurriedly they walked to the Musician, who thought he was getting the picture. He hated uniforms, even just work shirts with logos. Especially those shouting, Security! Such people had dealt him a rotten blow in the past. If these kids were in trouble, it would not be him giving them away. Definitely not to the two guys he was facing. They obviously were not police. Seeing themselves in front of what they saw as a longhaired yobbo, the Rangers approached with disdain.

Ahmed and Jack saw the Musician shaking his head in answer to a question. The *Cryslis* men were now in front of the panelvan, well away from them.

'Get into the Porsche,' Ahmed whispered to Jacq.

'Just do it.'

He moved quietly into the open. The Rangers had their backs to them. They sneaked into the car as silently as possible. But could not prevent the closing of the doors from being heard. Still, it was too late for the Rangers. Once behind the steering wheel Ahmed jammed the engine into gear and took off. The wheels spinning on the dirt of the embankment. Seatbelts and seat adjustment could come later. They raced away, around the hill. In no way could the Rangers stop them. All they did, was make a futile run to the road in desperation. They were stunned. That soon turned to anger. For a moment it seemed as if they might return to the Musician and get physical. It would take time they could not afford. They ran to the panelvan. Made a fast u-turn back towards Alice Springs and left the Musician stranded. The Director needed to be contacted. Stupidly, they had never taken the satellite phone from the pickup. Only had their mobiles handy. Mobile signals found little coverage out here in the open desert. Their boss had been right though in guessing these two would reach the highway. It had been confirmed at the roadhouse. An Indian boy had stood looking around fugitively near the pumps early morning.

At first Jacq was worried about the speed of Ahmed's driving. He pushed the car hard. But obviously he knew exactly what he was doing and enjoyed it. His concentrated and relaxed manner of sitting behind the steering wheel of this fabulous machine showed not a hint of nervousness. She had never seen a smile play on his lips for that long. Jacq began to relax also. Appreciate the speed at which the country flashed by. Arid and empty, with colours mostly shades of red and the occasional white from stone.

For Ahmed, regardless of their troubles, it was like a homecoming. He was happy to find his skills were still sharp, but was not taking risks. Most likely Jacq had never driven so fast, ever. He noticed her settling back comfortably into the leather seat after the first few minutes. It gave him an unexpected sense of pleasure. It felt as if being together in this Porsche was totally right and obvious. With him at the wheel and Jacq a passenger. If only it were that simple.

The road was excellent with very little traffic. The first half hour neither of them spoke and Ahmed was in heaven. Well almost. Their circumstances remained in the back of his mind like a nagging ache. They were driving way beyond the speed limit, but that couldn't be helped. Hopefully, the police had better things to do than pointing speed cameras – chasing offenders. He looked at the petrol gauge and quickly at the GPS.

Jacq opened the glove box. Perhaps she could find a road map and she did. It was a whole book full of maps with pictures and descriptions of places in

Australia. She found the pages they were travelling through. As the Musician had said, they were going south, in a somewhat easterly direction. Only at Port Augusta was an easterly turn possible. It meant a very long day's drive at normal speed. They were of course going much faster. Coober Pedy was a stretch over midway, she figured. They had no option but to follow the road and see what might happen. Unless the little notebook threw up further surprises. Right now, that seemed unlikely.

Ahmed asked her how far to Coober Pedy. It was easier that way, rather than being distracted by GPS.

'We need to tank,' he decided. The Porsche was unlikely to cover the distance to Coober Pedy. 'What's a place about halfway?' he asked.

Jacq looked at the map. 'Marla. I hope an alert hasn't gone out about us.'

Ahmed desperately hoped that too.

'We'll have to risk it.'

'Sure.'

They had to get to Coober Pedy and needed fuel. There was no option but to risk it.

'In Marla, I'll stay in the car,' Ahmed said. 'You tank and pay. Just tell them your father has a bad back, if anyone needs to know. The windows of this car are tinted. It's not easy to look inside. Put in the most expensive petrol available.' After a moment he added, 'And buy some more water and something to eat that will keep in the rucksack.'

Jacq looked at him sideways. Ahmed seemed to think ahead. For a moment she wondered whether to challenge his abruptness and decided against it. For all his skill as a driver, Ahmed would be under pressure. There was no denying that. She acknowledged what needed doing and studied the road map. The way east through the middle of Australia and beyond. What an enormous country. A short line on the map could be hours of driving.

Ahmed kept the car at high speed. They crossed the Northern Territory border into South Australia. He pushed along. Safe enough because of his skill, but fast. A sign showed that Marla was about an hour away.

A few miles before Marla, Ahmed slowed down considerably. It felt as if they were crawling along. It took effort keeping that speed and he engaged cruise control. He figured that if there were police about, it should be closer in to a town. They veered off the road at Marla into a large roadhouse. It was major stopover for travellers. Marla had few buildings but it included a regional police station and a hospital. The place was situated in the middle of nowhere with nothing but the Australian bush on the horizon. Jacq followed through with their plan. The Aboriginal at the counter took no interest in her. She had plenty of cars passing through and could not see the pumps from behind her till. A local man looked admiringly at the Porsche, probably wishing he could afford one. Few living in the desert could. It would be useless off the bitumen anyway.

The Musician began to hitch a ride to Alice Springs, by far the closest town. He was furious, not with Ahmed and Jacq, but with the Rangers. He walked a while along the empty road before finding a spot shady enough to wait for cars passing by. Cars were infrequent in the desert, particularly early morning. The first one ignored him. Obviously a tourist, or some selfish git. They had no idea about the danger of being alone here on the open road. The Musician swatted the flies from his face, cursing his luck. Soon after a car slowed. It was with mixed emotions that he saw the police in their customary four-wheel drive. Not possibly could he refuse help. As an explanation for his predicament he told the officer about giving two guys a lift and stopping for a pee. They had driven off leaving him stranded. The officer kept his idea of the story to himself and told this hiker to get in. They would talk further at the station

The Musician wondered why he had left Jacq and Ahmed out of his explanation. Perhaps because they seemed underdogs, like himself. Though obviously they were not short of a quid. Possibly also because he had no idea what those kids were up to and preferred not to be implicated. The less the cops knew the better, was his motto. It wouldn't surprise him if his car was found soon anyway. It was temperamental and needed careful handling.

That assessment was correct. Twenty minutes down the road a panelvan was seen stranded with a boiling radiator. The Rangers had driven it too hard. The Musician knew there was a large container of water in the back, but they obviously had not found it. While police car began to slow down the officer checked with the Musician whether the van was his. Indeed! It was. He followed the officer walking over to the Rangers. They were barely able to control their anger when faced with the guy who had made them lose the Porsche. And an awful lot of time also.

Before anyone could speak, the Musician angrily shouted at the men. I gave you a lift, and you dumped me. He said it twice to give them time to notice the hidden message. He was sure that these Rangers would rather leave the police out of their activities as well. For a second they looked at him with surprise. Then cottoned on. They recalled what the Director had stressed more than once: no police.

'Sorry mate,' one of them grunted.

The officer asked the Musician whether he wanted to press charges.

'Nah. Just get them away from me,' he said. 'I'll sort my van. I've got tools and water.'

The policeman accepted that without comment. He wrote down the van's registration number for the record. Undoubtedly, the owner of the old vehicle would not be stuck for long. Wondering whether to check the car's roadworthiness he decided against it. It seemed okay. The man was having enough trouble already.

Without the driver of the stolen vehicle pressing charges the officer liked to forget about the whole affair. There was not much he could do anyway. No one had got hurt and that was the main thing. That the guys in a Rangers outfit would have asked for a lift from a hippy in an old car, he doubted. Still, he couldn't be bothered with it and would drop the men off in Alice Springs. There they could sort themselves out. All he wished to know was where they were from. Learned it was *Cryslis*. The emblem on their shirts had already told him that much. He would write it into his report.

The road they travelled seemed endless, to Jacq. Mile after mile through a desert that could be monotonous or change shape and colour surprisingly. The sun now stood high in the sky. Ahmed was grateful that the windows had been tinted. The air- conditioning was on climate control. Jacq looked drowsily at the landscape. Sleeping in a cave had not been too bad. But the comfort of her luxury seat made keeping her eyes open difficult. The seat felt like a cocoon against troubles. Of which they had plenty. She dosed off intermittently.

Before reaching Coober Pedy the desert became pockmarked with mounds of whitish dirt. It was like a lunar landscape, Jacq thought. She had learned from the roadmap that Coober Pedy was the opal capital of the world. Test drillings and the shafts of actual mines pierced the earth creating heaps of sand and rock. A few hundred at least. She could only see some. Many were small. Larger hills might have mining equipment nearby. Jacq had read that in the town itself the houses often were under ground. Dug into a hillside to escape the summer heat. A dugout church and hotel were on offer and tourists could visit old mines underneath the town. It was the perfect place for buying opal. She had no time for that, Jacq mused wryly. Surely, Coober Pedy would not be their final destination. Jacq had no idea. For now the challenge was to travel east, escaping the Director.

Talking it over, they had decided not to use the Porsche any further than this town. It would be too risky. There might well be an alert out for it. The best approach would be to park the car at a decent hotel and walk away. With any luck no one would take much notice. At least, initially. By the time questions were asked, they should be well on their way again. That was the plan. How they were to leave Coober Pedy? Of that, neither of them had a clue.

A suitable hotel was soon found. They left the car behind the building without drawing attention. Ahmed kept the keys. Just in case they had to make run for it. He walked away from the Porsche with regret. It irked him that it belonged to the Director. He could have inflicted some damage to anger the man, but didn't have the heart. Never intentionally mess with a Porsche, he believed. It was midday and hot.

***

The Director was irate about the stealing of his car. He feared the worst and tried not to think about what could happen with that youth driving it. Contacting the police would only bring unhelpful questions. He decided to phone a *Cryslis* graduate who owned a nationwide security firm. The man visited the Temple every year.

The Director explained that two students from overseas had run away and needed bringing back. They were driving his Porsche and most likely to Port Augusta. This statement drew some questions. The Director remained evasive. He was asking a favour and was aware of that. It would be helpful not having to explain.

Favours were the oil that lubricated networks of any kind. The owner of the security firm was pleased to be of help.

CHAPTER 14

JACQ AND AHMED were on edge. Unsure whether someone from *Cryslis* might be out looking for them. Even though fairly well concealed, the Porsche would attract attention. It was that kind of car. Perhaps the Director had contacts in this town. They needed to be seen here as little as possible. Carrying the rucksack, including two tennis balls, they walked to a large roadhouse. It had a take-away and restaurant. The main street had a wide strip of dirt on either side and offered no shelter. There was no vegetation in Coober Pedy to speak of. The town was a dust bowl. Proper Wild West country, Ahmed thought. Had the cavalry made a charge, it wouldn't have surprised him.

Coober Pedy survived from mining and tourism. From traveller seeking something very different. It was also an obvious stopover when travelling from South Australia through the Centre to the Northern Territory. Jacq found it all messy and dry. But learning about opals would have been great. They made haste without running. In outback Australia people only ran in an emergency. Emergencies attracted attention. Ahmed and Jacq needed to avoid that. They reached the roadhouse fairly quickly feeling much less exposed once inside.

A large four-wheel drive with a double axel caravan was tanking at the browser. Ahmed busied himself scanning the street through the shop window while Jacq was buying lunch. The owners of the van entered to pay for fuel and ordered sandwiches. They looked a retired couple. Standing close by Jacq overheard them and learned that their destination was Port Augusta. This immediately rang a bell. She urged Ahmed to follow her outside. As they hungrily bit into their salad rolls, Jacq told him where that caravan was going. To the next large town. The one from which they could begin to travel east properly.

'Perhaps the caravan is open,' Jacq suggested. She walked around the large car casually and tested the door. Ahmed, a little behind, also tried to look unconcerned. From the restaurant they were now invisible.

Their luck was holding. Surprisingly, they found the door unlocked and without hesitation stepped inside. All as if it were a most natural thing to do. It raised no suspicion from the man tanking next to them. It was a nice, well equipped van. Everything shone cleanly. Obviously the owners took pride in it. Jacq and Ahmed badly hoped the couple had no reason to check inside. Fortunately, all the blinds were down against the sun. They sat on the benches eating their rolls and waited. Soon car doors were opened and shut. The engine started with a grunt and the car drove off.

Pulling a van that carried two fugitives.

Having finished lunch Jacq took the liberty of stretching out on the bed. She felt guilty about it, but overruled that sentiment. Rest was essential, as much of it as possible. She left her feet sticking out over the edge not to soil the cover.

Ahmed got on the floor on his back. Vibrations made resting uncomfortable. Road noise droned in his head. He found a cushion and that helped. So far, they had escaped detection. They were weary but determined. Whatever came next, it simply had to be. East was Port Augusta – for now. Ahmed and Jacq dosed off with intermittent periods of wakefulness.

After a few hours the car stopped at a rest area in the middle of nowhere. It was time for a cuppa. Ahmed and Jacq scrambled up. Car doors opened. They were stuck and desperately hoped the owners had no need to enter their caravan. But no such luck. There was nothing for it but to face the music. It could be playing an angry tune.

As a woman in her sixties readied herself to climb in, the last thing she expected was two young people staring at her.

'John!' she shouted urgently. Startled at Ahmed and Jacq standing together dumbstruck. A burly man arrived within seconds. 'What's up?'

His wife beckoned him to have a look. 'There's

two kids in the van.'

He poked his head through the door and looked at them briefly. 'You'd better come out and explain yourselves,' he said, stepping back.

Ahmed and Jacq obeyed slowly. Ahmed was first, holding the rucksack. Jacq felt her face going red from embarrassment. She looked forlorn.

'Okay. Explain.' The van's owner folded his arms and stood tall. His wife, a nurse, saw that clearly these kids were under stress. She had an eye for those signs.

'John. Why don't you make some tea for the four of us?' she suggested. 'I will take these two to that bench area over there.' It was only a few steps away.

John looked at his wife without comment. She usually knew what she was about. They were only young, he thought, nice looking too. The girl was close to tears.

Jacq and Ahmed followed the woman subdued and wondered what was next. They sat on the bench in silence looking over another stretch of desert and low bushes. John arrived with four cups. Jacq sensed their hosts would be caring rather than aggressive. She was grateful for that. Ahmed had gone defensive with that closed look on his face. Jacq had come to accept it as normal when he was under pressure. His dark brown eyes were wary.

'What's your story?' John asked, offering them a biscuit. Like his wife, he had made up his mind to be considerate. Ahmed looked at Jacq, who decided to explain. It would be best to keep it simple and similar to what they had told the Musician.

'We were travelling with some guys from Alice Springs yesterday and didn't trust them. We left them late last night at Coober Pedy. Ran away and found an old car to sleep in. Eager to get to Port Augusta we overheard you at the roadhouse. Maybe there we can catch a bus.

'There is a terminal there,' John agreed. He was unsure whether to fully believe Jacq. They did look as if they had slept in a car. Still, there would be no harm in helping them out. These two were well mannered and had the decency to be embarrassed. The girl's English was good. She came from Holland though. John's mother had been Dutch, bless her soul.

'We will take you there,' his wife decided. 'Have you got money for the bus?'

Jacq and Ahmed nodded in unison.

'Where are you headed?'

'Adelaide,' Jacq said. Knowing it to be unlikely.

'That will be easy then. My name is Rose and this is John, as you might have heard. Just call us John and Rose.'

The way in which Australians used first names, with people they hardly knew and of any age, was foreign to Europeans. It seemed impolite, particularly with older people.

Jacq made their introduction in response. 'I'm Jacq and this is Ahmed.'

'Good,' Rose concluded. The matter was settled. She was an embracing person. Jacq took to her. 'I'm sorry,' she offered apologetically.

'Accepted, no more said. You will have to sit with us in the car.'

Rose began to collect the mugs and walked off to the van. John headed for his comfortable vehicle. Ahmed and Jacq followed demurely, relieved to come out of a difficult situation so easily.

Rose was the talker. During the hours to Port Augusta John concentrated on the road keeping to the speed limit. The car was powerful and pulled the van easily. With a laugh Rose explained that they were classified as grey nomads, on their way around Australia. Last night, she and John had camped in the open desert. 'You should have seen the stars, millions of them. Looking at the desert sky in clear air, it makes you wonder.' The memory obviously gave her pleasure. 'Do you know anything about the stars and planets?' she asked

Ahmed preferred to be like John. He would leave the talking to Jacq.

Jacq remembered that night at Kings Canyon, where the stars had been so plentiful. In her desire to respond engagingly she said, 'Only the three planets of *Xrisis.*' She regretted it immediately and was just making conversation. Rose was nice doing them a big favour. Jacq would also rather just sit quietly, like Ahmed. She shouldn't have mentioned those planets, but so what. Few people would know of them.

For a moment Rose was taken aback. She said nothing, then turned and looked at Jacq searchingly. 'How do you know about them?'

'A story I read.' The question surprised Jacq. But she had better not elaborate.

'The myth of *Shalomat*,' Rose said. 'Fancy that.'

Jacq, now alert, said nothing. Ahmed suddenly stirred from a half slumber and began to listen.

'My grandmother gave us that to read. We were still children,' Rose explained. 'She was into ancient religions. Myths and stories like *The Epic of Gilgamesh*. She figured that *Shalomat* came from the Middle East.'

Briefly, Rose relived those memories. 'There was a riddle with it,' she continued. 'As kids we tried to make sense of it and couldn't. All we could come up with was that somehow the triangle needed to get into the circle. That was pure speculation and obviously nonsense. We had fun with it, for a while.'

Jacq took all this in with no idea how to use the information. But perhaps she could learn some more from Rose. 'You know about myths?' she asked.

'Well, a myth involves something basic in human experience that is presented in story form.'

That was the explanation given by Mr. Adams,

Jacq remembered.

'So, they're not true?'

'Depends what you mean by true. They always contain some kind of truth, something true about being human.'

Jacq remained silent. She only partly understood. What *Shalo* and *Cryslis* were about was people. That was true, Jacq thought.

'What about symbols,' she asked. Thinking of the Riddle they were trying to solve.

'Now, that's quite interesting,' Rose explained. 'You see that road sign up ahead with a kangaroo? Jacq did and they passed it at speed.

'That's a sign. It tells us about kangaroos jumping in front of our car. But imagine you are Australian and overseas and you see the kangaroo image on the tail of a Qantas jet. Then it reminds you of home. It opens up another world to you. Then the kangaroo sign has become a symbol.'

'So a symbol makes you feel you are connected with something?' Jacq ventured.

'Yes,' Rose agreed. 'You could say that. A life without symbols is pretty dull actually. In religion they feature prominently as a way into greater realities.'

'With the gods?' Ahmed joined in the discussion.

'Yes, or God. It depends what you believe in. There is a world we can see and one we can't. That's what *Shalomat* is about. If I remember correctly.'

'What do you mean?' asked Jacq. Any insight on the myth would be helpful. Rose seemed familiar with this kind of otherworldly stuff.

John chuckled. Rose was on one of her favourite topics in spirituality.

'There are all kinds of worlds,' Rose explained. 'There is the physical world, the psychological world, the psychic world and the transcendental one. The psychic world influences both the psychological and physical. It is a spiritual realm of good and evil. It has dynamics and structure. Tibetan Buddhism has a fair knowledge of that. Anyway, that's well beyond us simple people.'

Rose could have said a lot more but felt it would be unhelpful. She had no intention of wearing these young people out. They were tired enough already. That they suffered from mild exhaustion was obvious to her.

'*Shalomat* fits into the psychic,' Ahmed suggested perceptively. It sounded like India with its many gods and rituals.

'As a myth, yes. The story tells of an imbalance in how humans go about their business. There are psychic powers behind that. Christianity for instance refers to evil as the elemental spirits of the universe. Also there are guardian angels working for good. Every major religion takes those powers seriously in some way. The fight between what is good and what is harmful.'

Rose's comments came from years of interest in Religion Studies.

'What's the transcental world?' Jacq asked.

'Transcendental,' Rose corrected matter of fact. 'It is the spiritual world of One. Of being in unity and at peace. Of wholeness and rest. Religions recognise that realm as the ultimate. But each one interprets it differently. Judaism, Christianity and Islam believe in one supreme God. They focus on the transcendental realm predominantly. Christianity differs in that it believes in a personal relationship with Jesus Christ, who is God. It does a new thing in your life. You become part of a New Reality. Already now while still on earth. That New Reality finally will overrule and outlast all the other realities in eternity. That is possible because Jesus has disempowered evil in the psychic world.'

Rose was distracted by an eagle feeding on road kill. It was a massive bird. She still one more thing to share. Perhaps the most important.

'Every major religion believes in the power of love as the ultimate power of the One. Love is the supreme divine reality. It is interesting that love is also what everyone is hoping for in life. Even in the animal world affection is quite noticeable. That should tell us something.'

Rose had got carried away, as she knew. It was far too elaborate. But it was done now. And no harm done either.

Jacq's head was spinning. But it was interesting.

'The word *Shalomat* comes from the Hebrew idea of Shalom,' Rose added. 'Shalom means wellbeing for all. Quite beautiful.'

She then had a final thought. 'Even if you don't believe in any of this. It is clear that the world has lost balance. Many people are simply too one-sidedly busy with their lives.' Rose readjusted herself in her seat. The discussion had come to a close.

Jacq wondered about that comment. As if Rose knew about their mission. But obviously she didn't.

Ahmed was looking out of the window and got a nasty shock. There was a silver Porsche parked on the side of the road. It was a place where you would never expect such a rare car. He wondered whether it was waiting for them. In case they had driven on to Port Augusta themselves. Extra caution would be essential. His nerves began to play up again.

The conversation stopped completely and an hour later they arrived. In a sizeable town John and Rose dropped them off with their best wishes. Rose asked once more whether they had enough money. That was not a problem, they assured her. With mixed emotions Ahmed and Jacq watched those two fine people drive away. Again they were left to fend for themselves, and alone.

'We must talk,' Jacq insisted. 'Somewhere secluded.'

Port Augusta was not a busy place and they soon found a quiet spot.

'We need to buy jackets.' Jacq expected a cool night. 'And we need to split doing so.'

Ahmed told her about the Porsche. The less they were seen together, the better. Worry was their staple diet now, Jacq thought. She had better get used to it. They should move on as soon as possible.

'East from here is Broken Hill and further east is Sydney,' she told Ahmed. 'I learned that from the map in the Porsche.'

He gave it some thought. 'Tomorrow the Riddle needs to be fulfilled, whatever that means. We'll never get to Sydney by then. We must take a bus to Broken Hill. Let's find out.'

Jacq agreed. I will put my hair in a ponytail, she decided. If anyone was looking for them it would change her appearance a little. She found a few elastic bands in the rucksack and in no time had her hair tied up. With combat classes she had always worn it like that and riding horses.

'You just wait here for a minute,' she suggested. 'I'll find out about a bus to Broken Hill and when it's leaving.'

Jacq walked quickly to the bus depot around the corner. Ahmed decided to open the little notebook once again. Not that he expected any "news" for it gave up its secrets very slowly. Nothing extra had appeared.

Jacq arrived back disappointed. 'There is no bus to Broken Hill from here,' she reported glumly. 'We would have to travel via Adelaide.'

That simply wasn't an option. Far too much out of their way down south. They followed through on the idea of splitting up to buy those jackets. Jacq had noticed a shopping street. They would meet again in half an hour at the same spot. Ahmed hated the very thought of splitting up even though it had been his suggestion.

'You take the rucksack,' he suggested. 'I'm Indian and more easily spotted. Your combat skills are better than mine. And let's get money out of an ATM.'

Jacq took the rucksack without a word and slung it over her shoulder. What a mess!

'You look different,' Ahmed said, unsure whether he liked it. Jacq was donning a checkered blue and black jacket. He had seen them worn by country people in an Australian Outback magazine. Not that here was much wrong with it. It was different and shapeless. Perhaps that was on purpose.

'That's the point. No use looking as expected, like tourist. I'm now Australian, mate.' She grinned. 'It is actually very comfortable. And look at you!'

Ahmed was wearing a Ford racing jacket, mostly

black with some blue. It had taken his fancy. 'You look not at all inconspicuous.'

He shrugged his shoulders. 'I'm Indian,' he said. He would hardly go unnoticed whatever he wore if people were asking. Though he had seen other Indians about. 'And I used to race a Cosworth.'

'So what's the plan?' Jacq wondered. They were sitting on a bench next to each other.

'I have an idea. But I'm not sure whether it will work,' Ahmed said. 'Have you seen those large trucks on the roads? They're massive.'

Jacq could hardly have missed them. The trucks moved huge loads around Australia. She cottoned on right away. 'You mean, we hitch a ride?' It might be possible.

'Either that or take a taxi. That will cost.' It could be the option when all else failed, but would raise questions. Ahmed was not keen on it.

Jacq thought it through. She didn't really fancy sharing a cab with an unknown truck driver. That is, if you assumed all such drivers to be untrustworthy, which made no sense. They had a job to do and preferred the far horizons, on possibly near empty roads. That would be the life of the Australian truckie. The Europeans were always stuck on busy highways.

'Where do we find a truck to Broken Hill though?' she wondered.

'At a truck stop,' Ahmed replied. 'One of those

roadhouses that have food and showers and plenty of space to park a large rig.' He had thought it through.

'So where is that?' Jack wished to know.

'I'm not sure, but we can easily find out.'

'How?'

'By getting a taxi to take us there.' It was the obvious answer.

Jacq smiled, and nodded her head. 'Okay,' she said. Got busy on her phone looking for a taxi service.

Soon they arrived at a large roadhouse. A number of trucks were parked on one side. Passenger cars drove in continually to fill up at the browsers. In the distance Ahmed and Jacq could see the mountain ranges of the Flinders. Port Augusta had access to the sea and is the most northern port in South Australia. It was the main hub for the mining industry, the taxi driver had told them. Inland, hours away, there were significant mines. Uranium, gold and other metals. Jacq and Ahmed stepped into the restaurant wondering how to proceed.

'I wouldn't mind some hot chips,' Jacq said being not that hungry. 'And a large coffee.' To stay awake, she thought. 'How about you?'

'Just a burger,' Ahmed replied. 'With the lot, and a coffee.'

His brain was working overtime at how to find a truck to Broken Hill. Perhaps he should simply ask whether there was one at the roadhouse. No point in being secretive when it was counterproductive.

Jacq ordered their meals while Ahmed observed the staff at the counter. The woman serving Jacq seemed friendly in a kind of homely way. He decided to take the plunge.

'I wonder whether you can help us,' he said brightly. The woman had just taken Jacq's payment and looked at this young Indian in his Ford jacket. They were not local these two. Probably from overseas. But they seemed nice. She waited.

'We need a lift to Broken Hill. Is there a truck that might take us? We can pay.' A mild panic struck Ahmed. But he managed to look little concerned.

'There is no bus you see, as we had hoped,' Jacq added, giving it her best smile.

'That is true,' the woman admitted. She looked at them attentively. It wasn't a request she got every day. They were both too young, she felt, to be introduced to just any driver. If she wished to be bothered it. Her first reaction was to just shrug it off. Then she remembered that Sally was eating her dinner in the corner at the back. Sally was alright, mother of a twelve year old boy. She could offer the lift, if she was interested. Bit of extra money.

'Ask Sally,' she suggested, pointing out a solid looking woman in a coat with reflective stripes. 'She might be able to help. It's up to her, of course.'

Jacq said a warm thank you and made for Sally's

table. Ahmed followed.

'Hi,' she said, 'how are you?'

Sally looked up from her dinner and gave them both a quick glance. 'Hi.' On her head she wore an old dark blue cap with the letters NY. Ahmed knew it to be from the New York Yankees. Sally waited for what was next.

'Would you mind giving us a lift to Broken Hill?' Jacq asked. She found this Australian woman a bit unnerving.

Sally put some steak in her mouth and continued to chew. 'Why would I do that?'

'Because, we're stuck. There is no bus from here to Broken Hill.' Honesty seemed best, up to a point.

Sally seemed to give it some thought.

'What are you running from?' She had learned to be nobody's fool and concluded that these kids were nervous about something. 'From the police?'

'Heavens no!' Jacq exclaimed. She was taken aback by the question.

The female truckie looked at them standing there together, not at all cocky. They're okay, she thought, and something was bugging them. Their reaction to the police question had been genuine. Should she probe further or let it be? Or simple refuse to help.

'We're happy to pay,' Ahmed offered.

The school fees were due and having them in her cab would be no bother. They looked knackered and were bound to fall asleep. But Sally gave her answer some time, took another bite of dinner.

Jacq and Ahmed were becoming uncomfortable.

'Three hundred dollars,' Sally said. 'Find a table and follow me when I leave.' She felt to have made the right decision. Didn't mind their company. She would be nice to these young people.

***

After his unsuccessful search by air, and the loss of his Porsche, the Director kept up an angry pursuit. He organised a charter plane to Port Augusta. The youths would have travelled through that town. It was logical when coming from Alice Springs. Unless taking dirt roads into the never-never. That his Porsche had not been spotted by the one waiting was confusing. The young thieves may have ditched his precious car or crashed it. But they would be running on.

The owner of the security firm had arranged for that waiting Porsche. The man didn't have offices in smaller towns like Port Augusta, but a retired friend lived there. He owned a Carrera, had some spare time, and was willing to help. In intercepting Ahmed and Jacq, that had been to no avail.

The charter plane was free later that day and the Director touched down early evening. He considered his options. The place to start would be the bus terminal. He enquired whether there had been a blond girl and Indian boy travelling through. The girl was Dutch. No Indian, was the reply. There had been a blond girl with a slightly foreign accent. She asked for a bus to Broken Hill. But there wasn't one. It was her alright, the Director concluded. So, they were heading east. But how? Perhaps they could find a lift. Order a taxi even, though that would be expensive. Needed checking. He contacted taxi services. His second call confirmed that a young Indian and a blond girl had ordered a ride. Not to Broken Hill, but a major truck stop on the southern edge of town. Bingo, the Director thought, and took a taxi to that roadhouse. Spinning the story of being an uncle of the girl and looking for her, he discovered they had asked about trucks to Broken Hill. And probably found one. Which truck, he didn't know. The woman he talked to knew the drivers but not their vehicles. His spirit lifted. This was tangible information. The thought of those kids travelling holding the *Cryslis* almost choked him. He had to get it back fast or would be doomed. His job was at stake, his life even. The Director had no illusions about that. He wondered whether his security contact could arrange a look-out in Broken Hill. A call told him that the man had no connections there. The Director then asked whether it was possible to hire the Porsche of that retired friend. Money was not an issue. That could that be arranged, no problem. A little later the silver Porsche arrived. After dropping the owner back home, the Director drove to a luxury motel and settled in for the night. It was too late for a pursuit. There would be no benefit in leaving for Broken Hill right away. Those youths were unlikely to travel on from there tonight. If he made a start before sunrise, he could be at the Hill early morning.

CHAPTER 15

AHMED WOKE UP to a droning noise. It took him a moment to remember that he was in a huge truck. It was moving through the night. Instinctively, he reached out for the rucksack at his feet. No problems there. He would have liked to shift his shoulders, but Jacq was leaning against him sleeping. The panelvan came to mind. Particularly jumping into the back of it. It had shown him a lot and he was mulling it over. Something good in stressful times.

Outside it was pitch-black. Ahmed had no idea what the country they were driving through looked like. Whether it was different from what they had seen earlier at dusk. The truck lights shone far into the distance, but no wider than the embankment. The quality of country roads in Australia was pretty good. If you considered how little traffic actually came through.

They had followed Sally to her truck. It turned out to be a big rig. With a sleeping compartment behind the cabin and a large trailer on the back. Climbing up into the cabin had been fun. Sally told them to strap in and that she would have a chat later. Once she was out of town and through the pass in the Flinders. That suited Ahmed and Jacq fine. They would focus on the scenery in the dying light. Sally worked the truck through its many gears getting up to speed. Out of town they took a left towards the mountains and into the pass. It was fabulous country. Very old, with bluish grey rock against ochre. The usual Australian vegetation. The leathery leaves stopping evaporation so that heat and dry times could be survived. They looked dullish, almost dark grey. At dusk particularly so. The grasses were spindly and thick. Australia must be among the best places in the world, Jacq thought. She forgot about sleeping and kept her eyes glued on nature. The steep rock walls they were winding in between. One day, she would be back, that was for sure.

At Wilmington, a small township in the Southern Flinders, there was a dogleg in the road. It became an easy ride after that.

'So, where're you from?' Sally wished to know. She would keep it nice and easy. Whatever was bugging these two, it was not her concern.

'Holland,' Jacq replied.

'UK.'

'Never been to Europe,' Sally commented. She had been right in thinking they were tourists and not New Australians. 'Been to the States though.'

'New York.' Ahmed ventured.

Sally smiled. 'You've noticed my cap.' She had enjoyed visiting the Big Apple with a friend 'Went to a

Yankees game, I did.'

'What was it like?' Ahmed had been there but not to a baseball game.

'Bit like cricket. Nothing much happens and then everything happens.'

'Yeh,' said Ahmed. 'The Ashes.'

The Indian guy is English, Sally reminded herself. 'Do you play cricket?'

'A bit.' Ahmed had played at school but never much. His games were boxing, rugby, and car racing.

Jacq knew nothing about cricket. Hardly anyone played it in Holland. She'd had enough of this sport talk. 'Where did you learn to drive a truck?' she asked.

Sally had been waiting for this question. 'I'm from near Barcaldine, in Western Queensland.' She chose not to tell that Barcaldine was the birthplace of the Australian Labor Party. A nice monument had been erected, in remembrance of that. Right over the old tree. The timbers up high were draped with chains that clambered together in the wind like a chime. 'Grew up on a station,' she said. 'A super large farm.' Foreigners had little idea of the size of properties in the outback.

'How large is super?' Jacq enquired.

'Some stations are larger than half of Holland, I imagine,' Sally ventured. It seemed a safe guess. The Dutchies came from a small country. That much she knew. 'Anyway, in the bush you learn all sorts and start driving machinery young. It's sheep and cattle country.'

A station half the size of Holland, Jacq thought. That's Australia for you. 'So you ride horses,' she suggested.

'I sure did as a kid, but not anymore. Horses are still used but mustering is done with bikes now, or quads, or even helicopters.' Sally thought of the good old horsy days. It mostly ended before her time. 'You ride?' she asked Jacq. Something in the voice of the girl made that seem right.

'Yes, love it.' Jacq thought of Dappervoet and felt sad.

'But how did you get to drive a truck?' Ahmed interrupted. That question was still unanswered.

'My boyfriend. He did, and taught me. Then later on, I got my license.' She didn't reveal that they had got married, with a child. That fairly soon after he had disappeared over the horizon. Their son stayed with Sally's mum these days.

'This big a truck?' Ahmed asked. It would have been quite a feat for someone learning.

'At first, yes. Then bigger.' Sally could still smell it. 'He drove a road-train cattle rig with possibly two trailers. One more than this truck and the cattle on two levels. A double-deck, it is called. With sheep you could use a triple-deck.'

Those were the days. Young and randy. Sleeping in hay, sometimes literally. The cattle, restrained in their holding pens, mooing all night. They would arrive in the yards at dusk for early morning loading. Good times. It couldn't have lasted and didn't.

Ahmed was impressed.

'The roads were worse than this,' Sally continued. 'Afterwards, I worked at open-cut mines with dump trucks. The top of their tires way above my head. It was too restrictive, driving to and fro the same route. Good money though. But I prefer the open road.'

'Where are you headed?' Jacq asked.

'Townsville,' Sally answered. 'Four days drive.'

It meant nothing to Jacq, just another town, far away, in this huge country.

'You better have a kip,' Sally suggested. They had talked enough, even though it had been short. These two were exhausted.

Jacq stirred against Ahmed's shoulder and grunted softly, still quite asleep. The rig trundled on, mile after mile. Ahmed was fully awake now and wondered how much longer to Broken Hill. He looked sideways at Sally who sat relaxed behind the wheel controlling the large truck with ease. Ahmed enjoyed this ride, the massive power of it. He tried to feel the truck. Get connected with it somehow, like with his Porsche. He could imagine that you would scream at city work once used to a trucker's lifestyle.

He thought about being on the run. Extra care remained super important. However much he tried to convince himself that all would work out, a nagging fear persisted. He was feeling on edge. The Director should not be underestimate. That Porsche near Port Augusta kept bothering him. So far they had been ahead of their pursuers. Surely the chase was on. It could hardly be otherwise. For they were carrying the *Cryslis*. Also *Shalo*, though no-one knew that. It could get very nasty. A thought Ahmed preferred not to dwell on.

'You better wake your friend,' Sally suggested with a smile. 'Twenty minutes to the Hill.'

The truck was not allowed in the main street of town. Too much noise. It had to take a parallel road. Just walk down the side street to the main drag, they were told. Where to find accommodation so late at night, Sally didn't know. It was not her problem. There was bound to be something available in this tourist town.

Jacq and Ahmed expressed their thanks and were left standing in the dark. They knew nothing about Broken Hill. It was sparsely lit and looked deserted. Would someone be waiting? If they were expected by truck, they would be sitting ducks, Ahmed thought. Nothing happened.

It was not that far a walk. The houses looked old. Broken Hill was an early settlement with a significant mining town history. A few dogs barked as they walked past and that was all. No people to be seen, just the noise of a car further out. Soon they arrived at the town centre. The pale light of streetlamps showed mostly shops. The Backpackers was right behind the bus terminal and advertised a 24 hours reception. It might be their last resort. Ahmed figured that if anyone were looking, they would check there first. He didn't feel like sleeping with other people in one room anyway. Jacq agreed wholeheartedly. They walked on through a town fairly well shut up. A hotel still had lights on in the bar. A man was leaving shouting thanks. Ahmed beckoned Jacq to follow him and stepped inside.

The bartender, who could have been the owner, looked at them with raised eyebrows. Not every day two under-aged young people walked in at this hour.

'What can I do for you?' he asked.

'We've just been dropped off by a lift,' Ahmed explained. 'Would you have a room for a night?'

The man scrutinised them. It was possible. In this tourist town all kinds of arrivals took place.

'I have got some rooms at the back,'

'One room. We can only afford that much,' Jacq insisted. No way was she going to be separated from Ahmed.

The bartender nodded his head. They seemed okay. Sending them back into the night would be heartless. There was no need. They would end up at the Backpackers.

'$120 for the night. And I need identification.' That wasn't strictly necessary. But he preferred some details, just in case. They were rather young to be out and about at midnight alone.

Ahmed and Jacq produced their passports and paid the money. One English, and one Dutch, the bartender noticed. The young fellow was not from Asia. His accent so obviously middle class English. Handing over the key to room seven he directed them around the corner into the side street. They would find the motel rooms there. Departure no later than 10 o'clock next morning

The room had a double and single bed, a breakfast bar and a bathroom. Everything simple and comfortable. Ahmed and Jacq were grateful for this proper place to sleep.

'I'll take the single,' Jacq decided, and tossed the rucksack on the bed. 'And, I'm having a shower.'

She wearily rummaged through the rucksack pulling her hair free of the ponytail. That felt better already. She could not be bothered undressing in the small bathroom. Ahmed just stood looking as she stripped off top and jeans. The graceful movements of her body, even though she was exhausted, made his stomach ache. The waterhole flashed through his mind. Ignoring his gaze Jacq grabbed a towel off the bed and stepped into the bathroom. Ahmed threw himself spread-eagled on the double. Knackered and miserable. He tried to stay awake for a shower but failed.

When Jacq reappeared, feeling much better from a long hot drenching. Ahmed was fast asleep. For a while she stood considering this handsome Indian. His face looked anything but peaceful. It was half buried into a pillow. The matted black hair in need of a wash. Without him they wouldn't have got through the day, Jacq knew. She lingered. Her thoughts and feelings tumbling about. She felt uprooted and in need of solid ground. Touching base, any sort of normality, with Ahmed. But it was impossible. A pang of compassion hit her. Also desire. It really hurt.

Jacq took a deep breath and stretched up high. Took to her bed sliding under fresh sheets that felt like heaven. Soon she was wrestling with her dreams.

***

The Director had not slept at all. The audacity of stealing the *Cryslis* kept his anger burning. He left Port Augusta before 5 am giving the Porsche a workout. A speed camera would be unlikely so early. What almost caught him was a large kangaroo. Suddenly it hopped in front from behind a bush. The Porsche almost came to grief. Luck and his driving skills averted an accident. The car slid into a spin he could only just control. This reminder that wildlife was active at sunrise made him slow down slightly.

After Skippy, the journey was uneventful. Taken up with his thoughts on catching Ahmed and Jacq, the Director noticed little but the bitumen. He arrived at Broken Hill when shops were still closed and found an eatery for breakfast.

***

Ahmed opened half an eye some time during the night. Sleeping fully dressed on top of a bed was not comfortable. He should have a shower and clean up. Tomorrow, he told himself not wanting to wake Jacq. He stripped, pulled back the sheets, and soon fell asleep again.

Well after sunrise he showered. Stood for a long time with his face up to the steaming spray of water. The pleasure of getting clean and being soothed was great. Ahmed would happily have showered longer but couldn't afford the luxury. Today their mission needed completing. But they had no idea how. It was The Day of the Riddle. So many questions and too few answers by far. Mr. Adams had stressed that he should not doubt. It was easier said than done.

Ahmed stepped from the bathroom with steam billowing after him, rubbing his hair dry. Jacq was up already refreshed after a good night's sleep. She was sitting at the small table. The sphere of *Shalo* and the

Cryslis in front of her. Also the small notebook and the key. The two tennis balls were on the floor. The *Cryslis*, no longer at its place on the psychic grid, had lost some of its lustre. Jacq gazed at the small golden sphere and triangular crystal pyramid deep in thought. If answers were to be found, it had to come from these two objects.

'What's on?' Ahmed sat on the bed looking at Jacq.

'We need answers,' she replied. 'There's no point in going on otherwise.' She kept her eyes on *Shalo* and *Cryslis*. The round and the sharply pointed.

'The answer is in the Riddle.' Ahmed thought that obvious. 'That's what we need to fulfil somehow. Can you read it out again?'

Jacq opened the little book.

'When triangle becomes circle and ripples are created from a symbol of halves will balance be restored through chaos.' She spoke softly, thinking it through.

'What clues do we have besides that Riddle?' Ahmed asked.

'Well, three actually.'

Jacq had considered that. 'Seek the sunrise, which we think means going east. Today is the only day in which the Riddle can be fulfilled. And, Petrus told us that from what the sphere was taken, it needed to be returned.'

Ahmed gave it some thought, without getting any further. 'No extra writing in the book?'

Jacq shook her head.

'Do you remember what Rose said about signs and symbols?' she asked.

'Sort of,' he answered hesitantly.

'She said a symbol is an image that can speak of something else.'

'Yes. She did.' Ahmed was not much help here.

'Okay!' Jacq would reason it through logically. 'According to the myth of *Shalomat* we are busy with a task that has worldwide repercussions. We are in Australia and let's assume that the symbol, a symbol of halves, is also in Australia. What Australian symbols do we know of?'

'The kangaroo, I suppose.' That much Ahmed did remember from Rose's conversation.

'Yes, and the Australian flag, for instance,' added Jacq.

'Uluru?'

'Is there a major symbol in the east though?' Jacq persisted.

Ahmed searched his mind. An Australian symbol in the east? 'The Sydney Opera House, perhaps?' That would be a symbol.

Suddenly, Jacq sprang up, knocking her chair over. 'I've got it!' she shouted excitedly. 'It's the Sydney Harbour Bridge. Got to be! Two almost half circles on each side with a road in between.' Jacq was now convinced of it. At last a clue she could believe in. 'We need to go to Sydney. And there's water there. The sphere was taken from the water and must return to water. And water can create ripples. It has to be the Bridge!' Jacq could hardly contain herself. She gave Ahmed an excited hug and a spontaneously kissed him on the lips. Unexpectedly, and too fast for him to respond. Next, she turned to pick up the chair.

Ahmed, stirred by Jacq's enthusiasm, also felt his spirit lift. She was right. The Sydney Harbour Bridge. It had to be true. It was an Australian symbol and the best they could come up with. Now they had found their destination. 'What about the rest of the Riddle,' he asked. 'What about a triangle becoming a circle? What do you make of that?'

'I don't know,' Jacq admitted. 'Let's worry about that later. Let's go to Sydney.'

Sydney was an enormous distance away. Too far to reach by road in one day from Broken Hill. They needed to be at that bridge today. The day that the three planets of *Xrisis* were aligning. It could only be achieved by plane. Was there a flight however, and could they get tickets? Ahmed consulted his mobile phone. It didn't take long to find the airport and he punched in the number. Jacq hovered next to him.

Soon Ahmed had finished his enquiry. 'There's a

flight mid-afternoon. Tickets are available from the travel agent in the main street. That's easiest.' It was encouraging news. Nothing worked like having a plan. They talked it over.

'We must split up again,' said Jacq. 'If anyone is looking they're expecting an Indian and a blond girl. I am less noticeable. You should leave purchasing the tickets to me.'

Ahmed didn't like it. Surely there would be Indian looking people in Broken Hill. But Jacq was right.

'I shall wear a ponytail again, get those tickets, and then have my hair done.'

'Your hair done?'

'Yes.' Jacq didn't enlighten him. 'You must find a spot to hang out at where people are unlikely to search for us. A library maybe?'

Ahmed nodded.

'Okay, let's meet midday at the library. There is bound to be one near the town centre.' Jacq was in full flight now. Energised by these sensible ideas. 'You can buy yourself some breakfast on the way. Also, get some more money from an ATM again, just in case. '

They packed up the rucksack and slid the two cosmic objects back inside the tennis balls. Left their room close on 10 o'clock. Jacq returned the key at reception, while Ahmed walked away trying to look untroubled. He was not in a great mood. He disliked libraries almost as much as separating from Jacq.

Jacq, munching on a chocolate bar, passed a hair salon. It didn't look busy. She had decided to get her hair done first and then buy the tickets. It would be safer. The hairdresser was competent and quick. Jacq tried to relax while trained hands busied themselves with her head. The scissors were making a modern cut, of that she need not have worried. People in the heart of Australia kept up-to-date with contemporary fashion. Jacq looked in the mirror and smiled. 'I like it,' she told the hairdresser while settling the bill.

Leaving the shop she looked towards the travel agency a few doors down. That look gave her a nasty shock. Out of the agency stepped the Director. Oh, my god, Jacq thought. She stopped dead in her tracks. The Director came her way and Jacq had nowhere to go. He was too close. She couldn't run, for it would raise his suspicion. She had to tough it out and hope for the best. As a last resort she might try to disable him with a well-placed kick and then escape.

The man strode towards her aggressively. His shoulders slightly bent like a rugby player ready to tackle. Jacq kept her eyes away from him and just walked by. He never even gave her a glance. He had a vague picture in his mind of what the two students looked like from their Temple visit. He was searching for an Indian boy and a girl with longish blond hair. That Jacq was no longer that but a short-cropped brunette, he could not know. She had hated seeing the blond locks fall to the ground just some minutes ago. Like an offering for *Shalo*. Still, being a brunette made a change. It had definitely saved her right now from a bad situation. Her heart was racing from that brutish man brushing by. As a future actor it should make little difference what she would look like if a role demanded it. Today that meant the blond hair gone. Her symmetric face suited most hairstyles anyway.

Jacq wondered whether to chance getting those tickets. She would simply have to. It was the only way they could arrive at Sydney that day. They were on the right track with that Harbour Bridge idea. Act just as normal, Jacq told herself and stepped into the agency. An older woman sat behind a desk. She looked kind. Jacq breathed a little easier.

'Could I purchase two tickets to Sydney please, for this afternoon?' she asked.

'Certainly.'

The girl was from overseas, the woman thought. A man had just left looking for a blond girl with shoulder length hair and an Indian boy, who were from overseas. This couldn't be her though.

'Where are you from?' she asked Jacq, as she busied herself with the computer. She dealt with a lot of tourists here in Broken Hill.

'East Germany,' Jacq said. She had decided how to tackle this one. If the Director had given their details, she needed to be careful.

'Two tickets?' the lady confirmed

'Yes please. One for me, and the other for a friend from Switzerland.' Jacq used her real name Jacqueline as on her credit card. Also Ahmed's proper name. Terrorism had tightened security checks and possibly at Broken Hill airport. She would pay by card as tourists normally did to avoid raising suspicion. Cash might be a bad idea. The lady took the details without hesitation. The Director obviously had not asked for them by name. The tickets were issued without difficulty.

Ahmed found the library easily. It had computers for him to waste time on the internet. Also, it featured a coffee shop. He answered some emails and did a search on the Sydney Harbour Bridge. Just for interest sake. It might come in handy. When Jacq arrived at midday, his interest was in a car magazine. Scanning reports on the latest models.

'Hello.' She broke his concentration.

Ahmed looked up, and was shocked. What had happened to the blond hair that he so adored?

'You like it?' Jacq teased him with a faint smile. She expected Ahmed to find the change difficult.

'You look more, Indian,' he said. That's what came to mind.

'And that's a bad thing?'

Ahmed shook his head. Nothing with Jacq would be a bad thing. The way he looked at her unsettled

Jacq. In a good way. She changed the subject.

'I bumped into the Director.'

'Where?' Ahmed became immediately alarmed.

'Passed right by him at the travel agency.'

'And he didn't see you?'

'No. It was scary, but he overlooked me. I am no longer blond, of course.'

That was a sure fact. Ahmed was still coming to grips with it. Jacq was no less attractive. 'We could be in trouble?' he concluded glumly.

'Yes,' Jacq agreed, 'we need to be very careful.' Ahmed digested the news. 'Let's eat,' he suggested. 'But not here. I am sick of this place.'

'Is that a good idea?'

'We can walk through the car park behind this library. It connects with the main street. There is a place on the corner where we can have lunch. We should be okay there.'

Jacq was aware of that place and agreed. They could chance it.

'We can sit away from the window,' Ahmed said, as they walked to the small restaurant. He seemed to have checked it out. 'If the Director walks by he cannot easily see us.'

It seemed fairly low risk but Jacq was still jittery.

They sat down near the back with a corner view on both streets. Enjoying his food Ahmed saw a silver Porsche come to a halt and a blurred impression of the driver. It gave him a jolt. He alerted Jacq as the Porsche crossed over. The Director was too close for comfort.

They had to split up again and stay that way. The library, much to Ahmed's disgust, remained his best option. Jacq would remain undetected in other ways. She would order a taxi to drop her the airport. That taxi could then pick up Ahmed at the library. At the airport and during the flight they would not know each other. As they separated, Jacq handed Ahmed his plane ticket.

***

The Director had busied himself all morning with the whereabouts of those youths. He had no idea where they were, or whether they might have moved on. There was little choice but to start asking around without raising suspicion. They must have stayed somewhere overnight. On his walks he came across the Backpackers and checked whether a young Indian boy and blond girl had booked in late last night. The careful look of the receptionist highlighted the danger of such questions without authority. He explained to be an uncle of the girl and responsible to his brother overseas for her wellbeing. She had decided to start travelling alone with a new friend from India. At sixteen that wasn't a good idea. All plausible details, perhaps, but the story still raised suspicion. Also, he needed to keep is impatiens well hidden.

The Director imagined that, if those two actually were in town, they might travel on by plane. It would be the fastest way to disappear over a distance. He checked with the two travel agencies that sold tickets. Again he was received with suspicion. Broken Hill was a large town, but small enough for people to whisper to the police about someone they didn't trust. That needed avoiding. At both shops he drew a blank. He walked on like a bear with a sore head. There was no tall blond girl on the footpaths as he strolled about town, nor an Indian boy. Not anyone, who raised his suspicion. He noticed some Indian people but not Ahmed. In what other way might they leave Broken Hill, he wondered? By bus possibly and he decided to check that out. These investigations took their time. He was getting increasingly irate. Perhaps he should stick to finding whether they had arrived here in this town?

Surely they would have slept somewhere and if not at the Backpackers then where? There were many possible places in Broken Hill. It catered for the large number of tourists. They visited galleries of the local artists, some internationally famous. And Silverton, a popular movie set location. Once dropped off by truck, those youths wouldn't have walked all that far in the dark, the Director imagined. Looking around, he noticed a hotel further on and wondered whether his luck might change.

The woman at reception remembered the young people from what her boss had said. The friendly girl had returned the key. The Director saw recognition in her eyes. She put the shutters up insisting that no information about guests would be forthcoming. However plausible the reasons. That was fine by him. He had his first breakthrough. They had been in Broken Hill and most likely still were. He drove the silver Porsche slowly through the shopping street looking about. Perhaps he might find them. With no such luck he decided to check out local flight times. Took a short drive to the airport. Perhaps the culprits were there even. The next flight, he learned, was to Sydney this afternoon. If those youths had booked a seat, it would be easy. Just get to the airport before departure and spoil their plans. As run-away thieves they would not wish to attract attention. It was worth a try. He could again check at the bus terminal. But had they decided on that, it would have been an early bus. He had covered that already. There was no option but to keep looking and have a late lunch. At least those students had no idea of him being around.

***

Jacq left Ahmed at the library and wandered about in Broken Hill. Fairly convinced now that she would not be spotted. The Director had not recognised her. He had hardly seen her at *Cryslis*. With a changed hairstyle and colour she should be safe. Still, she remained alert.

Walking the major streets at random she passed the Broken Hill Art Gallery. Decided to step in for a visit. Not a bad way to spend some time. The Director was unlikely to turn up here. The gallery was beyond the shopping area. It displayed mostly contemporary art, much of it by Broken Hill painters. But also some older pieces. Jacq liked the large vintage staircase that led to the first floor. She would have gladly viewed the displays longer. But had to remain on the move, just in case.

Unexpectedly, Jacq spotted the silver Porsche. Neatly parked in a quiet side street. The shiny car gave her the shivers. It was proof that the Director was close. Her first impulse was to quickly move on when three teenagers hanging nearby gave her an idea. They looked street smart. Their manner typical of their age. Just loitering, not in a hurry to be anywhere fast. She conveniently forgot to be not that much older herself. Jacq crossed the street, approached them boldly, and got three stares. The banter stopped.

'You want to earn some money?' she asked. They looked at each other with a grin.

'How much?' one asked, obviously the alpha male.

'A twenty.'

'For what?' Twenty dollars was okay dough.

'Easy. See that Porsche?'

Of course they had.

'It's my uncle's and I hate the bastard.' Jacq spoke vehemently. She would have been horrified had she known that the Director actually was pretending to be her uncle.

'So?' The leader of the group played it cool.

'I need two tires let down.'

The three teenagers smirked. They looked at Jacq without comment. That would not be difficult.

'I'll give you ten now,' Jacq suggested, 'and the rest when it's done.'

'Okay.' The leader stretched out his hand for the money.

Jacq discovered that she had only a twenty dollar note.

'That'll have to do then,' the leader decided. 'Just give me the twenty up front.'

Jacq did and he directed his troupes with a shake of the head to get on with the job.

'We could run now. Could leave the car alone,' he teased. Trying on some fun with this chick. She looked like what he hoped for soon. Jacq was tense and not in the mood for this.

'Not with a busted kneecap, you won't.' She stepped in closer. Instantly, her eyes were ablaze.

The teenager raised both hands, palms open. He became careful. This was not a girl to meddle with.

Soon the Porsche was parked tilting on an angle with two flat tires on curb side.

Jacq disappeared around the corner once the job was done. Not wanting to be anywhere near that car when the Director returned.

As discussed, Jacq ordered a taxi to the airport, only a few miles away. She paid for her fare and for Ahmed. Making sure the taxi drove to the Library immediately. Half an hour later he walked into the terminal noticing Jacq, but ignoring her. It was a tough job. Still, being together again in the small departure lounge was great. He didn't know about the flat tires and wondered anxiously whether the Director might turn up. They exchanged glances. Jacq rubbed her lips with her thumb. Ahmed took it as a sign of encouragement – thumbs up. He winked back, feeling better now.

***

The Director enjoyed a good lunch. But another fruitless walk through the main streets of town got him irritated again. They had to be somewhere! When he rounded the corner and saw the Porsche well and truly stranded, his temper flared. He kicked one flat furiously. Swore under his breath knowing that those two had spotted him after all. For this was sabotage. Now he needed a taxi. He became further enraged when that took longer than expected. His plan of intercepting Jacq and Ahmed as they made it to the airport, if that was their intention, went badly wrong. He would be lucky to arrive at the terminal before the plane took off. There was no option but to try.

***

They were close to embarking and the check-in gate was open. Ahmed briefly looked towards the entrance and saw a taxi pull up sharply. He was horrified to notice the Director getting out in a hurry. Quickly he moved near Jacq and whispered, 'The Director's here. Get onto the plane. Don't let him see you. I'll sort this.'

Already in line Jacq moved through the gate and feared for Ahmed. Obviously, he was trying to have her gone before the man came close. Carrying the rucksack she changed her way of walking to slouching with her head down. Quite unlike her usual posture. Few would have thought this was the girl who could sit so proudly on a horse. The Director had no hope of recognising her. He detected Ahmed instantly.

Ahmed braced himself. Their enemy had found them, their cover had been blown. He stared at the man, defiantly challenging him. He sensed an intense hatred coming his way. It was powerful opposition. Ahmed forced himself not to run. Now was not the time for signs of weakness. After a few seconds, he calmly turned and began moving through the gate onto the tarmac.

This audacity almost made the Director lose his very fragile composure. Every fibre in his body screamed for action. He wanted to grab this insolent Indian with his dark confronting stare. But he had no authority in this airport. Apprehending him meant drawing attention. Getting a seat on that plane was the only answer.

He approached the sales counter to learn that all 34 seats were fully booked. It added to his fury. He was unaware that Ahmed knew of it. Had asked at his seat allocation. Therefore he could be so defiant. The Director's anger reached boiling point when in the distance he saw a slender dark figure climb the stairs into the cabin. With him goes the *Cryslis*, of that he had no doubt. The girl was nowhere to be seen and probably on board by now. They were in this together and would stay close. It was smartest to concentrate on that Indian. He would be spotted easily in Sydney. He had found them and knew their destination. That was a positive. Sweat was pouring down his back from sheer frustration.

CHAPTER 16

AHMED LOOKED OUT of the window while the small jet took off. He could see Broken Hill clearly. Its huge dumps of slag and towering head frames of the mining industry. Beyond town was uninhabited. The light sharpened each colour and the shadow of hills. From dusty green and grey, to red and tones of pink. Many artists made Broken Hill their home. A number of well-known films had been shot here on location. Ahmed remembered reading about that in the Library. Perhaps one day he would be back for a real visit. There was nothing below but open country with a few dirt roads making straight lines. The day before yesterday they had stolen the *Cryslis*. It seemed a long time ago.

Certainly the Director would have a welcoming party waiting for them at Sydney Airport. It was unlikely they could pick out Jacq from amongst the crowd. They would focus on him. Somehow, that trap needed avoiding. Perhaps he could just run for it. Not a good idea. It would draw attention from airport security. Perhaps being held for questioning. Losing precious time. A separation from Jacq might happen as well which was unacceptable. Ahmed couldn't bear the thought. He briefly looked at the headrest of a seat up front. Where Jacq was sitting, completely out of his sight. But a way of escape had to be found. Ahmed tried to dose off for a while, relax the tension in his body. Fat chance.

Ahmed sat next to a solid man, who exuded the calm of someone not to be meddled with. He was reading a magazine that gave Ahmed an idea. It was a sports publication.

'You play sport?' he suggested friendly. The man looked at him sideways.

'You could say so.'

Ahmed was reluctant to ask further. He didn't wish to appear nosy.

'Do you play sport?' the man questioned in turn. He had sensed both nervousness and strength in the young guy. It was intriguing.

Ahmed thought it best not to mention car racing. It might seem snobbish. 'Boxing and rugby,' he answered. At school he had always been in the first team for rugby.

'Union or League?' If the boy played, he would know the difference.

'Union.'

The man looked at Ahmed again. 'I am a League player.'

'Is that your job?' It sounded that way.

'Yes, I play in Sydney for the national league.'

Ahmed said no more. His plan was working so far. But it still could easily come to naught.

'What position do you play?' the man continued the conversation. The Indian seemed a nice boy. As a professional he had a soft spot for young players. Rugby was a tough and courageous game.

'Depends,' Ahmed told him. 'Fly half at times.'

They discussed rugby, its popularity, and the rivalry between England and Australia. The man called Andrew, was clearly doing Ahmed a favour. 'Where're you off to?' he finally enquired.

'Near Sydney Harbour,' Ahmed answered trying not to give away too much.

'You live there?'

'I've got family there.' Not true, but Andrew was not to know.

'Well enjoy.' The big man ended their talk and carried on reading.

***

The Director, unable to follow his prey, asked at the airport how he might fly to Sydney still today. Not from Broken Hill, he was told. But he could take the flight to Adelaide in just over an hour. Then book with one of the major airlines for Sydney that evening. It was good advice.

Before boarding he asked his security contact

whether a few men in civilian dress could to be posted in Sydney at the exit for internal flights. An Indian boy would be arriving soon from Broken Hill and needed intercepting. This should happen quietly and without fuss. The boy had to be taken unobtrusively. Police and airport security must be avoided. The Director was adamant on that point. They should also look out for a girl with longish blond hair.

His security contact assured him it was unusual but shouldn't be a problem. An Indian youth, on a small commercial flight from Broken Hill, would be quickly spotted. A girl with blond hair might be more difficult. They needed to be very sure about her, before they could approach. Many girls had blond hair. Perhaps the two young people might walk out together. The Director doubted that very much. But catching one of them would be a start. For this one send me the bill, he said. In a slightly better mood he boarded his plane for Adelaide.

***

The seatbelt sign flashed on for landing. Ahmed and Jacq were looking down on Sydney spreading out below far and wide including the Harbour Bridge. It had been a long time since she set foot in a major city, Jacq mused. Whenever she had heard of Sydney, she always imagined visiting the place. Now she would in circumstances that were unlikely to bring joy. The Director would have arranged a welcoming party, at least for Ahmed, that was a certainty. The man had contacts to make that happen. Jacq knew that *Cryslis* always would have connections to solve whatever problems it might be facing. It was amazing that they had made it as far as Sydney. Waking up in that cave near the waterhole yesterday morning was not even two days ago. So much had happened since. Yet even now they were just scratching the surface in solving the Riddle. Sydney Harbour Bridge was their destination. It had to be right, though it was still only a guess. All the way from Alice Springs they had been flying blind. If they didn't find the answer to the Riddle today, they could drop the whole shebang. It would be over and a relief. Jacq was worried about what might be waiting for them when arriving in Sydney.

The plane landed smoothly. Soon its passengers were allowed to disembark. Ahmed managed to walk briefly beside Jacq explaining softly that she had to find a taxi. Wait for him at the outside exit closest to the baggage collection area. When he comes through, she should beckon and have the taxi ready to drive off fast. He couldn't say much more. It would keep them together for too long and might reveal they knew each other. However different her looks, they should stay well apart. Jacq would escape scrutiny, free to follow up on his instructions. But she had no idea what was happening. Imagined Ahmed had plan. Involuntarily, she firmed her grip on the rucksack. Ahmed made sure to stay near Andrew, who knew his way about.

As the only Indian on the plane, the Director's security men spotted him immediately. They would wait for the right moment. It had to be near the exit, outside of the building. Making their way through the doors into the fresh air they allowed a pretty brown-headed girl with a rucksack to step out before them. Jacq had decided to amble through the luggage collection area slowly. Just to familiarise herself. She walked outside slightly ahead of two solidly built men. There was something about them that made her nervous. Could they be on the lookout for Ahmed? She should ignore them and get on with finding that taxi. Hopefully, Ahmed's plan of escape was a good one.

The security people paid no attention to Jacq. The girl they were to look out for, if she was even about, was blond. They had been told to concentrate on their main quarry, the young Indian. He was now waiting near the baggage carrousel.

'Against whom are you playing this weekend?' Ahmed asked Andrew. If he picked up their conversation again, he might be able to stay close.

'Against Melbourne.'

'Hard?'

'It's always hard. You would know.'

'Yep,' Ahmed admitted. He did know. If only Andrew knew of his predicament.

Andrew collected his luggage and began to walk to the exit. Ahmed remained in step with him.

'No bags?' Andrew queried.

Ahmed shook his head. He looked at Andrew frankly.

It was that look. It convinced the rugby player the boy was asking for help. He was not sure what it was about, but Andrew liked the kid. He began to suspect there must be a good reason for this Indian staying in tight. Unless the police or airport security got involved, he would look after the young guy. 'Hang tight,' he grinned with a knowing smile, much to Ahmed's relief. Thank god, his plan was working.

When Ahmed and Andrew exited the airport Jacq was waiting in a taxi a little further on. She waved frantically. Ahmed spotted her and took off. It was then that two men came away quickly from the side trying to block his path. Andrew at that point dropped his travel bags, half expecting something like this, and was onto them in a flash. His speed was incredible for such a big man. The assailants were taken completely by surprise. They could not take this opponent without creating a huge disturbance. Even then, they would most likely come off the worst for wear. The capture of Ahmed, who made it safely into the now speeding taxi, would have to wait.

'Where to?' asked the driver. The girl had asked him to be quick. She never mentioned her destination.

'Some eating place near the Harbour Bridge,' Jacq instructed. 'Somewhere near the water.'

'We need to talk,' she told Ahmed. He was trying to calm down after his escape, grateful to Andrew. Sometimes good things happened unforeseen.

I'm sure they needed to talk, the taxi driver mused, aware of the near abduction of the boy. He had seen it all before in his many years of ferrying people through the city. This was a minor bit of kafuffle that brightened his day. He would keep this trip in mind though, if ever a report were requested.

***

During his flight to Adelaide the Director gave the situation some further thought. His anger was still smouldering fiercely. Why were these kids flying to Sydney? That question kept running through his mind. It had to be because of the Riddle, absolutely so. He was only too aware that on this very day the planets aligned. It would be the most important day of his life. So much was at stake and the survival of *Cryslis* depended on it.

For years the Director had known the myth and

the Riddle of *Shalomat*. But he could never figure out what it meant. It hadn't been that important. He knew the Riddle from memory and slowly considered each word with urgency. Certain that the strange sentence held the key.

When he mulled on the word 'symbol' something nudged his brain. What exactly did 'symbol' mean? He was educated enough to know the answer to that question. A symbol of halves the Riddle spoke of. He began to list Australian symbols and arrived at the answer: The Sydney Harbour Bridge. It had to be so. Needless to say, that discovery excited him greatly. He felt an urge to start walking through the aisle of the plane, full of nervous tension. But he contained that impulse for the small jet had hardly an aisle to speak of. Remaining calm was important. Something else was beginning to dawn on him, something very significant. Catching those kids was not essential after all. All he needed to do was make sure they stayed away from the Bridge. The Riddle stated clearly that ripples were created from a symbol of two halves. Without access they could not possibly fulfil that, whatever the infuriating sentence might mean overall. It was a simple and logical deduction in typical *Cryslis* fashion. A moment of glee broke through his dark mood. Like a ray of light in a thunderstorm. But of course they needed catching to get the Cryslis back. He would place it the temple with no-one any the wiser. Taking them captive should not be difficult. At last the Director could smile a little. It was a smile to freeze a furnace. After landing in Adelaide he was briefed very apologetically about Ahmed and Jacq's escape. The girl still was around, it seemed, and no longer blond. It didn't matter. He asked his security contact to guard every access to the Bridge at both ends till midnight. Don't let them get near it in any way, he stressed. And of course, capture them. At midnight *Cryslis* would have won a mighty victory. This last thought he kept well to himself.

***

The restaurant where Jacq and Ahmed were dropped off was near the water and within walking distance of the foot of the Bridge. They found a table in a corner away from the street. It was dinnertime and rather busy. Nobody gave them a second glance. They felt reasonably safe, but not at all hungry. Eating on a nervous stomach was never easy. Yet food was essential, if they were to last into the night. Though neither of them had any idea what the next few hours until midnight would bring. For all their persistence and hard work they were none the wiser. The Riddle remained a closed sentence, mostly. They were near the famous bridge over the Sydney Harbour. But they could just as well give up their quest for want of guidance. The situation seemed even crazier here, than it had in Broken Hill.

They should at least eat something. Settled on a dip and a bowl of wedges, plus coffee to stay awake. The tension of outsmarting the Director was taking its toll. Ahmed wearily wiped his face with his fingers. As if to restore sore eyes. Jacq felt exhaustion settling over her like a blanket. She slowly began to retrieve the two tennis balls from the rucksack. Under the table she pressed out *Shalo* and *Cryslis*. She also pulled out the notebook and the key.

'What are you doing?' Ahmed asked alarmed.

'The answer is with them,' Jacq pointed out. 'We've got a few hours left to solve it. I want to know whether they give me ideas.'

Ahmed was giving her a dubious look. Still, in Broken Hill that approach had worked. There was no harm in trying again.

Jacq took the *Shalo* in one hand and the *Cryslis* in the other. She considered each. 'Do you remember what Rose said,' she asked.

'She talked heaps,' Ahmed replied a bit confused.

'Yes, but about the circle and the triangle in the Riddle.'

'Something like you must put one into the other,' Ahmed offered. The sphere looked absolutely solid to him, totally of one piece.

'Yes,' Jacq agreed. 'That was the gist of it.'

Rose had spoken of putting the triangle into the circle. 'Like this,' she said and began to bring *Shalo* and *Cryslis* slowly together. At the last moment she made them touch with some force.

Ahmed looked alarmed.

To Jacq's complete surprise, and absolute shock, the sphere of *Shalo* split open into two equal halves. They almost slipped out of her hand. She placed them carefully on the table. *Shalo* was not solid at all, but hollow.

Ahmed was stupefied.

'That is nice,' a voice commented from above. They looked up totally confused. The waitress had brought their food. 'Where did you get it?'

'At the market,' Ahmed had the speed of mind to answer.

'Cute.' The waitress placed a plate with pita bread and dips, plus a bowl of seasoned deep fried potato wedges with sour cream and chili sauce, on the table. 'The coffees will be soon,' she said moving on to the next customer.

'Triangle fits into circle, *Cryslis* fits inside *Shalo*,' Jacq whispered in wonder. The two objects had never touched each other before. When it happened, *Shalo* revealed its secret. The hollow inside of the sphere was the exact shape of the *Cryslis*. Jacq did not doubt for a second that it would make a perfect fit.

Ahmed was lost for words coming to grips with

this turn of events. His mind was racing, considering the consequences.

'Look, it fits perfectly,' Jacq said excitedly. She placed one half of *Shalo* over the *Cryslis*, then fitted the other against it. There was only one way of doing this.

'Amazing,' said Ahmed. 'Do it again.' It felt good to see the *Cryslis* neatly disappear.

But Jacq couldn't do it again. *Shalo* would not open, however much she tried. There was no line of any sort to be seen to suggest the sphere could come apart. *Shalo* had absorbed *Cryslis*, once forever, it seemed.

It brought them some joy amidst the hustle and bustle of the restaurant. They were not shooting into the dark. The Riddle was working, quite incredibly so. That sentence was not just a fanciful statement of ancient imagination. While these thoughts tumbled through their minds in a moment of exhilaration, the joy soon was replaced by weariness. Jacq and Ahmed felt completely exhausted. What else was to come? This whole adventure was demanding far too much.

'What do we do now?' Jacq wondered tiredly, once the excitement of their discovery had worn off. They were still no further in knowing their next move.

'Look inside the notebook,' said Ahmed as he slowly bit into a potato wedge.

Jacq did, expecting to read the same sentences, once again. How wrong she was. A new one had appeared. Her eyes widened in shock and disbelief. She was horrified. Clearly written it read: 'Throw *Shalo* off the top of Sydney Harbour Bridge at the yellow line.'

Her resolve to remain positive and keep up the fight came apart. Her world crumbled about her. 'I cannot do this,' she groaned softly dropping her forehead onto the table. 'I can't.'

The whole weight of the last few days, and the months of being under cover, was now crushing her. Please have pity, were thoughts that tumbled through her mind. She was asking for mercy from whoever was behind all this. Why should she have to pay this price? Feeling her wellbeing collapse like a pack of cards? Her stomach was cramping up violently. Steel bands were beginning to form around her head. To the top of the Bridge. That was a huge climb and undoubtedly dangerous. How could they ever manage it? They were too late anyway. It was getting dark outside. Only someone insane would even think of attempting that bridge before midnight.

Quickly Ahmed pulled the notebook from Jacq's hand. Her reaction struck him hard. What on earth was happening? As he read the sentence, he too was dumbfounded. He looked at Jacq, seeing her suffering so badly. This was cruel. It was ruthless this mission of theirs. They were in danger from the Director. Fully at the end of their tether. Now this next crazy instruction. The whole saga was becoming more than ridiculous.

Ahmed became very angry now and felt completely justified. A sense of complete helplessness hit him hard. His feelings were aching for his friend, who was so totally out of reach.

For a while they sat without speaking, oblivious to their surroundings. The food was left untouched. Not that anyone noticed. Every table in the place was busy with its own story.

'Let's go for a walk. Come on,' Ahmed finally decided. He straightened himself up. 'Come on,' he said again, gently urging Jacq. He took the notebook, the key and *Shalo*, dropping them into the rucksack. Ahmed needed fresh air, something to lift his spirit. If they were to get caught, he wasn't even sure that he cared. Then it would all be over. Almost certainly, it was already. How could they possibly succeed, feeling so wretched, and having only a few hours left?

Without giving it thought, on autopilot, they walked towards the twin towers of the Bridge at the north bank of the harbour. Two slender figures slightly slumped. The girl hanging onto the boy's right arm. A good distance away they stopped and had a look at this place of their failure. From faraway Europe they had come to solve a Riddle that was insurmountable. Forlornly, they stared at the giant structure before them. The huge pylons and the run-up to the Bridge that approached over some arches built from stone.

Ahmed knew that the Bridge could be climbed. He had discovered that on the internet in Broken Hill. A company took people up regularly as a tourist adventure. He remembered looking at the route of the climb in some detail because it had seemed interesting. Not imagining for one moment that they would be instructed to attempt it. The climb began at a door in one of the arches under the run-up. Ahmed could actually vaguely see that door in the distance. There was a man lingering in the vicinity only just visible amongst the shadows. It could only mean one thing. The Director had figured out the significance of the Bridge also. Ahmed softly told Jacq about the importance of that door and how access was now impossible. It was only fair that she should know. That information hardly seemed to register. It was urgent to retreat and not be captured.

They hastened their steps into a quiet area with some greenery. Jacq hanging onto Ahmed. He stopped and put his arms around her rather firmly in a hug. Willing her to be strong. It broke a dam inside of Jacq. She began to cry violently on his shoulder. Deep sobs, while he gently stroked her short brown hair. Their heads were touching. They held each other like that for as long as it took. Ahmed was regaining some of his composure from this caring. The feeling of Jacq's shaking body made him strengthen his back. He had to regroup and look after her. She was so much more important to him than defeating *Cryslis* would ever be. If allowed, he would hold her tight like this for the rest of his life. The sobs on his shoulder were getting quieter.

Eventually, Jacq released herself. 'What shall we do?' she asked wiping her eyes with the back of her hand. Her cheeks were streaked with tears. How many times had that question been raised before? This time though, it referred to the steps to be taken now that they had given up.

'Let's sit down.' Ahmed pointed to a bench.

They sat down, silently together. In spite of all that was happening, or not happening, Ahmed could not fully accept that everything had been in vain. It didn't make sense. Not if he considered how far they had come, with so little to go by. He reached into the rucksack for the notebook. But on second thoughts decided against bringing it out. It had brought them nothing but grief today. Instead he took hold of the sphere, which was no longer hidden in a tennis ball. They had been discarded at the restaurant. The sphere felt warm and strangely encouraging as Ahmed put both his hands around it. A mysterious energy seemed to be working on him. Through his hands and into his body. He was beginning to feel better.

'Hold the sphere for a while,' he told Jacq some time later. After hesitation, she reluctantly accepted it. She had come to despair of *Shalo*. Was totally gutted and not interested anymore. Ahmed's quiet insistence made her wonder though.

As she closed her fingers around the little ball, she began to experience something very strange. Her mind was thrown back vividly to when she had looked at the *Cryslis* in the Temple. Standing in a circle with the others. The memories of that time were now flashing through her mind. What she had felt at that moment returned to her soul. It was all intensely abhorrent. It hurt and made her cough for breath. As if she had not suffered enough. She saw her life's potential under the power of *Cryslis* with absolute clarity. The ruthless, linear and pointy approach to success. Jacq was gasping for air. 'Oh, my god!' she groaned. 'Oh, my god!'

Ahmed was shocked. This reaction was not what he had expected. He tried to take the sphere from Jacq, but she would not let go. All he could do was to keep his hands over hers in concern.

The encouragement Ahmed had felt now began pulsing through Jacq. It came in waves, again and again. She gripped *Shalo* so hard that her knuckles went white. She was oblivious to that. The sensation of warmth and energy seemed to last for ages, though it wasn't that long. She sat quietly, head down, with Ahmed still holding her hands firmly. He could only conclude that there must be a power at work beyond normal human capacity. It was encouraging and also frightening.

After considerable time, Jacq whispered, barely audible. 'We have to do it, Ahmed. Somehow!'

When Ahmed had held *Shalo* feeling its energy, he had thought the same. But Jacq's reluctance in accepting the sphere, and her violent reaction soon after holding it, had made him unsure. He would not have mentioned giving that bridge a go. Jacq, with so much thrown at her emotionally, would be the one to decide the future of their mission.

Ahmed was reminded of the gods *Sophius* and *Igod* in the myth. They were never sure whether they were playing with the spheres or the spheres with them. He could wholehearted identify with that feeling right now. The play was being orchestrated from somewhere else.

Jacq remained seated, slumped forward staring at the ground. Mysteriously, she felt much better now but for a hollow sensation in her stomach. Perhaps it was a lack of food, or the aftermath of emotional turmoil. Perhaps it was both. Just sitting quietly on the bench would be fine for the moment. Sharing the thought with Ahmed that somehow they should try to climb that bridge seemed no less crazy now than before she had felt the sphere's emanations. It seemed best not to try and figure things out yet. Just to rest a while. A sense of that mental fog she had experienced after the Temple visit was returning.

Ahmed was confused also. Security was guarding

the Bridge. Surely at all access points. And the night was ticking away. Soon it would be midnight with the Day of the Riddle behind them. Even if somehow they could get onto the Bridge, it was too late already. He had no idea how long the climb would take, but it was a considerable task. They could not possibly get to the top before midnight. Their mission was over. Nothing made sense.

***

The Director arrived in Sydney later that evening. More at ease now the contest weighted heavily in his favour. He could afford the time to hire a car rather than take a taxi to the Bridge. An expensive Audi was available. It didn't come close to his Porsche, which to his delight had been located unharmed in Coober Pedy. That young Indian must have good driving skills, he admitted grudgingly. He would have loved driving back to Alice Springs, but the *Cryslis* was needed at the Temple quickly. Beating that riddle was only a few hours away, at midnight. Thus far the two youths were nowhere to be seen. But he'll find them. His phone rang with a number he didn't recognise. It was the rich man. Hearing that voice, the Director cut the connection immediately. His mood darkened. He could not deal with that guy right now and would sort it later. He was to lose his job anyway. The fight was personal, between him and those infuriating young pests. That he was contacted right now showed the rich man knew something was up. His temper hit rock bottom as he drove the Audi to the Bridge.

***

Sitting on that bench together, well away from the Bridge, Ahmed grappled with his confusion. As a last resort he reached into the rucksack for the notebook. Not that he expected it to be of much help. So far every sentence had meant more trouble rather than a solution. With an involuntary shudder he found that another line had been added. In poor light Ahmed apprehensively brought the page closer to his eyes. With no idea what to expect he read: 'When does this day end around the world?'

The words made his head spin. With rising excitement he shook Jacq's shoulder and handed her the book. She accepted it reluctantly. With her quiet withdrawal now disturbed, she read the new entry a number of times. 'What does it mean?' she asked, hoarsely giving the book back, no longer interested.

Ahmed's brain was working overtime. Suddenly he understood. 'I know!' He stared at Jacq. 'What time is it in Holland right now?'

'Don't know,' Jacq shrugged. 'Much earlier.'

'Exactly,' Ahmed explained. 'Just think about it. The myth of *Shalomat* concerns the whole world, not just Australia. Around the world 'today' is not over at our midnight here.'

Jacq took a while to cotton on. Finding a way out of her mental fog. 'You mean we can do the job tomorrow?'

She was perplexed. Suddenly she understood it too and for the first time that evening was feeling some hope. Very early in the morning here in Sydney meant that Ellie in Amsterdam might just be getting ready in bed the previous day. It was so obvious, once you knew.

'Yes,' Ahmed agreed. 'We can do it at sunrise!'

There was that word again.

'Seek the sunrise,' Jacq whispered.

The Aboriginal lady at Uluru had said it. So had Petrus. They had come to Sydney on that knowledge. Now it had a second meaning. She could only wonder at the ingenuity of it all.

'The Director won't figure this.' Ahmed was struck with the beauty of the idea. 'At midnight he will call off security.' Hopefully that was so. 'Then we'll have access to the Bridge. It's got to work. It's too neat to fail.'

Excitement returned with their circumstances now completely changed. 'I'll tell you something else, Jacq,' Ahmed said. 'That key we have, is to open the door to the Bridge. I'm sure of it.'

Jacq had all forgotten about that key. They sat in disbelief for a while digesting this revelation. Earlier all was lost and now there was new hope. It was a rollercoaster ride of feelings Jacq would never wish to have again ever.

'It's still a big job,' Ahmed concluded. 'We need some sleep.'

But where?

Jacq nodded in agreement. The encouragement by *Shalo* had been a help. But if she would have to climb that bridge at sunrise as weary as she felt right now, she would never make it. Even after a good sleep it remained to be seen.

A campervan, one of those vehicles tourists hire to travel around Australia, drove up to park at the kerb in the distance. A man stepped out and began walking toward them. Ahmed and Jacq tensed up, ready to run. Never would the Director and his minions take them captive. Well away the man stopped and waved.

'It's Mr. Adams,' Jacq whispered in complete astonishment. She saw him walking down the street leaving the camper unattended.

CHAPTER 17

AT THE BRIDGE the Director learned that no attempt to access had been made. Jacq and Ahmed had not been sighted. He got back into his car and waited for midnight. Time was creeping by slowly. In spite of being confident that preventing access to the Bridge was pivotal, he remained edgy. Too many surprises had happened. His enemy, the force of *Shalo*, should not be underestimated. The slightly hazy darkness around about him and little illumination at the foot of the Bridge, accentuated his foul mood. He knew that the rich man would not leave a cut-off call unanswered. He was deeply tired.

When midnight came, nothing had happened. The Director was relieved. No longer able to sit still in his car he walked to the water's edge. He stared out over the magnificent Sydney Harbour under lights. It reflected all he believed in. Wealth, success and humanity's victory over the earth. The power of *Cryslis* was now established unchallenged, he believed. He had won. If only it felt that way. He had defeated the Riddle of Shalomat. The only person in the world to do so. He simply was too exhausted to care. He had to get the *Cryslis* back still. The Director thanked a few security men nearby and drove to his hotel. A whiskey was all he craved after.

He didn't sleep much. Close to sunrise he figured to curb his restlessness with another visit to the Bridge. It might lift his mood and bring a sense of victory. He had, after all, won the battle against *Shalo*. When the Bridge came in sight he parked a good distance away at the waterfront for a full view. The sun would be coming up transforming it from a sombre structure into the shining icon of Australia's history. Reflecting people struggling towards nationhood and identity. All was beautiful in the still and cloudless morning with no wind to speak of. The Bridge looked majestic and strong, reaching over a wide expanse of water. The Director got out of his car. He began to feel better.

It didn't last. In the distance two slender figures, one darker than the other, were purposefully making their way to the brick arches at the foot of the Bridge. It could only mean one thing, surely. But it made no sense. Still, it was happening. The Director's fury returned instantly. So did his exhaustion. His mind exploded with anger.

At that very moment an expensive limousine with darkened windows drew to a halt and blocked his path to the Bridge. A man stepped out from the front passenger seat. He opened the door behind it. The window of the other back door slid down. 'You fool,' the rich man spat out towards the Director. A menacing voice from a darkened cabin. 'Get in.'

Already confused, the Director's mind took a tailspin. He became completely incoherent. No way was he getting into that car. All he could think of were those two at the Bridge. Whatever was going on there, it had to be stopped. He had to escape this rich geezer. He jumped around the back of the limousine and ran.

'Leave him,' was the command to the body guard. The rich man had no idea why the Director ran towards that bridge. 'Take that Audi back and take his gear out. Leave no trace. We'll deal with him soon enough.' The limousine drove off as silently as it had arrived.

***

An hour before daybreak Ahmed's alarm went off. He and Jacq had found everything laid out in the van last night including energy drinks and food to bolster their strength. They had forced themselves to eat before finding their beds. Fell asleep well before twelve knowing that midnight was no longer significant. Now a peeping alarm urged them into a new day, much too soon for their liking. Still tired, but feeling better, they crawled out from under the blankets reluctantly. In the confined space of the van Ahmed let Jacq slip into her jeans and top first. Even when not her most energetic self, Jacq never lost the x-factor, he thought. She rummaged in the fridge while he got dressed. For breakfast they had an iced coffee, a banana with muesli, and water. Forcing the food down.

'I would like to throw *Shalo* off the Bridge,' Jacq said. She had thought it over and wouldn't budge in that it had to be that way. Whether she had enough energy to manage the feat, she didn't know.

Ahmed looked at her carefully. He had thought that perhaps the task might be his. Jacq had been so exhausted last night. He was feeling tired as well, but not too bad.

'I have to.' Jacq looked at him with determination and weary eyes. It was not a request he could refuse, that much Ahmed understood. He was just worried about Jacq's stamina for the job. It would be a huge climb. A thought crossed his mind.

'Are you afraid of heights?'

'No.' Jacq shook her head. 'I've climbed rock in the Andes. Height is not a problem.' It had been on holiday with her parents the year before. A great time of steep walks, rope climbing and a bungee jump. Height never bothered her.

Ahmed relented. Jacq was to go up first with him keeping an eye on her close behind.

'I will tell you what I remember about the climb from the internet,' he said.

They would enter the door in one of the brick arches under the run-up to the Bridge. Inside there was a staircase that led to a catwalk. That ran under the actual bridge to a huge pylon – to the tower, and around it. Then they would face steel ladders onto the top of the bridge's arch. Quite a climb. From there it was a matter of walking to the highest point of the arch, where he presumed the yellow line to be, and throw *Shalo* into the water far below.

Jacq took this information without comment. It sounded like a lot of work.

'With *Shalo* in your pocket you might be stronger than you think,' Ahmed encouraged her. He fervently hoped this to be so. 'Put it in your jeans, not your jacket, close to your skin.' Perhaps, staying in touch with *Shalo* that way might help.

It was now time to go. Jacq took *Shalo* from the rucksack and put it in her right pocket. The side of her throwing arm. She gave the key to Ahmed. They took their money, credit cards and passports, but left the rest of their possessions behind. They would pick up the rucksack later. Jacq and Ahmed were nervous and quietly tried to muster courage as best they could. This climb would be the end of a long mission. Of all they had accomplished, surely the hardest task to achieve. At first light they left the van and began their walk to the Bridge tower. The day was perfectly calm. Perhaps *Shalo* could control the weather as well, Ahmed wondered.

They were on the eastern side on the north bank.

Nobody was about at the brick arches so early in the morning. Some cars were travelling overhead making their run-up for a crossing. At the door Ahmed fished the key out of his pocket and inserted it. Unsure of what would happen. The lock turned without effort. His guess about the key had been right. As he opened the door and looked into the space behind he noticed a sensor up high. The tower was alarmed. Something they should have expected. The Bridge obviously should not be accessed without security clearance. He told Jacq to run for it as the place was wired. Bells must be ringing somewhere, not far away. She found the staircase as Ahmed had predicted and hurried to the top. It led to a narrow steel catwalk under the run-up. Cars above could be heard but not seen. Jacq felt *Shalo* burning in her pocket, on her upper thigh. It was a strange sensation. There were handrails on either side of the steel pathway. She tried to walk in a way that made grabbing a rail less necessary. It was not easy. The possibilities of slipping were very real.

Ahmed followed closely on Jacq's heels. She was fast, he had to admit, but obviously pacing herself. There was a long way to go. A climb like this when tired was asking for troubles. Hopefully, it would be okay. In the distance he could hear the wailing of sirens cutting through the morning peacefulness of the city. The police were on their way.

At the pylon of the Bridge the path turned 90

degrees. Moving through it, Jacq looked back down the catwalk. The shock of what she saw made her stop involuntarily. Ahmed almost slipped from not bumping into her. Something was amiss. He looked back as well. Coming towards them at considerable speed was the Director. In their haste they hadn't closed the Bridge door. The Director in pursuit was a horrible discovery. They could no longer pace their attempt at the climb. It had to be a full-on effort.

Making extra haste around the pylon, with fear griping their stomachs, they came to the other side. It showed a steel ladder that seemed to rise up for ever. It was also steep, almost vertical. With a grunt Jacq grabbed the rails and started to climb. With catlike movements ever higher. Her muscles were burning and she ignored it. No one was going to stop her, not now. By nature she was a long distance athlete rather than a sprinter. This aptitude would help but made the task no less formidable.

Ahmed felt his strength wane midway up the ladder. He was lagging behind and hated himself for it. He ground his teeth. The presence of the Director, now also climbing up spurred him on. Surely soon the police would not be far behind. Ahmed's arms felt on fire from the pulling and balancing. He reached the top of the ladder and entered the path on the arch of the Bridge. Jacq was ahead. The enemy closing in fast behind.

The Director felt a mad rush of energy that he would not have thought possible. Not that this fact crossed his mind. All he could think of was these kids and their danger to him. His anger was exploding like a volcano. His eyes were bulging out of his face from effort in catching up with them. That certainly was happening. He figured the girl was the main target. Something about her made that obvious to his now insane mind. What she was trying to achieve, he didn't know. His thoughts were far too incoherent to make sense of anything.

Jacq was placing her feet carefully on the broad metal strips that formed the path on top of the Bridge. It offered the friction needed to move up the incline. If she placed her shoes slightly over the edge of each strip, it became a foothold against slipping. She was grabbing the handrails and pulled and stepped as fast as she could. Her muscles were on fire. She just kept on stepping ignoring her hurting legs. There was no time for the fabulous view of the harbour. Jacq held her eyes firmly on the ever rising path. Hopefully, she would get to the yellow line before the Director caught her.

Ahmed heard the man panting hard close behind. Somehow he needed to be stopped. While climbing on he looked over his shoulder. The sight of an angry brute exuding violence and ferocity confronted him. With good reason Ahmed got very scared. This man was dangerous and out of control. What it might mean for Jacq to fall into his hands flashed through his mind with alarm. It made him stop and fired his determination to face this goon boldly.

Plant your feet firmly, boy. He remembered that advice from Rugger as essential in any serious scrap. Ahmed's feet found their best possible hold on the stepping strips. His back foot up because of the rise of the Bridge. It was not ideal.

The Director came upon him with disdain. He hated this Indian, who had shown him up so badly over the last few days. A hard swipe of his powerful arms should pulverise that menace. It was only a boy facing him after all.

Ahmed saw the wild intention in the man's eyes and readied himself. Diving under the flailing arms he landed two hard punches, one quickly after the other, into the pit of the Director's stomach. With a grunt of pain the man stopped in his tracks and growled deeply with animal ferocity. The punishment dealt out would have stopped most men, at least for a while. But not the Director in his present state. He would have preferred grabbing that young Indian and throw him over the railing. Between the steel bearers to a certain death. But the girl was running away up ahead. There was no time. He straightened up and stepped past

Ahmed giving him an enormous clout to the side of his face. Ahmed's boxing skills allowed him to fend off the blow and glide mostly away from it. A large fist clipped the back of his head and he lost his footing. The Director hurried on.

Ahmed slumped down holding on desperately to a post of the handrail. His strength, after more than two full days of struggling across much of a continent, gave way. His heart yearned after Jacq. He tried to get back onto his feet. He could see her ahead behind the Director's broad back. With a groan of frustration and utter helplessness he slowly let himself slide face down onto the cold steel of the Bridge and began to cry. Because of the uselessness of it all and his love for Jacq who was in deadly danger. And there was nothing he could do.

Two police officers soon arrived to find a young Indian totally exhausted and clearly in deep distress. The manner in which he had tried to stop that violent character up ahead had not escaped them. The kid had courage. One of the officers, a woman, remained with Ahmed. She helped him sit up slowly while the other officer climbed on.

Jacq felt her herself slowing down. It was a lengthy struggle and the yellow line just didn't show up. She began to despair of making it in time. The Director was getting nearer and nearer. She feared for Ahmed and desperately tried to block that out of her mind. The yellow line was all that mattered for now. It had to be.

Shalo was burning in her pocket. Never in her life, with every sport she enjoyed, had Jacq been so near the limit of her endurance. That she was still stepping one foot after another totally surprised her. Every muscle and bone was aching. Her stomach was a mess and breathing difficult from exhaustion. Still, she kept grabbing the railing. One hand after another. Again and again, pulling along for dear life. And her life was at stake, with that madman after her in hot pursuit. Like an ultimate sacrifice, Jacq thought grimly – giving your life for *Shalo*. She was determined for that not to happen.

The reason why she was on this bridge at sunrise spurred her on. Well beyond what would normally be possible. All she had learned about *Cryslis* and *Shalo*, came to mind. She considered her love for Ahmed and the absolute importance of their mission. Unless she collapsed in a heap, she would keep on climbing. If only it weren't so hard. Her eyes were beginning to lose their focus.

The metal stepping strips changed into a full steel path near the top. It made walking easier though still a massive struggle. Jacq was coming to the very end of her stamina. Her knees were only just functioning. The thought that crawling might be better crossed her mind. It prompted an urge to take *Shalo* out of her pocket. There were no more steps and a one-handed approach to walking was possible. She needed only her left hand on the railing. Holding the sphere in the other was making a difference to her level of energy. Jacq had no idea why.

At last the yellow line came in sight. At a distance for the yellow was painted on the handrails as well as the path. Jacq was hugely relieved that her climb was almost over. Still, would she make it in time? The Director had now come close enough to hear his erratic breathing. He would catch her before the line where she had to throw the sphere. Jacq was sure of it. There was only one way. A last desperate attempt. She decided to stop and confront him.

The Director's face was terribly contorted. Jacq saw it immediately. His eyes were incoherent. Clearly, he was out of his mind and super dangerous. He stopped before launching into his attack.

The girl held a golden sphere in her right hand, he noticed. Just visible between her fingers. Instantly, he knew it was *Shalo*. Here on top of this huge bridge this kid was holding that sphere. Despite his madness, the magnitude of what he saw flashed through his mind with absolute clarity. He stood rooted in his tracks, heaving and grunting, transfixed by *Shalo*.

It allowed Jacq precious seconds to assess the man. She placed her feet with a firm hold in the position needed for combat. The Director shook his head as if clearing a fog. Like a bull confronting a red cape. He began to approach. Jacq could see he was insane. Called on her training not to be side-tracked by impressions your opponent might give. Focus on movements alone. Courageously, she let him come in close. She was now in a zone of total concentration. Holding onto *Shalo* for composure. Knowing that her feet would do the damage. The Director would not expect that. At that moment all she had learned in combat skills came to her naturally. The relaxation, the timing of an attack and the purposefully directed force of it. Later on she wondered how, in her state of exhaustion, it could have been possible. But it was. With a perfectly placed upward kick at the low point of the kneecap she stopped the Director in his tracks. In agony he grunted and buckled, hanging onto the rails but nowhere near collapsing. Jacq was facing the resistance of a madness that didn't respond normally to pain. Still, it gave her precious seconds. She turned and ran the last steps to the yellow line. The man limping after her on one leg. With the railing for support his busted knee didn't slow him down much. But enough for Jacq to find her balance. With all the might she could still muster, she hurled the sphere of *Shalo* in a wide arc. From the Bridge towards the rising sun. It seemed to fly of its own accord. Well beyond the power of her throw. Its golden colour reflected the early sun rays beautifully, down and down into the water below.

With the anguished cry of someone completely mad, the Director clambered after the sphere. Over the railing onto the steel beyond. Incredibly, he limped along a bearer. One good leg dragging the other. Until he lost his balance and toppled silently out of sight.

Jacq stood transfixed holding the handrail for dear life. Her mind was a vacuum. All was a blank. She was too exhausted to think of anything. Not even the sudden death of the Director before her eyes. All she saw was a faint glow of golden ripples spreading wider and wider. Far in the distance where *Shalo* had ended its flight. Jacq couldn't take her eyes off it. Slowly the phenomenon faded out.

She slumped to her knees quite content just to sit. At the top of a major Australian symbol. There to be left alone and at peace. Jacq was beyond caring and did not feel victorious at all. Soon a deeply concerned police officer was crouching beside her.

With police support Ahmed and Jacq made their way to level ground. That they had survived the ordeal helped a great dealt in regaining some strength. Their impossible mission was behind them. And neither of them had got seriously hurt. They were taken in for questioning grateful for a car seat to slump into. It was obvious to the police that these young people were in a bad state. Difficult questions could remain for later.

The receiving officer at the station recorded their possessions. Considerable money, credit cards and passports. They were tourists. A doctor was called for who diagnosed that they were healthy but highly stressed. Badly needed resting. Being juveniles they should be treated with extra care. Don't hold them without clear evidence of a serious crime, was the advice.

Mr. Adams had arrived at the station explaining that he was a lawyer from Adelaide and uncle of the girl. Having business in Sydney he had taken her and her English friend along. She was family from overseas. He had received a phone call from the girl early this morning asking for their hotel name which they had forgotten. She and her friend had been on a night out and got lost. She had not wished to wake him earlier. That she had been out that late had been against his wishes. He had told her to hang tight till he arrived to pick them up. But they were not to be found. He waited, tried to phone her, but couldn't get through. That had worried him to the point of desperation. And then he saw them driven away in a police car. He wished to speak to his niece and her friend, both together in private, please.

The police saw no reason to refuse this request. They were not sure about that story, but it could wait. The man who had jumped off the Bridge, and why, was of more concern right now. They had found his badly broken body but nothing to identify him. They thought he might have left a car behind, but couldn't locate it. There was a key in the door of the Bridge and the police had no idea how it had been obtained. The investigation was continuing.

A female duty officer asked whether Ahmed and Jacq were willing to see a Mr. Adams. They gave a nod. Another surprise, but for the better. He appeared wearing a tailored business suit. It was quite a change from his stable clothes. Still, it was a relief to see him. He exuded kindness and confidence.

Mr. Adams found them in low spirits and had no time to change it. Of more importance was for them to have a believable story and know it well. All Ahmed and Jacq wished for was a good sleep. But they understood the need for a convincing explanation. Their real story no one would come close to believing. Telling that, they could find themselves at this station for a long time.

Mr. Adams explained that presently he is a lawyer and Jacq's uncle. He had come to pick them up after her call. If the police queried the whereabouts of her phone, well she had lost that during the chase. He suggested, that while waiting for him at the arches under the Bridge, they saw a man opening a door. He stepped inside leaving it ajar. When Jacq decided to look in, just to see what was behind the door, the man had grabbed her. He pulled her in and blocked the doorway. Upon which Ahmed had thumped him hard into the kidneys making him lose his grip. Jacq had run away up the stairs making her escape. Ahmed, sidestepping the deranged man, had followed suit. Out of his mind, he came after them. For whatever reason, he had his sights set on Jacq. They had no idea who he was and were traumatised by the whole event. Mr. Adams then gave them the name of a luxury hotel. They had rooms there, already for a few days. If the police wanted to know. Those rooms had actually been booked. Jacq and Ahmed were told their room numbers. As their lawyer Mr. Adams was going to inform the police of their explanation. Perhaps that would be enough. There might yet be questions. But they were juveniles and their story showed that a crime had not been committed.

Despite their weariness Ahmed and Jacq could appreciate the cleverness of the tale. It could have happened and was easy to remember. Hopefully though, they would not be questioned much.

The police were considerate. Ahmed and Jacq were briefly checked on the story. When both confirmed it, they were released into the care of Mr. Adams. The rescuing officers agreed that the now dead man had seemed very unstable and was clearly dangerous. The youths could not be blamed for that. Why he had been at the Bridge with a key and finally climbed over the handrail onto the bearers, the police could not figure out. Psychologically imbalanced people could do strange things. Perhaps the presence of the police themselves in pursuit had pushed him over the edge. One officer had been gaining ground on him rapidly. The girl may have thrown something into the water. The officer couldn't be sure with the man blocking his view. He had given most of his attention to the path and keeping a sure footing. There was no reason for holding the young people at the station. They had suffered enough.

Mr. Adams drove Jacq and Ahmed to the hotel. He handed them their door cards and the rucksack. 'We'll meet this evening at 7 o'clock,' he said. 'At the restaurant below for dinner.'

Standing in the corridor before her door, Jacq began to insert her card into the lock. Ahmed gently took her arm and she turned to him. He did not know what to say. But his eyes told it all. His great relief that she was safe and what he felt for her. Jacq placed a hand on his wrist preventing an embrace. She softly kissed him long enough give it real meaning. Then she rested her forehead briefly against his shoulder. 'Knock on my door at 3 o'clock,' she whispered. Her short cropped brown hair smelled faintly of salt. She stepped back and opened the door. It closed behind her with

Ahmed looking at it briefly.

That afternoon he found a refreshed Jacq waiting. Ahmed felt much better himself. The surreal nature of the last few days was already beginning to fade. It was surprising. He graved normality and would shy away from any kind of adventure for a long time. Jacq had decided they were in desperate need of new clothes and should go shopping. Ahmed happily agreed. However, first he wanted to discuss an idea about leaving Sydney. The sooner they could fly overseas the better. Whatever the police had in mind, and it may well be nothing, he would rather leave Australia in a hurry. His father was visiting India and they could join him for a holiday. Ahmed had enough relatives in India to make life comfortable without his dad. But a parental presence would make it easier for Jacq's parents to have their daughter joining him.

Jacq was delighted with the idea.

They should cover their backs, Ahmed explained. Jacq was to phone their Business Studies teacher for her to tell the Mentor that they were fine. They would be visiting Ahmed's father in India. The teacher should confirm with the Mentor that was fine instead of them flying to Frankfurt. The teacher must let the Mentor know that their parents might check with him about that permission.

Ahmed figured that their parents didn't know

about them running away. The Mentor should have informed them immediately, but waited. Ahmed's plan about India would help him cover up that negligence. He would be relieved that they were okay and agreeable. Ahmed stressed that Jacq should not allow the teacher to ask questions. Just say we're fine, nothing to worry about, and hang up.

Jacq took a deep breath. She followed through on the idea. Spoke slowly and firmly for her message to be clearly understood.

'Please give me a glass of water.' Jacq felt as if needing to wash a bad taste out of her mouth. What she had told the teacher was sort of true though not really. The next call would be worse. She needed to phone her mum.

Ahmed had guessed correctly. Their parents believed them to be at *Cryslis* in central Australia. Her mother was ever so pleased to hear from Jacq, who felt rotten being unable to tell the truth. They chatted briefly. She assured her mum that it was okay to leave *Cryslis* for India. Permission had been given. This would be her final lie in the service of *Shalo*, she decided. Absolutely! She fervently hoped it to be so. After careful questions about where she would be, there was no problem with the suggested holiday. Her daughter was a level-headed girl, Jacq's mother knew. Having friends around the world could only be good. Jacq needed to leave a contact number and address details. Those particulars were soon forwarded by SMS.

Ahmed booked tickets to Delhi for tomorrow early morning. He left a message for his dad, who was unavailable. It should not be a problem.

The shopping took a while in lifting their spirits. Jaq wrestled with pangs of guilt about that call to her mum. Still, life was returning to normal. It offered neither fear nor restrictions. Time passed quickly. They got back to the hotel just before dinner with Mr. Adams.

The table had a waiter especially assigned to it. Jacq bought something nice to wear that afternoon. Quite a change from the jeans she had lived in lately. Ahmed could hardly keep his eyes off her. He didn't look too bad himself, Jacq thought. He had the gift of wearing almost anything with an ease that made other people jealous. Ahmed was not aware of it though. That made it all the more attractive.

Mr. Adams soon noticed the affection and was quietly pleased. At least, they had gained something positive from their adventure. He held no illusions about how hard it all must have been. Sometimes young people had to carry the future. In this case, that had been true. There was nothing he could have done about it. Mr. Adams never asked about their mission, only expressed his thanks on behalf of *Sophius.* On behalf of the whole world actually, though nobody would ever know what heroes they were. Fine by me, Jacq thought. The very idea of being a hero made her cringe. Ahmed, having avoided attention a son of the very rich for years, felt the same.

They ordered from a superb menu. Ahmed opted for wagyu beef and Jacq for Australian barramundi. Today, they actually felt like eating.

'Why us?' Jacq still wanted to know.

'I don't know,' Mr. Adams admitted. 'I have no idea. But it was obviously the right choice.'

'We can't go back to *Cryslis*.' Ahmed knew that to be a problem.

Mr. Adams explained that he would visit their parents. Ahmed and Jacq could rest assured of not being reprimanded or face difficulty. How he would manage that, they could not imagine. But the manner in which it was said, with a quiet tone of complete authority, erased all doubt. There remained a lot of mystery behind the quest of *Shalo*. Always would, Jacq thought. Mr. Adams suggested that soon their adventure would be a distant memory. He asked for their firm word never to speak of it to anyone. The notebook had been taken from the rucksack and he would keep it.

Ahmed had a final question.

'The Riddle has now been fulfilled. But I don't understand the words about restoring balance out of chaos,' he said. Mr. Adams looked at Jacq.

'I do,' she admitted. 'I had the same question and figured it out this afternoon.'

She thought of the golden ripples in the water spreading wider and wider. Ahmed, in the care of the police, had not seen that. How spectacular it was. But she had told him about it.

'So, what is it? What does restoring balance out of chaos mean?' Ahmed wished to know.

'My brother is studying quantum mechanics in the US. When still at home he had a book on chaos theory. How the flutter of a butterfly's wing affects the whole earth.'

Ahmed had heard of that at school. He cottoned on fast. Remembered Jacq telling him about *Shalo* hitting the water. 'You mean that *Shalo* creating those ripples is a sign that eventually its power will spread everywhere?'

'Yes,' Jacq agreed. 'The balance *Shalo* brings, will be restored in years to come.'

Ahmed looked at her admiringly. Trust Jacq to figure it out.

'Well done,' Mr. Adams said. 'The powers of the gods are subtle. Like undercurrents in the psychospiritual nature of our world. When the *Cryslis* was found long ago, it began to introduce people to its power. They became instructed in systematic *Cryslis* philosophy. The mystery of its inner glow and the building of a Temple added to the fascination. It has been very effective in a superficial way. Excessively cognitive to the point of becoming harmful. There is much more to a life well lived than *Cryslis*.'

Mr. Adams paused and looked at them. He took no pleasure in this explanation for it spoiled the mood a little. But Jacq and Ahmed needed affirming in how essential their mission had been. The value of the price they had paid. Neither of them said a word. This talk reminded of those evenings at the stables.

'I just like to confirm with you the importance of what you have achieved.'

Mr. Adams continued.

'You will not see a great change in the world right away, for the gods work slowly. *Shalo* in the open will make a difference though. The sphere will be drifting around unseen. A temple would diminish its powers. The influences of *Shalo* are solely subliminal. Unlike *Cryslis*, which has an organisation and a special system of education. *Shalo* quickens people's minds without that. It always has and it will become much stronger now. Simply because you. For you have fulfilled the Riddle of *Shalomat*.'

Mr. Adams smiled warmly and raised a toast. 'Well done!' he said.

The next morning they flew over the Sydney Harbour Bridge. What a symbol, Jacq thought. Did she see a faint golden sheen over the water? That must be an illusion. Sunlight playing tricks. She would never forget that Bridge. Nor would Ahmed. He briefly touched his head where the Director had given him a clout. I'll be back, both Jacq and Ahmed decided silently. What a country!

CHAPTER 18

THE RETREAT HOUSE on the mountain ledge was basking in sunshine. Not that the three people sitting in the living room with its extensive views took note. The Protectorate was confronted with a most serious situation. Until recently it would have seemed impossible. The *Cryslis* had been stolen and the Riddle of *Shalomat* might have been solved. They weren't actually sure. What that meant for the future they had no idea about. Thus far all seemed as usual, apart from a Temple without the object that made it one.

'So, we have no idea where the *Cryslis* is?' the woman asked.

'No,' said the leader. 'Probably, it was thrown off the Bridge into the harbour.'

'Because the Director fell to his death there?'

'Yes. And those two kids were picked up by the Police on that Bridge.'

The Eminent person had misunderstood why the Director had run away towards that Bridge. He kept it to himself. He could have deducted what was going on from the Riddle, but didn't. It would have made no difference anyway, he had decided. His mistake had been trusting the Director to keep him informed. That too, he never mentioned. His incredible anger about it had only just begun to abate. 'The police have no idea who he is,' he said. 'We can keep the whole event secret. I'm sure those kids have been told to shut up about it by *Shalo* not to complicate matters.'

'How could those kids have grabbed the *Cryslis*? It burns like napalm,' the other man wished to know.

'There can only be one answer. *Shalo* must have been involved. I have no idea how.'

His mystical powers had lessened with *Cryslis* lost. That was nobody's business either. Absolutely not! But something was eating away at him inside and it felt real.

'So, where from here?'

The Eminent man had thought it through many times. They should just operate as before. Nothing would change quickly and the momentum of *Cryslis* was by now near impossible to stop. The increasing use of technology in society weighed heavily in their favour. People were already glued to their phones every day. Multimedia was a massive influence. *Cryslis* graduates held key positions. *Cryslis* philosophy would prevail. The loss of the *Cryslis* should remain between the three of them. They would take a copy ornament that had been exposed to the original. Figure out some lighting to make it seem glow from within. Little power would emanate from it but giving the idea of power should be possible. By using vibrations that affect the brain and were beyond human detection.

'What about those two kids?'

'We could have them killed, but to what benefit,' the Eminent man said. 'They are no longer a threat. As you know, we never assassinate unless it becomes unavoidable. It creates unnecessary difficulties.' They agreed and ended their meeting.

Thank you for reading *SHALOMAT*
I hope, you have enjoyed it.
For more, see the next page
Kind regards,
Michael

About this book

Ideas by philosopher John Ralston Saul (*On Equilibrium*) and theologian Bede Griffiths (*A New Vision of Reality*) have been used. As are those common to spirituality and the human spirit.

Books by Michael J Spyker
Available at agapedeum.com

Trilogy

Meeting Emma

A journey of discovery in which Emma becomes familiar with the many idea of Christian Spirituality through the ages. It helps her towards the person she would like to be. This book has assisted many in coming to love the vast wealth of the Christians spiritual tradition.

The Primacy of Love

Jake hears about his father's ideas on God's Love from Baz while travelling the Simpson Desert. Their talks include the significance of eternal and universal love, and the relational. The story has been called a significant theological feat.

The Language of Love

Emma and Jake fall in love. JH introduces them to the real meaning of Eros well beyond merely sex. They learn about being a Friend of Jesus and the language of love. Emma and Jake set off camping in the outback in search of JH. They work out what it means to live intimately together.

Novels

Julian's Windows

A musician and a teacher of children with intellectual ability fall in love. He lost his wife. She questions her vocation as a religious sister. Country life in Victoria restores his soul. A holiday in Australia from Liverpool decides her future. The ideas of Lady Julian of Norwich are an integral part of this love story in a most natural way. Great fun and informative.

Shalomat

Jacq and Ahmed, 16 years old, are on the run through Australia on a quest with mystical dimensions. It draws them together. All seems lost but isn't quite. Young people and adults enjoy this adventure. It is partly a comment on the one-sidedness of modern society and uses ideas of spirituality and philosophy. Will there be a sequel, an appreciative reader asked?

Treatise

Science and Spirit

Science exists by the creativity of God. But where to find God within physics? Where in society, in which God has become irrelevant? An informed answer best includes knowledge of history, science, philosophy, theology and religion. Plus ideas about a way forward. A read of significance to enjoy.

Christian Living

Drawings and Reflections

52 short reflections and 15 drawings that lift the spirit. A brief story that sows an idea. A picture to enjoy. It is not so easy to stay focused in a busy world. A little help always comes in handy. There is nothing religious about this book apart from keeping Jesus in mind and living vibrantly.